dogs

Published in the United States by
Lorimer Press, Davidson, North Carolina
Printed in China

Library of Congress Control Number: 2010930201
ISBN: 978-0-9826171-4-4

This is a work of fiction. The characters and events
are inventions of the author and do not depict
any real persons or events.

www.lorimerpress.com

dogs

a novel

Abigail DeWitt

LORIMER PRESS
DAVIDSON, NC

2010

Infinite thanks to Judy Goldman and Susan Monsky for reading dozens of drafts of this book. Without them I could not have written a word. Judy and Susan were reading drafts before they were drafts, and reading right up to my final deadline.

Great thanks, also, to Tommy Hays, who read the book at a crucial moment and helped me see it through new eyes.

Thanks to the McColl Center for the Arts, the North Carolina Arts Council, the Tyrone Guthrie Center in Annaghmakkerig, Ireland, the Asheville Arts Alliance and the Lenoir-Rhyne Visiting Writers' Series for generous support during the writing of DOGS.

Thanks to Martin Richardson at North Carolina's Central Prison for helping me with early drafts; and to the Honorable Stephen Yelenosky and the The Honorable Judge Robert Perkins, who answered my many questions about judges.

Thanks, too, to Leslie Rindoks and Allison Elrod, the best publishers I could imagine.

Thanks to Jim, Galina, N and A.S. for their wonderful gifts.

Thanks to my mother and sisters for their years of encouragement.

Thanks to Jessi and Adrienne, who bestow such generous and abiding blessings.

And thanks to Sarah, light of my life, for her love and laughter, which inspire me every day.

In memory of my father, Bryce DeWitt, who, night after night, read to his children and grandchildren

And for Larry, always

…out of rock,
Out of a desolate source,
Love leaps upon its course.

—W.B. Yeats, "His Confidence"

What breaks my heart is the begging, the shamelessness of a dog's desire. A dog will follow you around, matching its pace to yours—only a little faster, a little more eager— even after you've pushed it away. Say no like you mean it and it follows you with its eyes, whimpering, thumping its tail.

I had two dog dreams when I was young. In one, my yellow dog, the dog of my childhood, is outside the sliding glass door, crying because it is pouring rain. Someone tells me to put him out of his misery, and only after I have held him up by the forelegs and pulled a butcher knife down from his neck to his belly do I realize that I could have put him out of his misery by letting him in.

In the other, my mother is going to feed me to the dogs because I have a terminal illness. I can hear them at the end of a long hallway: bone-gaunt hounds leaping and barking in a metal cage. They aren't vicious. Their barks are the barks of desire: hunger for sustenance, atten- tion, love, even. But I turn to my mother and stop her. "Wouldn't a gun hurt less?" I ask, because dreams are so innocent of their own symbols, because you can be a sixteen-year-old girl who has just learned what a phallic symbol is, a sixteen-year-old-girl who prides herself on catching every sexual reference the world has to offer and who will awaken in the morning thinking, *a gun, Jesus, I dreamt about a gun*; but still, lying asleep in your single bed where none of the boys you know stay longer than an hour or so, not get it: you can still think, of course, a gun. A gun would hurt less than a pack of hungry dogs.

I didn't understand those dogs at all, or the nakedness of their longing. They would never eat a human being.

Of the two dreams, the worst was the one in which I did the killing. I had other dreams in which I killed people—always innocents, children, unpopular girls at school—and for days afterwards it was hard to speak, I could barely eat. If I could go back, undo what I had done—but even in dreams, you can't.

Seventy-two years old and wide awake, my father killed a girl. No one would have called it murder; they didn't even say it was involuntary manslaughter. He spun out on an icy road and the girl, the fourteen-year-old hooker wannabe, his passenger, had failed to fasten her seatbelt. My father—that beautiful, noble man who presided over the 217th District Court, whose robes smelled faintly of eucalyptus, and upon whom all eyes gazed as he pronounced his sentences—my father said he was trying to get her off the street and home to her mother. He knew the family because I had once been the dead girl's mother's friend. Without that alibi—the years of Becky's and my innocent delinquency—what would people have thought of an old judge driving a make-believe whore? They thought it anyway, but not enough to accuse him of anything.

He's dead himself now—he died in the crook of my arm this morning—and now, if I want, I can prove what people only thought: assault, rape, reckless endangerment. But I knew it all before he died, before I had a bit of proof; I knew because I loved my father and because, when I was young, I was just like that fourteen-year-old girl.

I was born in 1959, in Austin, Texas, the fifth child of the Honorable Judge Henry Moore and of his French wife, Jeanine. My parents met in Normandy, in the middle of June, 1944. My mother's family had been killed in the D-day bombings and she was squatting on a pile of rubble, a thin girl with auburn hair, trying to dislodge a stone from the mound, trying, as she had been for days, to unearth the remains of her family. My father saw her, the sun lighting her hair, the edge of her dress, and it was the prettiest thing he'd ever seen. Those were the words he always used, *the prettiest thing I'd ever seen*, as if, after ten days of solid fighting, of the choking terror and the stench and the noise, she had been perched there, above the ruins of her own house, as his reward. I don't know if he helped her dig through the rubble, or if he took her right then, as she bent over in the sunshine. He always ended the story with those words, *the prettiest thing I'd ever seen*. He had two ways of talking, the Harvard and the Texan, and he always used the Texan when he spoke of my mother; it wasn't an accent, just locutions, *the prettiest thing, I'll be damned*.

He didn't have to fight; he'd been raised a Quaker, and my grandfather had been a conscientious objector in World War I; my father could have stayed home, too, but he saw what it had done to his own father to be a pacifist in a land of cowboys—or rather, what it had done to him and his mother, because my grandfather, from what I heard, never regretted a thing, and died young, leaving my father to spend his adolescence alone with his mother, a tiny, olive-skinned, beautiful woman who, after spending two decades disparaging her husband's cowardice—she was a Baptist—made herself sick from crying when her son joined the Navy. He was all she had, and he wasn't obliged: America didn't need his help to kill off some Japs, and the Jews had it coming to them anyway.

"No," my father said one year, when the subject came up at Christmas dinner. "It was clear what the Nazis were up to; it wasn't a time for pacifism."

"Well!" my grandmother exclaimed later, when she was back among her own friends. "After that, he ended up with the most awful French girl. You can't understand a word she says, and she just eats all day. She wasn't so bad when he married her, but now she is fa-*at*. Big as a house." She said that to her friends in Corpus Christi, where I was sent for a week's vacation. She lay on a chaise lounge in a bikini, because she was beautiful, tiny, barely wrinkled at all.

Around my grandmother, my father used his Harvard voice. He often disagreed with her, but his language was always proper, even elegant. It was an act of courtesy, because all she had ever wanted—until Pearl Harbor, when what she wanted was simply for her son to stay home— was for him to go east for school, to make something of himself, and to be courteous. He had beautiful table manners, he held doors and chairs as needed, he never wore a hat indoors. And he had, besides manners, principles. He did not believe in social or racial hierarchies, and that was the best of courtesy, where his father's moral convictions joined with his mother's conventions; there was no man he would not tip his hat to, no woman he would not give up his seat for. If, by accident, his manners failed him—if he didn't open a door for a cleaning lady—he apologized profusely, *I'm terribly sorry, ma'am, I didn't see*, his voice then almost like a child's.

But around my mother, my great, fat mother, he never apologized for anything—forgotten birthdays, missed meals, his own mother's cruelty. My mother stared at him sometimes, her expression perfectly blank, and then, the way I remember it, turned her attention back towards me. She held me on her warm lap for hours when I was small, in the back yard beneath the live oak trees or at the kitchen table. Once a week we went to church, and while she knelt, I leaned into her soft, coffee-smelling body and gazed at the crucifixion story in the windows. Jesus, my mother said, had given everything away—which was the opposite of the Pope, she added, as if she were taking me into her confidence: Jesus was the least of our brothers, but the Pope was a hoarding imbecile.

I pinched the loose skin of her elbows, patted the long, faded red braid that hung down her back. I meant to console her for the Pope's failings, but I also felt that her body belonged to me, and to me alone. My siblings came and went in the distant reaches of the house, but they were much older than I, and seemed to have no relation to us.

When I think of the early days, what comes to me is the smell of coffee, the hot shade of the live oaks and the stations of the cross. That was the world, the yard, the church, the kitchen, and within it, only my father in his dark robe, and my mother, already old, a Rubens going to seed. Now and then my grandmother's voice floats through, as querulous and repetitive as a blue jay's, but mostly what I hear are the backyard squirrels, and my mother's deep, rich murmur. There were morning doves, too, and bright red geraniums my mother had set in pots around the back yard to remind her of her childhood. The light was golden, mote-filled, and even when I turned five and was sent to first grade—a land of much taller girls who took turns carrying me around the playground—my mother and I continued our rocking afternoons, as if school were to be only a brief interruption, a few hours of clear cool lights and starched blouses in the middle of the long, hot, rustling dream of childhood.

And then, one day, there was a commotion of packing. Boxes and trunks and bags filled the foyer beyond the kitchen. Claire and Yvonne were going to Vassar. Claire had a mole, and Yvonne's eyes were closer together, but otherwise they were identical. I would have been seven when they went to college, but already I knew that Vassar was not

Radcliffe, that there had been a disappointment. I noticed that day how pointed their breasts were, and would have touched them, except that they were not the kinds of girls you touched. My mother went up to them, her fingers to their cheeks, but they shrank away; and I understood then that a whole family had preceded me, and that the house was full of that family's belongings, their complicated allegiances. My mother was wearing only her bathrobe, the way she often did unless she was going out, and I could see that the twins, in matching pleated skirts, didn't like to see her so undressed. They were watching my father, who stood perfectly still in a suit and tie, waiting for the good-byes to be over with.

"Break a leg, I guess," Ted said. He was red-haired, like my mother and me—the others were all dark, like our father—but Ted's skin was even paler than mine, as if he had been turned inside out. He was only two years behind the twins, but he seemed much younger. He picked his nose still, and he had a high, whinnying laugh.

"Break a leg?" Babette said. "That's stupid. That's only for plays."

"Well," Ted said, blushing. "College is a kind of theater."

Babette rolled her eyes. She was twelve, and beautiful, and she would roll her eyes and snap at anyone; my father loved her best of all.

"Well, then," my father said. "Let's move along, or you shall miss your flight."

And then, suddenly, Claire burst into tears. We weren't allowed to cry. My mother, soft and delicious though she was, did not believe in tears. Nothing since the war was worth crying about, and that was why we must eat leftovers, too, because she'd been so hungry during the war, leftover vegetables and leftover liver and brains; nothing must ever be wasted, neither grief nor cut of meat nor article of clothing—that was our only rule, never waste anything: hand everything down, clear your plate, be strong. But when Claire cried, my mother put her arms around her, and Claire held her back and then Yvonne was holding her, too, the three of them embracing as if they'd known one another all their lives, as if my mother belonged to them, too.

"That's enough," my father said, opening the front door.

When they were gone, Ted started to cry, his whole face blooming like a rose. My mother wheeled around to him. "*Ça suffit!*" she hissed, and then she vanished, slamming the door between the living room and the hallway.

"Don't cry," Babette said. "They'd probably let you into Vassar, too."

"It's a girl's school, stupid."

"Duh."

"You know what, Babette? You know what?"

"What, crybaby?"

"You don't know anything, that's what."

"Oh boy, that really hurts my feelings."

"Get out of here, Babette."

"Don't worry. I'm going. Come on, Molly. Let's get away from him." She took my hand and led me to her bedroom and I was proud because Babette liked me. The children's bedrooms were all on one side of the house and my parents' was on the other, and in between was an open expanse of kitchen and dining room and living room and den, where Ted stood, watching us march defiantly away. I wasn't sure what we were defying; I only knew that Babette's was a noble cause and that I was on her side. She opened the door to her room—it was white, and soft: a fluffy white rug, a white bed. She put a record on the turntable—I could look at all her things, she said—and she lay on her back and stared up at the album cover. I watched her for awhile, and then I studied her room. There was a shelf full of trolls and a jewelry box that sang and a bottle of pink shimmery nail polish, but better than all of these was the cheerleading trophy above her bed, a golden girl with hard, smooth breasts and a golden pom-pom; and her top dresser drawer, filled with smooth, neat stacks of 28 Double A Maidenform bras.

She laughed. "I didn't say my drawers," she murmured, but I could see she didn't care. She flopped over on her stomach, her eyes still glued to the album cover.

And yet it's not possible that, until that day, I was barely aware of my siblings. It's the way I remember it, as if they burst onto the stage the day Claire and Yvonne left for college; but years before, I'd dreamt about Ted. My mother was killing him, going about it in the same no-nonsense way she went about preparing organ meats, slicing some parts, wrapping other parts up in wax paper, keeping the counters clean.

I woke screaming and she came into my bed, her body hot with sleep, and I asked her if she loved Ted, and she said of course, she loved all her children. And so, like any child, I must have seen everything before I began remembering it.

If I was seven when the twins left home, I'd already had my first communion, with the white gloves and the veil, my first confession in which I confessed that all I really liked were peanut butter and jelly sandwiches. I had reached the age of reason, in celebration of which my mother bought me a big yellow mutt.

"He's like the sunshine," I said.

"Yes," she said, smiling. "He is a spoke? Ray? Of the sun."

"Ray," I said. "I could call him that. Or Buttercup."

"Buttercup?" my mother asked. "It is not cup of butter?"

I laughed, and spoke to her in her own accent. "Butt-air cup," I said, rolling my R. "It's a flower, Mama."

It made my mother laugh when I mimicked her, and I imagined her accent was a thing we shared, a private joke. She was old and fat and she had no patience, but she laughed at herself. It was an easy laugh, the laugh of a slender, red-haired girl who has suffered no losses at all.

"Buttercup will be company," my mother said. "Now you are big enough, so in the afternoon I will go out and pick up clothes for all the children who have lived the wars. But Buttercup will be here—and also Babette and Ted of course." She paused for a moment, and then continued: "To help people—it is the most important thing, Molly. I help the children to have clothes, you help me by being a good girl."

I ran my arms through Buttercup's long, soft coat—his nose was as high as my shoulder—and my mother told me to throw a stick for him. I threw, and Buttercup caught, running across the long sloping yard like a horse, I thought, so I climbed onto him, stretching out on his hot soft back, but he ran even faster and I slipped off, and that became the game. I threw my body across him, he ran, I fell, he nudged me up with his cool, leathery nose.

My father appeared out of nowhere. "I see you've made a friend," he said, and there was real pleasure in his voice, and I was so happy. I turned to look up at him, at his black, shiny hair and the way he stood so tall and straight in a suit and tie, even on a Saturday, and I wanted to say something, but I couldn't think of anything, and Buttercup, wanting to keep playing, jumped up and knocked me down against the picnic table. My father kicked him hard in the ribs and I felt the impact in my own chest, my heart dividing and multiplying, because there, on the far side of the yard was Buttercup, whimpering, and above me leaned my father, gazing at my forehead.

"Goodness," my father said. "That will need stitches."

And then my mother was beside me, holding my head in her lap, but I could not make Buttercup come to me, no matter how much I stared at him, thinking, *I'm sorry*, over and over and over again, *I'm sorry, Buttercup, I love you*, and I could not let my father know how grateful I was for his concern, because he was already back inside.

———————

In the afternoons, after school, while my mother scoured the city for clothes, I played with Buttercup. We chased each other around the yard and when I lay down, he nudged me, his thick breath a thing I loved, as I loved the scratchy grass beneath me and even, in those days, the damp Texas air, like a warm bath we rolled in as puppies from the same litter. Sometimes, when I pushed myself off the ground, he jumped on my back and humped me and I always let him, as he let me climb on his back, even when I was big enough that, straddling him, my feet touched the ground.

Once or twice a year, one or another of the girls who carried me around the playground came over to my house, or I went over to hers. There were birthday parties to attend, all of us dressed in our Sunday clothes and bobbing for apples, but for the most part what I remember of the second half of elementary school—besides the pride I took in my penmanship and in the gold stars that brightened all my papers—was the back yard, and Buttercup, and the sound of Babette and Ted, screaming and slamming doors.

Sometimes Babette hit Ted, clawing at his face or kicking him in the shins, and he fought back, the two of them as matched in strength as me and Buttercup, and that was the saddest thing of all, that Ted, who was in college now, was no stronger than a girl four years his junior. He hadn't gone away to college; he went to the University of

Texas, two miles away, living at home and taking his courses by correspondence. He did his chores—the table setting and dishwashing, the Saturday dusting and vacuuming—the same way Babette and I did—reluctantly—and the only grownup gesture he ever made was on Mother's Day, when he bought flowers. *Stop*, I wanted to tell him. *She thinks cut flowers are a waste, just make a card.* But I couldn't stand to hurt his feelings, and he never seemed to notice the thinness of her voice when she thanked him.

Once, towards the end of a school year, when it was raining, so that I could not play with Buttercup, I sat at the kitchen table, studying for a spelling bee, my stomach already light and eager, my shoulders buzzing, because I knew all the words—*intention, satisfaction, motion*—but suppose I forgot something? Suppose I made a mistake, standing before the class, saying the letters out loud? That was my great fear in life, not failing a spelling bee—though the thought of that filled me with waves of nausea—but how easy it was, even when you knew better, to make a mistake. In Sunday school—a dull, basement hour before mass when all I could think about was food—Sister John of the Cross had said it was impossible to commit a mortal sin by accident, but I did not believe her. I already knew everything was possible by accident.

"You'll never get out of here," Babette said suddenly, flipping through the TV Guide. She was talking to Ted, but I flinched. She never talked to me that way—I was the only person she never talked to that way—but still it hurt my stomach. Even our father, whom Babette adored, was fair game if he got in her way—for weeks now she'd been waiting up for him, pleading and yelling the minute he walked in the door because he wouldn't let her go out on a date with a seventeen year old, and she was fifteen, there was hardly any difference between fifteen and seventeen, and he was like a jailkeeper, he was ruining her life and she hated him; her voice wafted to me through all the slammed doors where I lay in my bed, drifting in and out of sleep through their arguments, his voice muffled and deep and certain through her jagged fury—but she never yelled at me and I was always welcome in her room, and I was glad of it, and guilty too; and that was another thing Sister John of the Cross would never have understood. She was married to Jesus, my mother said, an idea both creepy and fascinating, like her bald head. But whatever my mother said about Jesus, whatever Jesus himself said about loving the least of these, I knew that Sister John of the Cross had never liked having Ted in her class, and that she, like Babette, preferred me. She didn't seem to know that it was wrong to be favored, that it was as sinful a thing as being rich.

"You won't," Babette was saying. "You'll never get out." She slammed the TV Guide shut. "You'll live here in your stupid room till the day you die."

"It's none of your business what I do or don't do." He had been sitting at the table with us, with his hands clasped, doing nothing at all.

"Well it's pathetic is what it is."

"Yeah well you'll just find the most expensive college you can go to, won't you? You'll just waste all of Mama and Daddy's money."

"Maybe I won't go to college, stupid."

"That wouldn't surprise me. You probably won't get in anywhere."

"Well I'm not going to rot in this house, that's for sure. I'm not going to sit and rot here like some little old spinster. That's what you're like, you know? Like a little old lady spinster. You can't even get a goddamned date."

"Go to hell, Babette. Anyway, you're the one who can't go on a date. Daddy won't let you."

"I can too go on a date you idiot. I'll go on any goddamned date I want to. Anyway I said get, not go on. You can't get a stupid date. 'Oh, won't you go out with me? Please? I really like you—'"

He slapped her, hard, his own face reddening like it did when he was on the verge of tears.

"You fucking bastard, I'll tell Mama you slapped me," she yelled, but she was already gone, slamming the door to her bedroom. My heart was pounding, but in a little while I would go to her and offer to let her brush my hair. That always calmed her down.

"You're sweet," Ted said, his face still brilliant, though he wasn't crying. He slid over next to me at the kitchen table. "How come? How come you're not mean like the others?"

"I don't know," I whispered. Babette's room was the nearest to the kitchen, and I didn't want her to hear us talking, to think I was siding with Ted.

He smiled, his color fading. "You're just a little kid, I guess. You don't understand any of this, do you?"

I looked down at my spelling words.

"You want to sit on my lap?" he asked.

"It's okay," I said, still looking down.

My mother would come home soon. She would fry up some liver, she would re-heat a potato and cabbage casserole, and I would knock on Babette's door. *You're the only one I can stand,* she would say, and she would let me play with her cheerleading trophies—she had four now— while she brushed my hair, stroke after stroke until her hands stopped shaking. People at school remembered Ted; they said, oh, you're Ted Moore's sister—as if she weren't also the twins' sister, the twins, who had been the most popular girls in the school and whom, in her dark, olive-skinned beauty, Babette obviously resembled, but no one remembered them—and she had to work to have friends; she had to fix every queer thing Ted had ever said or done.

I would stay with her until her hands stopped shaking and then Babette, my lovely, wild sister who respected no rules and no authority, would come out with me and we would all sit down to dinner and she would eat my mother's cooking just like the rest of us, she would drink milk, she would pass what she was asked to pass, and she would only leave the table—and then only to do her chore—when the evening news was finished and Walter Cronkite had bid us all goodnight. My mother always put the news on for supper; whenever Walter Cronkite came to the part about Vietnam, she leaned forward slightly, her wide, pale face as hard and motionless as a statue's, her blue eyes glazed. I used to think we watched so we wouldn't forget how important it was not to waste anything, but now I think my mother turned the TV on just to keep Babette and Ted from fighting.

But that night we were spared. We didn't have to watch the news and we didn't have to eat liver; my mother didn't have to keep anyone from fighting. She burst through the door, laughing, while I was still finishing my list of words. Ted had been staring at me for several minutes, as though I needed a proctor, but at the sound of her laughter, he jumped up. "Andy, my man!"

Tall, lanky, with curly brown hair and eyes so narrow they disappeared when he grinned, Ted's only friend in the world, Andy Newell, strode into the kitchen with my mother and clapped Ted on the shoulder. "Ted," he said. "Look at you! Not a mushroom yet—though who am I to judge? The bowels of Widener Library and a sky that darkens at three in the afternoon are hardly better than college-by-correspondence. How are you?"

Ted laughed, his thin, horsy laugh. It was incomprehensible to us that Andy was Ted's friend. Andy had other friends, even girlfriends, and he was at Harvard now; but he and Ted had been best friends since kindergarten—it was Andy who had given Ted his name, when the other children on the playground made fun of him because his real name, Thierry, sounded just like what he was: teary—and all through grade school and junior high and high school they had been the two smartest boys in their class.

"I met him on the sidewalk," our mother said. "He has finished up his exams."

"Lucky you," Ted said.

"C'mon, what've you got left? Phys. Ed.? How do they do that by correspondence anyway?"

Ted swatted him on the arm and Andy, laughing, looked down suddenly. "Who have we here? What mayhem have you been stirring up lately?"

I blushed. "I've got a spelling bee tomorrow."

"A spelling bee?" He lifted me out of my chair and swung me onto his shoulders. "Fear not," he said, patting my knee. "You shall prevail." And then he swung me off again and set me on the floor. "My mother sent over piroshkis, Mrs. Moore. I don't know what you were planning for supper, but anyway you can freeze these."

"We will eat the piroshkis tonight if you will stay with us," my mother said, squeezing his arm.

"She's sorry she couldn't bring them over herself, she wasn't feeling well."

My mother shook her head sadly. "Your poor mother," she murmured.

"Yeah, well," Andy said.

Mrs. Newell, who was Russian, was a great cook, but she was always sick. I thought the friendship between Andy and Ted must have something to do with both of them having foreign mothers. Mrs. Newell left

Russia when she was five and barely spoke a word of Russian, but still there was that strangeness about her, a sense that she smelled different from the other mothers—women with lipstick and nylon stockings who seemed to take a narcotic pleasure in their own knowledge of house-keeping products and who, upon learning that my mother was French, always sent their voices up a few registers to exclaim how well I must eat at home.

Babette appeared at her bedroom door, straight across from the kitchen. "Hey," she said. With Andy there, she wouldn't let on that she was mad. She wanted Andy to like her and for a moment, watching her lean against her doorframe with her black hair hanging all the way down to the crook of her elbow, I thought she and Ted might give up fighting. With Andy there, the three of them could have fun together, and I could tag along, joining in whatever they did around town.

Andy's eyes widened for a second. "Hey yourself," he said, grinning. "What are you up to this summer?"

"France," Babette said. "What else?"

We all spoke of going to France for the summer as if it were a punishment. Other children got to sit around their pools, or at the very least their television sets, but we had to visit an old uncle with a port wine stain on the side of his face who had a chalet in the Alps. There were no other children around for miles, and though you could see Mont Blanc in the distance, there was not much to do besides play cards and go on hikes and we hated it.

That was the official version anyway. Secretly, I loved it. There were blueberries everywhere, and the cool, damp air, and because there was no refrigerator and no running water, all we could eat were picnic foods—bread and cheese and fruit and pastries. The chalet had electricity and Babette brought her 45's of Janis Joplin and Ike and Tina Turner and Cat Stevens, and with no one else to distract her, she danced in the granary with me for hours.

"Don't have your license yet?" Andy asked.

"I'm fifteen," Babette said.

"Oh well," Andy said. "Next summer."

Once we had a license we were free to stay home with our father and use our mother's car to get to a job, but for one more summer, Babette was stuck. Even if we promised to take the bus, our father didn't want the risk of one us being stranded and calling for a ride.

"Your mom sent piroshkis?" Babette asked.

Andy nodded. "I can't believe you're not sixteen yet. You look like you should be in college."

Babette grinned and gave a little shrug; then she straightened herself and walked towards Andy. They were just watching each other, like she was coming down a runway towards him, and my heart was pounding: she was going to steal Andy from Ted. They weren't going to be a threesome, she and Andy would turn away from Ted. She was looking at Andy like they shared a secret, knew some joke none of the rest of us knew, and I wanted her to go back to her room now, to stay there all night the way she did when I couldn't console her. My eyes stung, but she kept on walking towards him, smiling, as if there were miles and miles between her bedroom and the kitchen, and none of us said a word, each of us as riveted as Andy. I hated her and I hated Andy too, though a little less, because I didn't think he realized he would end up ditching Ted; but Babette wasn't stupid: she knew perfectly well she was about to steal the only person who had ever liked Ted.

And then, at the last minute, she stopped. She didn't even reach up to hug Andy. She looked over at Ted and scowled. "It's your turn to set the table," she said, and once more she was just a bratty kid, maddening and impossible.

I stared at her, transfixed. She had done it on purpose. She had deliberately made herself ugly. Andy was a college student—a Harvard student—handsome and popular and he liked her. He would have driven her all around town, let her do anything she wanted and all she had to do was keep smiling. But she had stopped because he was Ted's. I don't know how I knew this, but I was certain. I am still certain: Babette was the most generous person I have ever known, and her generosity terrified me, because I knew I could never be like her. I would never make myself unappealing just so that a boy who belonged to someone else wouldn't want me. I couldn't take my eyes off her, slumped in her chair, looking at no one.

That night, after Babette had done the dishes and Andy had left, after I had set a place for my father for when he came home—placing the plate and the cup and the silverware just so and writing up a menu for him—a menu I decorated with hearts and flowers and vines, *liver à la suprême, tripe superbe*, except tonight it was *Madame Newell's world-famous piroshkis*, sometimes starting over three or four times and hiding the wasted paper from my mother—Babette climbed into my bed. I had heard her through the wall that separated our two rooms, talking with a boy on the phone. She still had the princess phone my parents had gotten her for her thirteenth birthday, when she was a cheerleader. It was the only thing she'd kept from those days, besides the trophies themselves. Sleek and plastic, it sat by her incense holders and her collection of puzzle rings on an overturned crate, a bright pink missile to the outside world. "But why?" she had said. "I can sneak out. It won't matter—please. Please, David. Don't hang up, please. David?"

"Can I sleep with you, Molly?"

I burrowed into the crack between the bed and the wall, to make room for her and because I liked it there. She started to cry and after awhile I could see my mother's shadow in the crack at the bottom of the door. I willed my mother to go away, because Babette would only yell at her; because, even if she didn't, my mother would say, a little sharply, it's nothing, Babette. Nothing to cry over. Just a boy. And then, I was afraid, Babette would hurt our mother. I thought she would claw and hit our mother just like she did Ted.

My mother stood perfectly still, deciding.

After a long time, her shadow moved, and then it moved again, and she had gone; I took a deep breath, drinking in the salty smell of Babette's sobs.

And then, in 1972, they vanished. We had Easter dinner together that year; it was the last time I remember all of us being together—the twins, Ted, Babette, me, my mother and father and grandmother. The twins were home for spring break and for the first time I was embarrassed by them: they looked like Republicans. Babette, who could almost have been their triplet, had black hair down to her waist now; she wore pretty, embroidered blouses with nothing underneath and a pair of hip hugger bell bottoms she took pride in never washing. Claire and Yvonne still had short, teased hair in the kind of bouffant Babette hadn't had since she was fourteen, and they were both wearing flared pantsuits, the way, it seemed to me, Republicans did, trying to look mod without being hippies; I didn't know there were Democrats who dressed that way, too.

The twins had driven all the way from New York, arriving just in time to go to Easter mass with my mother and Ted and me. Babette didn't go to church at all anymore, preferring to stay home with Daddy. He'd never been to mass in his life, though he sat quiet and upright in the living room for an hour or two every Sunday, conducting his own private Quaker meeting—after the war he no longer felt that he could be a member of the Society of Friends, but he was still, in his own way, the boy he had been, and he liked an hour or so of pure silence. Babette said she liked that better than mass, too, though she mostly kept quiet by sleeping.

The five of us came home from church, and before we were through the front door, Claire said she and Yvonne wanted to make Easter dinner and my mother said how nice, thinking they'd prepare whatever meal she herself had been planning; but Yvonne said they'd just run and get a couple of things from the store first.

"We do not need anything," my mother said. She was holding open the door, waiting for us to pass through. Ted was standing next to her in a suit and tie, his red hair still as bright as mine, and too short to be fashionable, though it never occurred to me that he looked like a Republican. He was too sad and clumsy to belong to any group; and he didn't need to be standing there, waiting for our mother and the twins to finish their conversation; he ought to just go on in the house, and yet we both stood there, Ted and I, waiting. Next to our mother, with her large, mottled arms and the blue church dress she'd been letting out, inch by inch every year for decades, he looked like Jack Spratt.

"It won't take a minute," Claire said, heading back towards the car with Yvonne.

"But what do we need?" my mother asked, her voice suddenly high and soft.

A whole ham, as it turned out, and Pillsbury pop'n fresh dough biscuits. A new head of iceberg lettuce, bottled French dressing, instant mashed potatoes, frozen corn, red and orange jell-o for jell-o salad, and a jell-o no-bake cheesecake.

My mother stood in the kitchen while they carried in their armloads of provisions. She had watched them from the kitchen window as they came down the walk, an old woman, I thought, though she wasn't even fifty, and as she stood there, leaning her weight against the sink, her eyes glistening, I was suddenly terrified that she would die.

She pulled things out of the bags before Claire and Yvonne set them down. "This—" She said, holding out the box of mashed potatoes in one hand, the bottled dressing in the other. "This! We have, we have— *vous n'avez aucune idée!* I will prepare the dinner, you return, and return—" But she didn't expect anyone to return anything; she was terrified of shopkeepers. Her eyes welled up with tears and the twins just stood, wide-eyed and silent. "There are some kidneys in the Frigidaire," she said at last. "Perfectly nice kidneys. They have to be eaten today."

And then she disappeared into her room, staying there even when the doorbell rang and my father went to greet his mother. He bent down to kiss her cheek and take her coat, my size six grandmother with her Texan accent and her baby blue suit, her thick, gold jewelry. She was of course a Republican, not because she listened to the news and thought the Republicans were better equipped to run the country, but because her social clubs were all Republican. In the level of our political sophistication, my grandmother and I were perfectly matched.

"Where's Jeanine?" My grandmother demanded.

"Resting," my father said.

My grandmother arched her eyebrows. "Seems to me she ought to do a little less resting, a little more moving around. The reason I have kept my figure, Henry, is because I'm active."

"Well now, Mother. Come on in. Come and have a seat."

My father gave me her coat and put his hand on the small of her back, guiding her from the entryway around the half wall that separated it from the formal living room where he would sit with her until dinner was ready, asking her about her joints, her night vision, her breathing. He inclined his head towards her and nodded every now and then, as if he were a doctor. My grandmother was in excellent health but I believed she was as sick as sick could be because my father plied her so lovingly for news of all her organs and appendages and she

18

responded in such detail and at such enormous length.

"See?" my grandmother said. "See how my elbow makes this clicking sound? Now my knee makes exactly the same sound, and they're both on the left side, that's what concerns me, Henry. And when I have gas it's on the left side, and headaches, too, and I saw on the TV—" She broke off, catching sight of me across the half wall where I was pushing her coat into the closet. "Don't push that in like that, Molly. Take the other ones out and put mine in gently, it's worth a lot more than those other coats. That's right. Like that." She laughed. "New clothes have got to be treated differently from old ones, sugar. If people like me didn't take care of our clothes, your mother wouldn't have anything to send overseas and all those African children would still be completely naked. Oh don't look at me like that Henry. I'm not talking about colored people, I'm talking about pure blooded African children and they do run around naked. You still crying, sugar?"

She asked me that every time I saw her because when I was five and my parents sent me to visit her in Corpus Christi, I had cried every day and every night.

"Claire and Yvonne look like Republicans," I said, standing in Babette's doorway, where I had been sent to call her to dinner. She had her black light on, but she was buried beneath a mound of covers.

She pushed herself up with one arm. "What do you mean?"

"Like bouffant hairdos and stuff."

"Gross. Do you think they really are?"

I shrugged and she lay back down. "Is it really time?"

"Grandmother's here and dinner's ready."

"Fuck."

"The twins bought all this food. Like ham and mashed potatoes and stuff."

She sat completely up this time. "What did Mama say?"

I didn't like to discuss Mama with Babette, so I just shrugged. "I don't know. I think she just wants us to eat the kidneys, too."

"Well fuck if I am."

"Well I don't want to be the only one," I said.

She sighed. "You want me to talk to Mama? You want me to tell her you should get to eat what you want on Easter?"

"No," I said hastily. "No. Couldn't we just all eat a little of the kidneys?"

"No, sweetie. No I really can't. Not when there's ham and mashed potatoes."

"Please?"

"No—oh, God." She had tried to stand up too quickly. "I don't know if I can eat anything." She was sitting on the edge of her bed, holding her head in her hands. You could see her breasts through her grey tee-shirt, and her underwear was black and silky. "Fuck. Will you help me, Molly? Find a skirt or something I can put on and then I'll just go to the bathroom. Tell them they can start without me."

But my mother wouldn't, of course. She had emerged from her bedroom to preside over the ham all laid out with slices of pineapple and maraschino cherries and the kidneys nestled together in a casserole dish, dark and fragrant and shameful. There were circles under her eyes so dark it looked as if she'd been punched, but she said nothing, only that we should wait, and she stood at the foot of the table with a serving spoon in one hand, looking at no one, as if she might stand there all day.

My father and Ted sat with their heads bowed, the one so dark and handsome and broad-shouldered, the other so skinny and pale; but Claire and Yvonne and my grandmother played with their silverware and sighed and every few minutes craned their heads to see if Babette was coming.

"Let's begin," my father said at last. "We can't wait all day."

"Molly," my mother said. "Go to see if Babette is almost ready."

"No," my father said, and I thought how hard my mother tried to please Babette and how, for all Babette's tantrums, she preferred our father.

My mother sighed, the circles beneath her eyes seeming to grow deeper, and took my grandmother's plate, offering her a bit of everything except the kidneys, which she put on everyone's plate without asking. But Claire and Yvonne, chastened, asked only for kidneys and potatoes and though I expected my mother to say something, to reprimand them for wasting the ham, she didn't.

"I wanted to tell you all something," Yvonne said, smiling. "I've decided to go by Pat."

Ted laughed, showing his food. "What? Like the First Lady?"

"Like my middle name," Yvonne-Pat said irritably.

"I think that's very nice," my grandmother said. "It's much more sensible to have an American name if you're going to live in America. I always thought you did the right thing, Jeanine, by calling Marie Molly. Of course you could have just called her Mary, that's nicer than Molly, but American names are just better for American children. Remember when Ted had that awful name no one could pronounce?"

"Thierry," my mother said, grimly.

"Teary, that's right. Well, Ted is just an enormous improvement. What I don't understand is Babette—I love that girl, but I can not say her name without thinking Baboon. If it's short for Elizabeth, why not Beth or Liz or Lisa? Good for you, Pat. I for one am tickled that you have the same name as the First Lady. I know I stand alone that way, but *I* think it's an honor."

"I think it's an honor, too," Yvonne-Pat said, blushing.

"You do?" I blurted out, horrified.

"Oh Molly, don't you get started on things you don't understand," Claire said, laughing.

"So," my father said. "The two of you are Young Republicans now. Well! I suppose you have boyfriends who are Republicans. Forgive me, Mother, but in this case it hardly seems a matter of politics. These two have always done things in tandem, and now their ability to think or function independently has been further hampered, I gather, by the attentions of young men."

"Daddy," Claire began.

"Have you a boyfriend?" my father asked.

"Well, I—"

"And is he a Republican?"

"Yes, but Daddy."

"And you? Patricia?"

"It's not because—"

"Oh girls," my father said. "Girls. You're all the same. It's remarkable, really. When you're Molly's age, you can still think for yourselves, but then it's all over. A man comes to call, and you follow him blindly, in thought and deed. 'For a man's attention/ Brings such satisfaction/

To the craving in my bones.' That's Yeats, of course, and it's no surprise it took a man to say it.

"Now the exception, interestingly, are prostitutes. No, no, mother. Now, listen. I've had quite a few in my courtroom—naturally they're involved in all sorts of crimes—and I will say this for them: they think for themselves. They are not impressed by any man, not even the one who will determine whether they shall go to jail or be free. You never encounter that kind of toughness—that fierceness of spirit—anywhere else."

I listened to my father talk about the spinelessness of women, the fierceness of prostitutes, and I was pleased because he had singled me out, he had said that girls my age still thought for themselves. Ted was watching him gravely and I knew he was glad, too, to be exempted from my father's criticism, but he didn't realize that if my father didn't look down on him for being a girl, he didn't respect him, either. My mother, I remember, was simply gazing at her food.

"As a matter of fact," my father continued, wiping the corners of his mouth, "I have occasionally paid a prostitute for her time."

"Henry!" my grandmother exclaimed.

"For her time, Mother. I am well aware that in conversing with me, she is foregoing other income-producing—"

"Henry!"

My mother was quietly spearing a potato with her fork.

"It is worthwhile to converse with them, Mother. We could all benefit from it. We could all stand to learn from those who think for themselves, even if their thoughts are not always complex."

"Henry, I forbid you," my grandmother said, but just then Babette appeared, grinning wildly, and my grandmother jumped up and kissed her. "My very favorite grandchild," she said, as if she expected Babette to provide us all with a new topic of conversation. "You look just like something the cat dragged in, and you are late late late, but still I could just eat you up!"

The ham and potatoes and biscuits were gone, for we were all quick eaters; all that remained was some corn and, on every plate except my mother's and the twins', a lone kidney.

"Hey Grandma," Babette said, sitting down beside her. "Hey Claire, hey Yvonne."

"It's Pat," my grandmother said happily. "She's going by her middle name now."

"As in Nixon?" Babette asked, and she began to laugh hysterically, and I had to look down at my plate and focus on my kidney so as not to join her.

"Well," Ted said, clearing his throat. "I, too, have an announcement." He spoke formally, the way our father did, and I knew that, in fact, he was the best educated among us, that although he wouldn't leave his room to go to college, he read more than anyone. He could have quoted Yeats as easily as our father.

"I've decided to join up."

"Join what?" I asked, afraid for him, the way he spoke as if you could just join anything you wanted, without being asked.

"The Army?" my mother asked, her eyes wide with fear.

"Good for you," Pat said. "I think that's admirable."

"The Navy, actually, and I'm not a Republican," Ted said, coldly. "I'm not affiliated with either party. I simply think it's important to serve."

My father was shaking his head and Babette looked as if she might be sick.

"But Ted," my mother began, and then Babette let out a short, hard laugh.

"You're going to join up?" Babette asked. "The Navy?"

"The Navy, yes."

"The Navy. Jesus. Jesus, Ted. Why not just stay here? Why not stay here and kill people? Why travel so far?"

My mother reached across the table and slapped Babette, her fingers streaking across Babette's jaw. She had never hit any of us before, and though I loved Babette, I was relieved: whatever I had dreamed, my mother loved Ted.

"Well," Babette said, getting up from the table. "Fuck you all, too."

She slammed the door of her bedroom and I remember that my father closed his eyes and sat perfectly still, shaking in furious Quaker silence at the head of the table. My mother's face was as expressionless as if she'd suffered a stroke.

"My goodness," Claire said. "I didn't drive all this way to hear that kind of language on Easter Sunday."

Everyone was fighting then, even our grandmother, who said Babette just needed a whipping, as if my mother hadn't basically given her one. Mama burst into tears, and it was not a figure of speech: she seemed to explode, tears coming out of every pore in her body, but no one did anything, and I couldn't touch her with my grandmother there; I couldn't do anything with my grandmother watching.

My father spoke at last, his voice as calm as if he were in his robes. "I am deeply disappointed," he said, shaking his head. Pat said some fathers would be proud and Ted said, "Of what? A daughter who tells everyone to fuck off?"

I slipped away then, because I could not touch my mother. I went to visit Babette in her smoky, black-lit room, and she told me she was leaving, too, that she and her boyfriend had decided to move to Berkeley.

"Not that anybody gives a shit around here," she said. "I could kill myself and nobody'd notice. Except you, Molly. You'd notice, you're the only one. But I've gotta go, sweetie. Gotta hit the road."

CHAPTER

That summer we didn't go to France. My mother canceled the trip as if, by staying home, she could hold onto Babette and Ted. June was a month of slamming doors in which even my father partic- ipated, a month during which, out of an odd sense of decorum, everyone hushed as soon as I entered the room. I took to stationing myself outside their doors.

Babette was on the pill, and refused to go off. No one spoke of sex or virginity, and I wasn't sure if Babette and her boyfriend, Justin, had had sex. It might have been the pill itself my parents objected to. My mother said peel, wanting to know exactly how long Babette had been on it.

"And you weel not stop?"

"Then that settles it," my father said. "If that's the life she wants."

"Enree."

"No, Jeanine. I've had enough. I am washing my hands of this affair."

He washed his hands more easily of Ted. I don't remember any arguments between the two of them about the military; only that my father, home more often now since Babette was causing so much trouble, seemed more irritated than usual with Ted. Ted would go up to him when he was at the kitchen table, reading the newspaper or gazing out over a cup of coffee, and try to start some conversation—about basic training or military intelligence—and my father would just keep reading or gazing as if Ted hadn't spoken at all. And so Ted would repeat himself. He repeated himself until my father snapped, "I'm not interested in this," and then, blushing, Ted always looked over at me, as if I might know what to do next.

But as with my mother and the flowers, I couldn't bring myself to tell Ted the truth—that my father meant exactly what he said—and so I said nothing at all. I might even have looked away.

I wondered sometimes if what irritated my father most was Ted's plan to go to Vietnam, or that anyone should talk to him when Babette was on the pill. Only Babette, sulking all day in her room where my parents now regularly visited her, seemed to care that Ted was in danger. It was she who pointed out again and again that if he managed to avoid getting blood on his hands, it would be because he was dead.

Through the door I could hear my mother sighing. Once, she said, "That is the reesk a soldier takes," and her resignation terrified me. What had become of her tears at Easter Dinner?

I didn't know that her tears and her resignation were of a piece, that war was the only thing she was completely certain of—as if she had dreamed everything since D-day, even her own children, who could fornicate without conception.

"I can't believe you all are jumping on me about the goddamned pill when Ted's about to join the fucking Navy."

"You sound as if you've already joined it," my father said wearily. "The language you use."

"Enree."

They had the same fight every day and I sat in the hallway, riveted, the gold plush carpet growing between my toes. It was too hot to go outside; Buttercup lay all day beneath the picnic table, panting, and though I thought I ought to go out and rub his belly, try to cheer him up, I couldn't bear to miss the sounds of Babette's and my parents' voices, the sound, that particular afternoon, of Ted's. Ted mostly kept to his room, but every now and then he joined the fight. He had started it, after all: he'd told our parents that Babette was on the pill. Every afternoon for weeks, he'd watched her punch the little pink tablet out of its foil backing while she sat at the kitchen table, trying to decide what to watch on TV, what snack to make for herself and me, and now he had exacted his revenge. Only I don't think he thought of it that way. There was something besides loathing that bound them to each other, some furious concern; he was worried about her.

The night she realized it was he who had ruined her life (what had she imagined before? That I had?) she slapped him over and over until he grabbed her hands and she clawed at his face, tearing the skin; but now, with the four of them sequestered in her room, it was my parents she hated, for letting Ted do whatever he wanted.

I couldn't believe it—that she would forgive Ted, allow him in her room, where he sat like a third parent, admonishing her. I couldn't believe my father would tolerate Ted's presence in the midst of his battle with Babette. Somehow, by tattling on her, he had earned parental rights. Or was it because none of them expected him to live? I don't know. I didn't think of death; loneliness was the worst fate I could imagine.

"I'm twenty-one," Ted was saying. "That's the difference."

"So when I'm twenty-one it doesn't matter if I go on a killing spree? Doesn't matter if I get my legs blown off, but now, if I take a goddamned birth control pill—"

"That's enough," my father said. "I don't expect you to have any sense when it comes to boys, no girl does; but you are still a minor, and I will not permit you to abandon your studies nor, since you are so fond of calling a spade a spade, to screw around."

"Enree! Stop!"

"All right then, Jeanine. You solve this, you—"

He would storm out any minute now, so I slipped into the bathroom. I wanted to console him, to let him know that I at least still had principles, morals. I put the lid down on the toilet and sat perched on it, my knees drawn up to my chin. For a long time I tried to think of something I could do, some way to show him that the world hadn't gone to the dogs. That was what he said if he was home in time for the news: the world had gone to the dogs. He shook his head when he said it, his eyes glued to the television set—he didn't sit down or take off his coat, he just shook his head, and it seemed to me his heart was breaking. It must be terrible for him, who did all he could to see that the criminals who came before him were rehabilitated instead of punished, who stayed at the courthouse sometimes until midnight, and hardly ever rested. All that effort, and still the news was bad every night, still his children fought against him.

Once there had been a story on TV about a Japanese soldier who'd been hiding on an island in the Pacific for over twenty-five years, unaware that the war was over. I felt sick hearing about it. I hated it when people didn't realize what was going on, when they didn't get things; but then the TV showed a picture of a wild, scrawny man and Walter Cronkite said the soldier was ashamed, because he had fought so poorly for his emperor, and my father made a sound I'd never heard before. I looked up and saw him standing behind my mother with his hat and coat over his arm, weeping. I wasn't embarrassed to see him cry; it comforted me the way it comforted me when he worked late: somehow he would fix all of this, he would make it so that people didn't even have wars anymore.

But now Ted was going to fight the Vietnamese and Babette hardly cared about anything except boys.

And then it came to me: I would become a vegetarian; then my father would know that I was opposed to killing, and that I was too thoughtful to be boy crazy.

I left the bathroom and crossed the house, hurrying so that I wouldn't be intercepted by one of the others.

"Daddy," I said, knocking tentatively on his study door. "Daddy?"

"What the hell is it?" he asked, but still I pushed open his door. He was sitting at his desk, his face white with rage.

"I wanted to tell you, I'm thinking of becoming a vegetarian."

He glared at me. "Get out. Get the hell out, Molly."

I don't know where I went. My room would have been too far to reach in the time I had to vanish, the back yard too visible; all I remember is hours later, when the house was dark and silent, sitting on the floor of my bedroom thinking, *he thought it was about Mama's cooking. He didn't understand.*

It was very late and I hadn't eaten much supper. My mother had fried up some eggs and brains, but no one but I had come to the table.

I'd thought I'd have to eat it all, to make up for the others, but she was too distracted to notice how much I took, and all I'd managed was a spoonful. Anyway, I was a vegetarian now. I got up, thinking I'd fix myself a peanut butter and jelly sandwich—that was all I'd eat for the rest of my life, then he'd see—they'd all see—how serious I was—and I crept out towards the kitchen.

But Ted was there, on the phone.

I stopped in the dark and listened; he was on the verge of tears.

"I just thought, since I'll be shipping out. Well, just a movie then. Just one movie, Jesus. It's all I'm asking. Goddamnit." He stood with the phone in his hand, staring at it; then he hung it up and looked through the phone book. "Carol? Carol Wilson? It's Ted, Ted Moore, from high school. Yeah, I know it's late. Listen, I'm heading off to Vietnam."

The next two times, he got the girls' fathers. The girls were long gone and the fathers had no patience with him. He sat down at the kitchen table and put his head in his hands and wept. I stood in the dark, not making a sound.

By the end of June, Ted and Babette were gone. Babette had taken her GED and my parents, defeated, had let her go to Berkeley. She was living on Telegraph Avenue, above a Top Dog, where you could eat all the free condiments you wanted whether you bought a hot dog or not. She ate sauerkraut three times a day and never spent a cent.

Ted went to the Great Lakes Naval Training Center, his head so shorn and pink it looked raw, and when he left he cried, but no one else did, not even my mother. I dreamt about him all the time, but in the mornings I talked myself out of it: the Navy would be full of boys like him—who else, now that the draft was over?—and he'd make friends. Surely in the Navy he'd make friends.

I spent the rest of the summer alone, with no one to eavesdrop on. Sometimes I accompanied my mother on her trips around town, my feet up against the scorched dashboard of the Plymouth station wagon, our windows down to stir the singeing air; but the truth was, we both preferred it when I stayed home. My mother never minded solitude, and I hated driving around, helping her beg for clothes. Even if I stayed in the car, it was terrible to watch her work: a fat, shabbily dressed woman who, if she had to, could stand all day on some slender house-wife's front stoop, waiting for that housewife to answer her knock and gaze down at her, wide-eyed, almost alarmed.

I never said I didn't want to go with her, and she never said she liked to drive around alone, but more often than not she let me sleep, and left me sweet notes, saying she hadn't wanted to disturb me, and I should enjoy my vacation.

I worried about Ted in a constant, aching sort of way. Even if he did make friends, they'd all be geeks. He'd never *learn*. Then I remembered Andy Newell. Ted had a popular friend—which meant that it was all right, even natural, for me to prefer my sister to my brother. Ted wasn't alone and I could stop worrying. I could go in Babette's room and try on her clothes; I could entertain myself for hours rummaging through her shelves and drawers. I was relieved almost to the point of tears because I, too, was on the verge of a brand new life: I was about to start junior high.

My new school's very name sent pins and needles to my arms and sped up my heart beat: O'Henry Junior High, bridesmaid to the high school. I was done with elementary school forever. I was as small as a nine-year-old, my breasts as insignificant as my hip-bones, my skin as transparent as water, but Babette's room contained everything I needed to transform myself and I looted freely. I took a half-empty box of tampax which I wouldn't need for another three years, an old pot baggie containing seeds and stems, and two books: *The Kama Sutra* and *Everything You Always Wanted to Know About Sex, But Were Afraid to Ask*. I didn't take Babette's journals, but I studied them. They were mostly filled with elaborate line drawings she had made with her rapidiograph pen—whorls and petals and waves and cubes—but if she had had a date she wrote the boy's name over and over again and noted a few details. *Friday Steve and I balled by the lake, it was a full moon.* I thought about that word, balled, picturing a beach ball, though I knew it meant sex, and I wondered how close they lay to the lake, if the ground was wet, if the water lapped against them. I don't remember ever being told about the mechanics of sex—it seems to me I always knew, and knew the words for sex, even though what I pictured was simply an insertion, the genitals hairless and cartoon-like, but the lake was something new, and fascinating. It clarified for me that sex was a lying down proposition, though I don't know why, what clue it contained to any position.

I put the baggy and the tampons at the back of my sock drawer—I wanted to save the marijuana so I could share it with someone, but I read the sex books over and over. Or rather, I opened them over and over. Nothing in those books interested me as much as the idea of having a gym uniform and a locker combination. I liked having the books in my room—owning them, as I thought—and it was thrilling to see those words, penis and vagina, in print. But actually reading more than a sentence or two was impossible. I'd get stuck on the same incomprehensible passage for an hour sometimes: *"As a woman approaches orgasm the whole pace of her body accelerates. The heart rate zooms up to 160 or more. Respiration gives way to panting and groaning. Blood pressure can double. In the meantime, the pelvis is going wild."* Or: *"When the lingam is in the yoni, and moved up and down frequently without being taken out, this is referred to as the sporting of a sparrow and takes place at the end of congress."* I had no more idea what a pelvis was than a lingam. I didn't even like the pictures in *The Kama Sutra*, those expressionless, sideways faces, those soft bodies. But I loved the bindings, the covers, the books' presence under my bed.

Still, even such bounty wasn't quite enough, after all. I needed a few more objects before I could start junior high: makeup and a new outfit, neither of which my mother would ever pay for. My closet was full of Babette's hand me downs, clothes she'd worn in 1965, when she was ten: Snoopy themed tee-shirts, a red and black plaid jumper, a bright orange culotte jumpsuit, penny loafers. It could have been worse; if Babette had not regularly worn my mother down with demands for spending money, I would have been wearing the twins' knee-length kilts. Still, I needed something.

I called Mrs. Anderson, at the end of our cul-de-sac, and asked if she needed a babysitter. She had boys my age, but no girls to watch her two-year-old. I earned seventy five cents an hour reading to Trudy and watching over her in the kiddie pool in the back yard while the boys watched TV inside. I had to sit in the pool myself to stay half-way comfortable and I could see the pee slipping down Trudy's leg, but I was entertained by her baby voice and her feverish delight when she splashed me, and by the middle of August I'd earned twenty-five dollars.

I walked to the shopping center at Cassis, further than I'd ever walked alone, and though the air pressed down, scalding and damp, as if the sky were the exhaust vent of some giant Laundromat, I was happy. This was much better than France. Down to the end of our street, right on Mountain Laurel Lane, left on Mountain Laurel Drive, and right on Exposition. My head throbbed, but I was there.

I pushed open the door to the dress shop and a sudden icy breeze washed over me. But TOTS TO TEENS was small and the carpet was thick, the women's voices on the other side of the store hushed and dreamy; girls did not walk in there alone with heat-blanched faces and sweaty scalps. I felt shy, but I had come so far, and no one told me to leave. I lingered awhile near the big girl racks; I wore an 8/9, which was not so bad. It was better than 6X, where I had hovered for years. For awhile I couldn't quite see the clothes—sweat stung my eyes and I started to see spots—but then my breathing slowed, I was even cold, and I chose a beige polyester blouse with ruffles down the front, a brown polyester knit skirt, a pair of artificial suede brown shoes with hollow, two-inch heels.

I don't know what I was thinking. Nothing said Republican like my new polyester outfit and though Austin was still Texas, I'd grown up with Babette; I'd gone with her to the Drag, with its jewelry and incense selling venders, I'd even accompanied her to the campus free clinic once, though I hadn't known the purpose of our trip. Maybe I understood that Babette couldn't help me now, that as thrilling as the prospect of junior high was, it wasn't yet total freedom. The girls in my class would still be watched over by their mothers, their outfits scrutinized, and I wanted those girls to like me.

But more likely I couldn't tell what was wrong with that beige and brown polyester outfit, anymore than I knew what a sporting sparrow was. It was in earth tones, that was the cool thing, and the shop keeper, pretending to ignore the burst of heat and sweat I had brought into the store, assured me that it was very nice and that brown was such a good color for red heads. I bought a pot of strawberry lip gloss, too, and a little compact of pale blue eye shadow.

But I was sad on the way home. Time seemed to stand perfectly still, the way it does when the heat is unbearable. I pushed through the hot shadeless hour with my plastic bag swinging damply against my leg and I was sad because shopping was frivolous; I had never done anything against my mother before and now I had, and for what? Everything looked so pretty in the store, but now they were just things, and Babette would never come home and what would become of Ted?

When I got home I put the bag of clothes at the bottom of my closet and went outside with a glass of ice water to sit in the hot, scratchy grass near Buttercup. He came out from under the bushes to lay his soft head in my lap. After a while he licked my legs, my neck, the side of my face. It was sticky and warm and it did nothing to cool me down, but I would have liked him to lick me for hours, to absolve me of the sin of shopping.

A week or two before school began, when there was almost nothing left to do to prepare myself—I had my outfit and my makeup, my mother had taken me to buy whatever school supplies we didn't already have lying around the house—my father said I could come with him to the courthouse.

"When?" I asked, my chest already tightening.

"Tomorrow," he said, loosening his tie; it was a Sunday night and I'd gone to his study to say goodnight to him. My mother would come to my room and kiss me and then I'd stay up for a few hours, looking at my sex books and all my other treasures, or writing in a blank note-book I'd found in Babette's room.

"You'll have to behave," he added and I said that of course I would, I promised.

I'd been to the courthouse when I was small, with my mother, and I'd seen my father in his robes, but I'd never sat in on a trial before; I'd never gone there alone with my father, to watch him. I don't know what prompted his invitation unless my mother had finally told him that I needed some kind of activity—or perhaps he'd seen himself that all I was doing, besides babysitting Trudy now and then, was rummaging around all day in my room and in Babette's.

In the morning, we rode together in silence and I watched the way his hands rested so lightly, so knowingly on the steering wheel, and how the blast of the air conditioner raised the dark hairs on his wrists. I would have to spend the morning sitting quietly in the hallway until court was called to session, but I didn't mind. The benches in the hallway were hard as church pews and my feet did not reach the floor, grownups smoked above me, getting more and more impatient, and no one was happy but me, but I was, I was so happy.

When I had been sitting there for two hours and my bottom was asleep and my legs were numb, a woman dressed all in pink asked if I'd like to have lunch with her. Her fingernails looked like tiny rose petals and her bow-shaped lips matched the pink of her skirt; the pink of her blouse was darker. "I'm Miss Barrett," she smiled. "The court coordinator. Your father thought you might be hungry."

I was starving, but I didn't want to go downstairs to the coffee shop with Miss Barrett and be forced to make small talk about what grade I was in and what my hobbies were. I just wanted to sit where I was until court was in session.

"No thanks," I said. "I'm not very hungry, thank you."

Miss Barrett laughed. "Oh, baby. You will be. Come on, sweetheart. Let's get ourselves a couple of cheeseburgers."

I flinched, but clearly I had no choice; and, in fact, it wasn't so bad. Between tiny bites of her sandwich, Miss Barrett said I would just love junior high. I ought to try out for cheerleading, she said, because I had the exact right build for the gymnastics part of it. I could tell she was making up for having mistaken me for a little kid, and I was grateful.

She went on and told me that I must be so proud of my daddy, he was the smartest judge in Travis County, and so handsome, too. She blushed a little when she said how handsome he was and added that she'd been just terrified when she'd been assigned to him—she'd worked for criminal judges before, but never anyone with Judge Moore's reputation—but he was, really, the kindest and most considerate man in the world. You wouldn't expect that from a judge, would you, but he was. Did I know that if a defendant showed up without a coat and tie my father sent him home to change so the jury wouldn't be prejudiced against him? He cared about everyone, my daddy did.

I felt sorry for her because she was exactly the kind of girl my father had no patience for, and I could see that she was sick with love for him, so I told her that I really liked her nail polish.

"Why thank you," she said, wiping the corners of her mouth. "You'll be fixing yourself up soon enough. That's what junior high is all about. What're you're going to wear on your very first day?"

I told her about my new brown polyester outfit in elaborate detail— the little ribbon at the neck, the ruffles down the front of the blouse, the side zipper on the skirt—and I justified the triviality of our conversation on the grounds that Miss Barrett couldn't do any better, and she deserved our sympathy because she would never have the man she loved. Besides, she must be a good court coordinator, or she'd long ago have been fired, and so we all ought to be grateful to her.

"That sounds so pretty," she said, shaking her head, and then she said we'd better hurry on back. We went back upstairs and she disappeared into a side door and I took up my post on the bench again, licking around inside my mouth to taste the last of the cheese and ketchup and pickle, and my heart started pounding a little, because soon it would be time.

After a while the bailiff, an old man with a pencil mustache, came to tell me that court was about to be in session, that I could go and watch my father now. My heart started racing outright, but it wasn't fear. My father had sent someone to me twice, he wanted me to be there, so I wasn't afraid going through the wide doors and up the aisle between the chairs. I sat on my hands, leaning forward slightly, waiting, and though I was drenched with sweat, I smiled at all the other people in the audience, as if I were the hostess. Then, suddenly, there he was, in his black robe, such a beautiful man, taking his seat and inclining his head to all the people below him.

I thought I heard everyone gasp when he came in, but of course they didn't; it was just the sound of everyone rising and sitting back down again and the exhalation of beginning at last, the trial starting, the wheels of justice shifting into gear. My father listened to everything everyone said, even the endless repetition of names, the elaborate and pointless identifying of the defendant, the witnesses, the exhibits; he attended to it all, his wise blue eyes gazing seriously from beneath his dark hair, my father, the Honorable Judge Henry Moore, and when he struck his gavel I could feel it all the way down in my solar plexus.

The lawyers were nothing compared to my father. They were noisy and they gestured foolishly with their hands, as if they didn't know how ordinary they were, how like monkeys.

It was a gruesome case: a man accused of murdering his wife and infant son. The defendant had taken his seat with his face all sad and pock-marked, and all day I wanted to believe he hadn't done it. There wasn't anyone else who could have, according to the Assistant D.A., and yet, still, the man looked so sad, and his complexion seemed to me a proof of innocence, as if such an ugly man could only be a scapegoat. But my stomach hurt, because he probably had done it, and it was awful to look at him even from behind, to see his bowed head and to imagine him shaking his child to death and then strangling his wife. All the public defender had had to say in his opening remarks was that America had a great system of justice.

The defendant never took the stand that day—I don't know if he did some other day or if, by a miracle, another culprit was found and he was acquitted (or better yet, his wife and baby found, unharmed). The day I was there, three policemen testified, and the first was so nervous his mouth seemed to tremble. The Assistant D.A. seemed nervous, too, and I was glad of that. He kept talking to the first policeman about how the defendant had tried to run and the cop had knocked him down; I remember the exact words he said, because they didn't seem right, and later I repeated them to my father. 'Is it fair to say,' the Assistant D.A. asked. 'Did his conduct ensue this action?' What did that mean, I wondered, and what did knocking him down have to do with murder?

My father gazed out over it all, and when I looked at him, I didn't feel as sad. I knew he would make it all right, that he would be kind and fair, and his fearlessness—he was used to murder—gave me courage. Somewhere off in another room, Miss Barrett did her coordinating, and I was glad suddenly that she was so pink and foolish: things couldn't really be as terrible as they seemed. Cheerleading might be passé, but it was nice to know that I looked like a cheerleader, and that my new outfit sounded so pretty. I thought again of how much she admired my father, how the thought of him made her blush, and the case itself began to fade a little. For all I knew, Miss Barrett had gone home after lunch and was somewhere on the other side of town, watching *The Young and the Restless*, but I didn't think so. I imagined her on the other side of the wall, behind the dais, listening to every word.

In the evening, on the way home, I wondered if there was any way

I could ask my father about the case—but of course there wasn't; so I asked him instead about conduct ensuing action. He smiled. "Very good, Molly. You have an ear for grammar."

"What does it mean?"

"Nothing. An ungrammatical sentence is meaningless. To be proper English, the question should have been, 'Did his conduct ensue from this action?' But even that is a convoluted and pretentious way of speaking."

He was silent then, and I knew he didn't want to be disturbed. I wasn't grown up enough, interesting enough, for him to talk to, but I would be; why else would he have invited me to the courthouse? I wondered if eventually he would talk to me about the case—when I was older and it was all over. I wanted him to explain why a man would kill his own child. There might have been some reason he had to, some terrible thing that hadn't come out yet; or maybe it was an accident, all of it, the strangling and the violent shaking, and my father would explain that to me. He would sit me down and in his elegant, deep voice he would transform the man's helpless, pock-marked expression into something pure and noble. He would show me that no one had been killed, or even hurt, and that we all had only one purpose in this life, to make things better for one another; and that although we didn't always go about it in the right way, helping others was still our purpose, what we were all striving to do.

"I was thinking," I said, so he'd know I didn't mind the silence. "Maybe I could stay home on Sundays and have silent worship with you. Instead of going to church."

"Whatever you like," he said mildly, his gaze fixed on the stream of cars, and I could tell he wasn't listening. I wondered if he knew Babette had stayed home all those Sundays and I felt bad about making a plan not to be with my mother. But if I changed my mind now, I'd seem frivolous. Today of all days, I didn't want to annoy him, but I would miss my mother. I hated to think that she might miss me, too, though she'd never say. I loved her and wanted her to be happy; I wanted them all to be happy: my mother and father and Miss Barrett and the defendant and the blank-faced jurors whom I'd barely noticed and even the inarticulate lawyers.

But I could barely keep my eyes open. The man who had killed his wife and child was not happy and my mother was not happy, either; but my father was a good man. He had invited me to go to the court-house because I thought for myself. Soon I would be old enough to be interesting and my mother would be happy, too. I would walk to school by myself, to O'Henry Junior High, with long, cheerleader legs and golden breasts. Outside, the streetlights were coming on, and my head jerked up suddenly, but I let it fall back, let the car's air conditioner pour over me while I slept. When I awoke, we were already pulling into the driveway and everything was all right again: any day now I would be older, and there would be nothing to be afraid of anymore.

The night before school, I took a naked razor blade into the bath and gently scraped the hairs from my leg. How smooth it suddenly was, how perfect my skin—and then my leg seemed to open up and the water turned crimson. It was a beautiful color, and I wasn't afraid, but I called my mother anyway.

"Molly!" she said, seeing all the blood. I was sitting on the edge of the tub now, wrapped in a towel, and blood was still beading down my leg into the bath. "Molly, what have you done?"

"I shaved my leg," I said, and I forced a shrug.

"But are you out of your mind? What *where* you thinking? Molly!"

I shrugged again. "For school," I said. "For school tomorrow."

"But you are a leetle girl, Molly. You don't need to shave! *Vas!* Wipe your legs off and get into the bed. *Vas,* Molly." She paused, and then repeated more gently, "*Vas-y.* I will get the mercurochrome."

In the morning, dressed in a Snoopy culotte jumpsuit—it was too hot for brown polyester—my legs partially shaved and streaked with orange, I walked a mile up Exposition Boulevard to school. To take the bus I would have had to get up even earlier and drive all around town and I had thought it would be fun, walking to school; but by seven the air was already hot and humid, the traffic racing, and I was terrified of being late. I walked as fast as I could, half running along the edge of the road because there was no sidewalk. My book bag bounced against my leg and the roots of my hair were damp, my face oily. On one side of me were the glinting cars, on the other the chain link fence surrounding the Austin State School for the Mentally Retarded. The children were not yet pressed against it, gazing out, as I had seen them so many times from the window of my mother's car, but still the low, brick buildings terrified me.

What had I imagined? That the air would cool down overnight, that I'd walk along a broad sidewalk with my fellow students, all of us relaxed and laughing the whole way? That the state school, half way between our house and O'Henry, would have vanished? Babette once said our parents had gotten Ted from the State School and my mother, trembling and red-faced, sent Babette to her room without any supper, which only made it worse, as if Babette had told the truth. I hated going near there.

I don't know how I found the bathroom that first day, only that it was filled with smoke and that I stood at the sink, wiping my face with wet paper towels and patting my underarms dry. I smelled sour, and my eye shadow was all caked up; I looked nothing like any cheerleader.

A pair of older girls, both blonde and fat, perched on the dusty windowsills with their cigarettes, and stared at me but did not laugh. They never laughed, all through that long, hot fall, though I was there every morning, pulling towel after towel from the dispenser. Sometimes they even nodded hello, and I came to think of them as my friends, for I had no others. The girls who had carried me around the playground in elementary school now carried yellow or pink Papagallo clutch purses to match their buttery soft shoes. They had boy-girl parties to which I was not invited and they whispered feverishly among themselves in the halls. I had no place in their world: going to Tots to Teens by myself, feeling sorry for a murderer, having spent half the summer eavesdropping on my family—all of that was just queer.

Still, it was a surprise to me when, in October, the school held elections for Friendliest Girl and I wasn't nominated. In the afternoons, when the retarded children reached their fingers to me through the fence, I suppressed the urge to shy away; I'd never fought with Babette or Ted; I didn't tell on people. Who was friendlier than I? All week leading up to the announcement of the nominees, I had looked forward to hearing my name read over the loudspeaker. No one spoke to me or raced to my lunch table, no one phoned me up at home, but I'd been certain my name would be called.

And then, just before Thanksgiving, Becky Lopez dropped a note in my lap. It was a carefully folded piece of paper with the edges neatly tucked into each other, about one inch square and thewidth of two quarters. Now and then, Mrs. Morse, our homeroom teacher—a heavy, tired woman with a tight brown perm—snatched up a note from someone's desk and carried it to the front of the class to read aloud. When her hand darted out, a thrill passed through the rest of us—those of us who knew our secrets were not about to be revealed or who, like me, had no secrets—until Mrs. Morse, standing in front of the blackboard, unfolded the sheet of paper and read, *I like Brian* or *Pete is so cute*. A few children always giggled nervously, but once the secret was out I just felt sick, the way I did when a boy was being paddled.

The note was slipping between my legs, but I waited for Mrs. Morse to turn to the board before I touched it.

Mrs. Morse sucks. Write back!

My heart was racing, but I was not afraid.

Becky sat in the back with the boys, watching everything with her wide, brown, friendly eyes, speaking only if spoken to. Now and then she joked with one of the boys, but she never hung around the girls; still, I knew, from overhearing my parents, that her mother had threatened to sue the Austin School Board for keeping poor children out of honors classes. Honors classes at O'Henry Junior High were reserved for the residents of Tarrytown and Barton Hills, regardless of ability; no black or Mexican or poor white child had ever crossed their thresholds. Becky was three-quarters poor white, one quarter Mexican, but her mother had paid to have her IQ tested, and then, my father said, she had started making calls.

She sure does, I wrote, thrillingly. I folded the note back up and, on pretext of needing to sharpen my pencil, dropped it on Becky's desk.

The truth is, I'd never given Mrs. Morse much thought. She was cruel, but so were all the other teachers, and several of them looked exactly like Mrs. Morse. Three months into the semester, everything was still blurry to me; the only thing that stood out clearly was Exposition Boulevard. Inside the school there was so much noise—so many people rushing in different directions and lockers slamming and bells ringing—and though I was always lonely and always anxious about my makeup, what I mostly thought about was how to get to my next subject. I still sometimes got lost, and when I had landed safely in whatever room I needed to be in, I started right in planning my route to my next class.

Meet me after school outside the gym, she answered.

I looked back at her and she smiled at me—a wide, open smile that showed all her teeth, straight and even and stained—and though the gym, located in a distant wing of the school, was a room I rarely found on the first try, I grinned back, as if to say, *Sure, why not? I meet people all the time outside the gym.*

When I found her, long after the last bell, she was squatting in the grass, tying her shoe lace. She smiled up at me. "I thought you'd forgotten."

I shook my head and blushed. I was wearing the beige and brown polyester outfit, and the hollow heels of my shoes had been punctured along Exposition and filled with tiny bits of tar and gravel. I thought how relaxed Becky looked, in a boy's tee-shirt and bell bottom jeans and sneakers, and her hair tied back in a ponytail, as if she didn't really go to school at all, as if she had just dropped in for a look. "I got a little lost."

Her eyes widened. "Shit, girl. You still don't know your way around? I figured you were late for class so much because you had better things to do."

"Like what?" I asked, thinking of the kind, blonde girls who were not actually my friends, who stayed smoking in the bathroom long after I had patted myself dry and rushed out.

She laughed. "Anything. Anything would be better than sitting in those stupid classes. You want to do something?"

"Sure," I said, and then I offered boldly, "Want to come over?"

"Okay," she said. "I told my mom I might go home with a friend today."

How had she known, I wondered. Did she have lots of friends she might go home with? The boys in the back of the class? Or had she known it would be me? She must have. I felt a sudden tightness in my chest, and I thought how pretty she was, with her ponytail and her freckles, and how her voice sounded older and fuller than the other girls'.

We walked down Exposition together, single file, without speaking, because there was no sidewalk, and the cars were too loud, the dull sky too glaring. The retarded children were out, their fingers inches from my arm; but now I was not afraid, my heart did not pound the way it did every other afternoon. I could hear Becky behind me, laughing a little, not meanly. She was looking at the children, nodding hello, as if neither their slack faces nor the cage that held them was anything she had to worry about. They seemed no more nor less to her than any other group of people we might pass, and her business was with me, not them.

When we turned to cross Exposition, to get into the quiet streets on the other side, she handed me a piece of Juicy Fruit gum, and I was as happy as I have ever been. I had never done anything like this before, spent time with a girl my age without our mothers having planned it, without the hours of our play having been determined in advance.

"Holy shit," she said, when we turned onto Mountain Laurel Lane. "These are some big ass houses."

"They're not as big as the ones in the hills," I said, trying to ally myself with her: to let her know that I, too, possessed less than some.

"I'd like to see those," she said, walking slowly now and staring at every house we passed, at the lawns that remained mysteriously green and mowed though no one ever appeared in them—no one ever worked or sat or threw a ball in those yards—and the houses with their brick walkways, their faux columns and balconies, their little gas lamps by the front door. Our cul-de-sac was less formal than the rest of Tarrytown—the Taylors had a neglected though pristine basketball hoop in their driveway—but still we all followed the neighborhood custom of turning our front yards into still-lifes. No one would ever have grown vegetables or had a picnic in a front yard; no laundry would ever dry there. The one terrible exception was Mr. Wise. Old and dirty minded, with a yard full of weeds—he had lived in our neighborhood when all the other lots were fields, and he wouldn't budge—he sat in front of his house in a metal recliner, calling out greetings to the cars.

Even Becky didn't like Mr. Wise, rolling her eyes as we passed by.

"You got a friend with you," he called out. "That's good. Kids need friends."

I nodded and walked as fast as I could to my house, a low-slung brick ranch two doors down, and pushed the door open. I headed straight through the house and to the backyard where Buttercup was standing against the sliding glass door, whimpering. When I slid open the door, he licked my hands as intently as if they had been dipped in hog fat.

"Woah girl! That boy likes you," Becky laughed.

"Yeah," I said, picking up a stick and throwing it across the yard. "He gets so excited he knocks me down sometimes." I showed her the scar on my temple but I didn't tell her how my father had kicked Buttercup; nor did I tell her how Buttercup sometimes climbed on top of me and humped me for a couple of seconds. I almost did—I had a sudden desire to tell her everything I knew—but I didn't know how to explain my father's violence or the sweetness of Buttercup's attention.

We took Buttercup for a walk around the neighborhood—we had to pass Mr. Wise again, but this time he didn't speak—and then I showed Becky the house. I didn't show her my bag of stems and seeds that day, or my two books, but I showed her Babette's other treasures—her black light, her macrame—and I showed her my parents' room with the twin beds and the twin sinks; I opened the slatted doors of my father's closet and showed her the spare robe, the carefully pressed every day suits, the shoes all lined up with his shoe horns. I wanted her to smell the faint odor of eucalyptus, to see how neatly everything hung.

I didn't open the door to Ted's room; it wasn't a thing I would have shown anyone—the bare walls, the tightly made single bed—and naturally, Becky didn't ask. She gazed politely at what I did show her, drinking in the smoothly painted walls, the deep carpets, and I could have gazed quietly with her for hours; I didn't know what we were going to talk about, once our tour was over.

We went out to the back yard and sat on the picnic table beneath the live oak trees and I shrugged a little, smiling, wishing I had a secret to tell her.

She smiled back at me. "I hate the people at our school," she said at last. "Their fucking pink and yellow purses. It's like being in a damn nursery school."

"Do you think I'm a geek?"

"Nah. You dress geeky, but you're not a geek. You crack me up. 'Can people have syphilis their whole lives and not know it?'" she said, quoting a question I'd asked during sex ed.

"I wanted to know."

"That's what cracked me up. Everybody else is sitting there like some damn prude, and you just come right out with it. You're cool."

"I hate my clothes."

"Get new ones," she said, shrugging.

"Well, my mom's not really—she believes in hand-me-downs."

Becky laughed. "I'll hand you down some stuff then. I've got so much shit I've outgrown."

For weeks then, Becky came home with me almost every afternoon and we sat together on the picnic table, dressed alike now, in hip hugger bell bottoms and boys' tee shirts, though Becky filled hers more than I did—she was thin, but muscular, and she had more breasts than I had, the beginnings of hips. Becky liked to do things—she'd played volleyball and she planned to run track; she never tried to cut gym—but I think she was happy, after school, just to sit. We talked about who we hated and which teachers were the worst and sometimes she made me close my eyes so she could quiz me about the layout of our school. My sense of direction had become a joke between us and sometimes I deliberately failed the quiz just to make her laugh.

But often we were just quiet. We read a lot—books Becky had checked out of the public library, *The Prophet* and *Rosemary's Baby* and *The Strawberry Statement* and a copy of the *Baghavad Gita* she had picked up from some Hare Krishnas on the Drag. She liked to read everything—instruction manuals, sports books, the Bible, even—and she liked how silent my house was, how you could read an entire chapter of something without being interrupted.

At her home, she shared a bedroom with her mother—the other room was occupied by her brothers, Jack and Stevie, who were fourteen and nine—and there were newspapers, clothes, ashtrays, radios, sewing projects piled everywhere. The chaos was thrilling to me: someone was always calling out to someone else, different songs played on the different radios, the smell of tomato sauce and onions and tobacco hung over the kitchenette, and filtered in from the other apartments. When Becky and I went to her house, Becky's mother always offered me a donut and a glass of milk. I needed to put some meat on my bones, she said and though I said no thanks—my mother had told me to say no; they were too poor to feed an extra mouth—I liked the offer.

Mrs. Lopez, who worked in the bakery department at the supermarket and was young and pretty and plump, said no one could eat so little, it just wasn't possible, but she never pressed me. The Lopez's never took offense or got angry. Or rather, when they did, it hardly seemed to matter.

Once, Becky and her brothers and I were at her kitchen table—Becky and Stevie and I were cutting out coupons and Jack was supposed to be helping, but he was mostly playing with the scissors, seeing if he could balance them on one point, or pretending to cut off the tips of his fingers—and Stevie cut out an advertisement for something that wasn't a coupon at all.

"You see anywhere where it says five cents off, or fifteen cents off, or two for a dollar?" Jack asked. "That's just a dumb advertisement, stupid."

"I beg your pardon?" Mrs. Lopez said, wheeling around from the stove.

"Well, he doesn't know what he's cutting. He just cuts anything at all." Jack could have been Becky's twin, the same dark eyes and auburn hair, the same freckled nose, but Stevie was blonde and pale, like no one else in the family.

"And what coupons have you cut out?" Mrs. Lopez asked. "You think I can't see when I've got my back turned, but I've got eyes in the back of my head, boy, so you just hush your mouth."

"But Ma, he can barely read. I could read better than him when I was six."

Stevie's pale eyes were full of tears and he was gazing at his mother, but her eyes were fixed on Jack. "A lot of good it's done you, Jack Lopez. Look at you, pretending to cut off your fingertips. You preparing for a life of crime? Is that it? You're a smart boy, Jack, but if it wasn't for Becky I'd think poor people just deserved what they got."

"I just said—"

"Don't you just said me. You sit there and cut coupons and I don't want to hear another word out of you. I don't want to see you playing with those scissors, either, because I'll tell you what this kitchen is not, Mr. Jack Lopez. It is not a kindergarten."

Jack's shoulders were twitching and I thought he was going to get up and storm off.

"You hear? Jack?"

Jack sighed. "Yes, ma'am."

"No sighing."

"Yes, ma'am."

"All right then." She sighed herself and then suddenly she laughed, and Jack laughed a little, too, and it was all over, as if nothing had happened. Stevie was bent over the paper, carefully cutting something out, and Jack picked up his scissors, scanned a page and said, "I think we got them all, Ma."

"We, nothing."

"Well, it's not exactly a four person job, Ma."

"Then come here and wash these dishes for me, Jack. Make yourself useful for once."

I loved Becky's home, and the way her mother talked, but Becky said it was too damn noisy, everybody always hollering over everybody else, so we mostly went to my house, where my mother, out of concern for Becky and all that she lacked, had begun stocking the pantry with pop tarts.

Invite her to supper, my mother said finally and I said oh, okay, sure. Could we go ahead and eat early, before she and my dad got home? Becky and I were so hungry right after school, I said.

I had never lied before, but now I shoved two portions of meat and vegetables down the disposal every afternoon and toasted half a dozen pop tarts to share with Becky. I never felt a shred of guilt. Becky was too friendly, too pleased with me, for me to suffer any pangs of conscience. And the sight of my mother's food just made her laugh.

"Shit," she said, the first time. "All French people eat this way?"

I nodded, though I had no way of knowing.

She shuddered. "My mom would kill me if she knew we were doing this."

"My mom, too," I said, glimpsing for the first time the wild possibility that a mother's displeasure might be as harmless and ordinary as a bruise.

Later, after Becky had gone home—walking the two and a half miles back to her apartment in the dusk—my mother came home and while she ate I sat with her and did my homework. We didn't watch TV anymore—the news was long over by the time she came home now anyway—and she ate quietly, leaning over her plate, wisps of hair falling out of her braid around her face. When she was done and I cleared her plate, she said what a comfort I was to her, what a good girl, and I never thought, as I might have, *if you only knew.*

Except for throwing my mother's food away and passing notes, we broke no rules, but Becky said we were bad-ass girls; she meant that we were perfect just as we were, and nothing could hurt us. I said we should call ourselves The Sluts, and I showed her my sex books and how, if I got on all fours, Buttercup would hump me. She laughed; I was a pervert, she said, admiringly. Then she said it was cool to be so small— I could have passed for a third grader—that it was easier to hide when you were small; secretly I imagined myself as a bit of treasure she kept in her pocket, like a pebble or a piece of beach glass—a thing she might touch every now and then with her boyish, chewed up fingers.

Being sluts, we needed to discuss how far we'd go with the various boys in our class; for Becky, the prospect of 1st and 2nd and 3rd and 4th base—she always laughed when I said 4th base, though I didn't know why—was a rule-breaking opportunity—she'd sit on the porch swing where my mother had rocked me, peeling the bark off a twig, or chewing on it and say, lightly, "Yeah, I'd let Carlton or Jimmy finger-fuck me. They're okay"—but I took our plans seriously. What scared me most in the world—the one thing Becky could not help me with—was that I might graduate from college without ever having been on a date.

When I told her, she just laughed. I remember she tossed a stick across the yard for Buttercup; she could throw one all the way to the fence, as if it was nothing. "Why wouldn't you get a boyfriend?"

"I don't know what to say to boys."

"Hell, I don't think you have to say much."

"But some people—they never end up with anybody. They never get married or anything."

"Who'd want to get married?" She didn't know her father, and she hated her stepfather, who was mostly gone anyway.

"Well I mean even if I don't get married. I mean a boyfriend."

"You'll get a boyfriend." She said it as if everyone just automatically got one and I wasn't at all reassured.

"Some people don't. They just stay lonely."

"Who?"

I couldn't bring myself to say Ted, who, I was sure, was still a virgin. "People," I said. "Lots of people. I bet Mr. Wise never had a girlfriend."

She laughed again, her wide stained smile as pretty as any I had ever seen. "Don't be an asshole then. Don't be like Mr. Wise—or Mrs. Morse, either. I bet she's never gotten laid. Just be friendly and things'll work out. That's what my mom's always saying. It's corny, but it's true. You don't know what to say, just smile."

"I think there are a lot of people who aren't mean who never get laid."

She sighed. "You lonely now?"

I shook my head.

"Well, then," she said, as if that settled it.

But when Lisa White, who lived next door to Becky and was Becky's best friend before me—until Becky got sent to the rich classes and she, Lisa, started fooling around with Charlie Romero—decided she'd had enough of Charlie and that she'd rather join me and Becky in the afternoons, I knew I had been saved: Lisa would find me a boyfriend. Lisa had long blonde hair and grown up breasts and though she was plenty smart, she would never have been admitted to any honors class. Content with D's and C's and even F's, she never did a bit of homework. I'd seen her before next to her locker, standing perfectly still and looking into a little compact, as if the flow of bodies all around her—the school itself—had nothing to do with her. It was different from the way Becky stood back and observed; Lisa simply didn't see what she didn't like, and that was most of O'Henry Junior High. Rich boys as well as poor tried to talk to her, but Lisa couldn't stand rich kids. She wasn't a bit happy about me that first afternoon outside the gym when she asked Becky where she was going and Becky told her.

She stared at me, making a face. "What do y'all do together?" she asked, incredulously.

"Hang out," Becky said. "You coming or not?"

"But y'all are so different."

"Not as different as you and me. Make up your mind."

"But you and me are like sisters. Why didn't you tell me?"

"You were busy," Becky said, without bitterness.

"Shit," Lisa said, but she followed us out to Exposition, making a wide arc for the retarded children and fixing her gaze on the oncoming traffic, as if any one of those hot, shining cars might contain the man of her dreams.

At first, poking frankly around my house, she spoke only to Becky.

"Don't her parents ever come home?"

"She going to get in trouble if we finish up the pop tarts?"

"Her dad's a judge? Shit, that means she can do whatever she wants and never go to jail."

I almost interrupted then, to say that my father would never use his position that way, but she had already moved on:

"She smoke?"

"Why're you asking?" Becky said. "You got a cigarette?"

"I got a whole damn pack of Winstons."

"Who bought it for you?"

"Charlie's brother."

"I thought you were sick of Charlie."

"I can still ask his brother to buy me cigarettes, can't I?"

"Well shit yeah she smokes, what do you think?"

And so I did. The way I remember it, with the three of us sitting out in the yard, I never even coughed. It was as if I'd been born to it.

"I wouldn't of thought you'd smoke," Lisa said, eyeing me.

I said nothing, inhaling that soft charcoal-filtered air with immense pleasure. It didn't seem to me that our relationship had yet progressed to the point where she'd want me to answer her.

"Why wouldn't she?" Becky asked.

"You seem like a prude," Lisa said, still talking to me.

"What the hell do you know?" Becky said, mildly. "You thought Charlie Romero was a nice guy."

"He was nice," Lisa said. "I never said he wasn't nice. I just didn't like the way he went on and on about us going all the way. It got on my nerves, all his damn reasons why we should. I'd of done it if he'd of just shut up about it."

Becky nodded and we were quiet then, watching our smoke dissolve into the mild afternoon. It was the end of January, but for weeks it had felt like spring—the spring which, when it actually came, only lasted a day or two before the heat set in. That kind of weather still makes me crave a cigarette, even when I've gone years without.

"You want another?" she asked me when we were done. She shook one out of the pack and held it towards me.

"You going to smoke them all up today?" Becky asked.

"There's more where these came from. Go ahead, Molly. If you want one." It was the first time she'd said my name.

"Thanks," I said, taking a cigarette, though I was dizzy enough by then. "How much do I owe you?" I asked, remembering my mother's admonitions about poor people.

Lisa laughed. "These are free. Charlie's brother doesn't pay for them."

After that, she came over every afternoon with Becky and took me on as her pet. She studied fashion magazines as voraciously as Becky read, and more often than not, I studied them with her. We filled out all the surveys and though I mostly scored zeros—they were largely about boys and sex—she said that was all right, one of these days I'd bloom just like one of those sped up flowers on TV. I wouldn't know what hit me. The Sluts was a good name, she said, even though, personally, she didn't want to touch any more boys. But we were sure as hell bad-ass girls, she laughed—she, with her full breasts and blonde hair; Becky, with her bright dark eyes; and me. In my only picture from seventh grade, I am buck-toothed and scrawny, pale, like something that has never been outside. And yet there is a swollenness about my face, a puffy, cocoon-like quality, which is an ugly girl's best hope; and I have friends: on the back of my picture, in Becky's handwriting, are the words *one cool slut.*

I n the spring, Lisa took Becky and me into my parents' bathroom, whispering and hurrying as if we should hide; she was going to teach us to kiss. She could have taught us at the kitchen table—we would have been as undisturbed—but she wanted to go to the most secret, private part of the house, to make as little sound as possible.

"Come here," she said, and in the mirror above the double sinks, above my mother's hairbrush with its tangle of faded hair, my father's leather manicure kit, I watched her beautiful long hand cradle my head.

"Like this," she said, her tongue just flitting inside my lips. "It's no good if you use too much tongue."

I considered this. We had already had two spin the bottle games since my parents had gone for a week to help my grandmother recover from a broken wrist. I don't know why my mother went, unless she hoped for some kindness from my father, who'd never taken a vacation before, but she didn't object when I said I wanted to stay home. No one worried about kidnapping in those days. "I've got so much school-work," I told my mother, promising to call Andy Newell's mother if I needed anything at all. "I'd hate to fall behind."

I wondered, now, why too much tongue would be a problem. I'd thought that was the point of French kissing, to use your tongue, and if that was so, why wouldn't more be better? The boys I'd already kissed during our games—Mike and Bobby Taylor, Becky's brother, Jack—hadn't used a bit of tongue and I wasn't sure whether I'd actually made it to first base or not.

"You can put your hand on the back of their necks, too," Lisa continued. "Charlie really liked that." Her fingers were cool and smooth against my skin, but suddenly she straightened up and pulled away. "One of these days," she said, tucking my hair behind my ear. "One of these days I'm going to give you a decent haircut."

Becky sat on the bathroom counter, watching us. Lisa had said she would show us how to kiss, but I didn't think she was really going to show anyone except me.

Becky hunched forward, her legs swinging back and forth. Her gaze was tolerant, patient: the world interested her, in all its oddness, its variousness: the taste of pop tarts and cigarettes, the sight of two girls kissing, the silence of rich people's houses.

Lisa leaned down, stroked the back of my neck and put her mouth to mine so I could show her what I'd learned. Her hair fell across my face, smooth and gold.

"That's good. You'll be a good kisser. Just don't rush it."

She didn't say anything about Keith Miller, the goal of all my lessons, but it was she, knowing I had a crush on him, who had invited him over for our third spin the bottle game. None of us had set foot in O'Henry since my parents had gone out of town. Becky and Lisa hadn't been home once. What they told their mothers and how they kept the school secretary from calling their homes I have no idea. I could imitate my mother's accent perfectly and though I'm sure I sounded like a child, the accent still fooled everyone. My teachers thought I was in Corpus Christi. Becky might have forged a note explaining that she and Lisa had head lice, or impetigo; her handwriting looked just like an adult's.

Other than my occasional calls to Mrs. Newell to let her know I was okay, there was nothing any of us had to do. We watched TV half the day, smoking cigarettes even indoors because there would be plenty of time to air things out before my parents got back. Charlie Romero's brother had started stealing beers for us, and Lisa and I would split one because I didn't like the taste and Lisa didn't want to get fat, but Becky could drink them like sodas and barely get drunk. In the afternoons, Jack Lopez and the Taylor boys from down the street came over for spin the bottle. Lisa didn't have much use for Mike and Bobby Taylor—she thought they were immature—but they were nearby, so we invited them.

There may have been other boys, too. Though Lisa would have kissed Jack, I can't imagine Becky or Lisa kissing either of the Taylors, with their smooth, blond, unformed features. I did; at some point during that week, obeying the rules of a game we had devised, Mike Taylor and I closed the door of my bedroom and on my blue bedspread, with my stuffed animals arranged beside us, we tried to go all the way. He didn't say much, but I felt like I knew him, because of the hours I'd spent with Trudy in her kiddie pool—not that knowing him really mattered, that wasn't the point of the game. We took our pants off and he lay on top of me and rubbed his soft, dry genitals against mine. It seemed enough, and though I wasn't sure if I'd gone to first base, I was confident I'd fucked a boy.

Still, it's hard to imagine Lisa so much as holding hands with Mike or Bobby Taylor, so there must have been other boys; but all I really remember is Keith Miller, his sandy blond hair and his doe-brown eyes, his chapped lips. His hands were short and calloused and he used to drum his fingers lightly on his desk at school.

How was it that Lisa invited him to my house? How did she know him, one of the richest kids in the school? He was in the same classes as Becky and me, and though Becky sat in the back and joked with the boys, they were not boys like Keith. Keith's friends were mostly girls, the popular, wealthy girls who won the contests, whose families went water-skiing on the lake with his, girls he had grown up with and whose expensively outfitted parties he attended. But Lisa had invited him and asked him if he liked me and he'd said yes.

It's hard to believe, even now. Whatever became of me later, I was ugly then. I didn't know it yet, but still. And yet of all the rich girls, I was the only bad one; he must have seen me as a trailblazer.

I liked him because he was cute, because of the girls he was friends with, but even more, because he was, like Becky, without snobbishness or meanness. If he had never told Lisa he liked me, if he hadn't agreed to come over, it would have been an ordinary crush; but that a cute boy who could have gone out with any girl would overlook my geekishness was as startling to me as if he'd had two heads. I needed to hear it over and over.

"I told you. Yes. He said yes. I am not making it up." My kissing lesson finished, Lisa was trying to put gloss on my lips.

"Why shouldn't he like you?" Becky asked from her perch on the counter.

"No boys like me."

"Mike didn't seem to mind you too much," Becky said, matter-of-factly.

"You know what I mean."

Lisa held the wand away from my mouth. "I can't put this on if you keep talking. Anyway, it's not true, about boys not liking you."

"What do you mean?"

"Boys think you're all right."

"Who? Tell me."

"Steve White, for one. And Justin McCrae." They lived in Lisa's and Becky's apartment building; I'd never even spoken to them.

"Why? What did they say?"

Lisa sighed. "I knew you'd want to know."

"Well, duh," Becky said. "Don't start some damn thing you're not going to finish."

"Well it's kind of nice and kind of not-nice."

"Okay," I said, amazed that Keith Miller had said he liked me, that other boys should speak of me, that anyone besides Becky and Lisa and the Taylor boys might recognize me in a crowd. "Whatever they said, I want to know."

"They said you had a dog-face, but a great body."

I didn't know what a dog was, I'd never thought anything about my body except that it was little.

"You do have a really cute body," Lisa said. "You've got perfect boobs."

I stood there in my parents' bathroom, while Lisa waited to finish my lips, and Becky swung her legs against the counter, and I saw, through my tee-shirt, that my breasts had grown, that they were no longer buds, but distinct and firm as two peach halves. The training bras I wore—old ones of Babette's I put on for the same reason I wore eye shadow, because all the girls did—were so worn and stretched they didn't bind me. I had managed to grow breasts without realizing it, and I stared at them now, neither pleased nor displeased, but curious: what was it about breasts that changed how boys saw you?

And then I looked up and saw my face, as raw and bony as Ted's, and I knew what a dog was.

"Was Keith there when the other boys were talking? Did he say anything?"

"No Keith wasn't there." She laughed, " Keith doesn't exactly hang around those boys. But Keith already said he liked you, okay? You're driving me crazy."

I didn't want to drive anyone crazy, least of all Becky or Lisa. I was quiet then, closing my eyes so she could put eye shadow on. I felt sick to my stomach, and my hands were cold. I didn't want to have to talk to Keith Miller, or show him around my house or anything. I just wanted to get to the part where we were kissing, and I would put my hand on the back of his neck, I would just barely flit my tongue inside his mouth.

Keith showed up right after school, when Lisa had told him to come. He rang the bell and I could see him through the kitchen window, wearing a baseball cap and staring down at the ground. I asked Lisa to please answer the door, and she said I should go, that he was coming to see me and I looked really cute but I said I couldn't do it. Becky, seeing that I was on the verge of tears, said, I'll go, and let him in and greeted him the way she greeted all boys, as if they were just regular people and then he was there, standing in the kitchen, touching something on the counter—the telephone cord? A napkin ring?—the way he always did, fiddling with something on his desk or in his pocket. He chewed his fingernails and his hands were a little dirty, always fiddling. That was all I knew about him—those nervous habits that were visible for all to see, and who his friends were, and that he said he liked me. I didn't know if he had siblings or what his parents did or if he played sports. I had noticed that he had a sore on his lip that looked just like the stage one syphilis sores they showed us in the sex ed movie and when he walked through my front door, I thought, well, I will just go to the free clinic on campus next week and if I've caught it from him they will give me penicillin. There would be just enough time to get treated before I went to France in June.

The other boys came then and I spun the bottle and it pointed straight to Keith Miller. He scooted across the green shag carpeting to where I sat between Becky and Lisa and I leaned forward slightly. I didn't put my hand on the back of his neck, our tongues barely touched. But I loved his dry, chapped lips, like parchment paper; I loved the faint pressure of his mouth against mine.

And then, suddenly, all the turns were used up, the boys went back to their houses and once more it was just Becky and Lisa and me with our soap operas and our cigarettes. We sat in the kitchen with our bare feet on the table and the television flashing dimly before us, the air filled with smoke, and my heart seemed too big for my narrow ribs, my arms too skinny for all their longing happiness. Keith Miller had leaned his face towards mine, he had kissed me. For a few seconds, I had been everything to him.

Somewhere in the midst of our blissful indolence, Mrs. Newell dropped by to check on the plants. In the nick of time, Becky and Lisa fled to my room and I threw the cigarettes in the trash.

"You home, Miss Molly?" she called from the front door, sensing my presence. "I was just coming by to see were you watering the geraniums."

"I didn't feel well today," I called back, weakly.

"You got a fever?" she asked, marching straight through the cigarette reek to where I stood, frozen, and putting the inside of her wrist against my forehead. She was a big, husky woman with iron-colored hair and a man's voice, but her wrist was pale and soft.

"Nah, you're okay. Three o'clock flu, huh?"

"The three o'clock flu?" I asked, wondering when she would notice the trash, overflowing with beer cans and cigarette butts.

"You know. The one that ends at three o'clock." She laughed and I was mortified to be accused of any deception I had not actually committed.

"Fix you a sandwich?" she asked.

"No thanks," I said, my sense of mortification turning indignant: I would never have made up a flu that vanished at three o'clock. "It's my stomach that's upset," I continued, forgetting the trash, and wanting to remind her that, fever or no fever, it was still possible to feel sick. "I'd better lie down," I added, heading thoughtlessly to my room where, had she followed me, she would have found Becky and Lisa crouching behind the bed, stifling laughter.

But she didn't follow me; she went out to the back yard and looked over the geraniums, which I had, in fact, neglected.

Several minutes later I found her, watering the plants. I had told Becky and Lisa about our conversation and Lisa, weak with laughter, had said, "Oh man, you should of said yes to the food. I'm sick of those damn pop tarts."

"Mrs. Newell?" I said. "Actually, I am kind of hungry. Would you mind making me a couple of sandwiches after all? Maybe three?" Any one of us was perfectly capable of putting something between two slices of bread, and yet the idea of feeding ourselves seemed impossible.

Mrs. Newell laughed. "That three o'clock flu. Leaves a body pretty starved, doesn't it?"

For whose benefit did she think I had had to feign weakness for eight hours? Had she forgotten that I was here alone? Her blood was so full of alcohol she would be dead within a year, but I didn't know that. I figured she was just stupid. And yet, still, the sight of her pale wrist, as she lifted the watering can to water one last geranium before going back inside to make my sandwiches, made my chest sore.

"Lettuce, cheese and tomato okay?" she asked, brushing her wrist across her forehead.

"That would be great," I said. "Thanks."

I spent my last day of freedom alone, cleaning every nook and cranny in the house, and when my mother came home, disappointed by her week with my father, and saw how the house shone, she said what a wonder I was, *une merveille*. She could pretty much leave the house in my hands from now on, couldn't she?

I wasn't sorry to go back to school. I would have been content never to see Keith Miller again, to be able to hold the memory of our kiss intact forever; but, failing that, I wanted to see him as soon as possible.

It was, of course, a terrible day. He didn't look at me and all day I was overcome with waves of nausea; but that afternoon he called. "Molly?" he said. "This is Keith."

I stood in the kitchen, beads of sweat rolling down my sides.

"Listen, I was wondering. Do you want to go steady?"

Through the sliding glass doors I could see Becky and Lisa, trying to blow smoke rings.

"Sure," I said.

"Great," he said.

And then, since there was nothing left to discuss, we got off the phone. After that, he didn't call anymore and we didn't speak at school.

Poor Keith Miller, upon whom, because he was kind and had a nervous, boyish beauty, I heaped all my longing, all the loneliness of my childhood. He seemed an answer to everything, that innocent, tow-headed boy who, having come to my house and kissed me, having asked me to go steady, had spent all any twelve-year-old boy might have of a capacity for romance.

He didn't call me, but I called him. I called him every day for a week or two, crying. He always picked up on the first ring, afraid no doubt that someone else in his family would hear my ragged voice. Did he not like me anymore? I asked. He didn't know, he said. He liked me fine, it wasn't any big deal. I cried till I was choking on it, till snot ran down my face, till my eyes ached. To risk his hatred was better than not hearing his voice at all.

At school, I looked away from him so that I wouldn't burst into tears, but all day I felt sick. My eyes were sore even when I wasn't crying, my body ached, I couldn't eat. I wanted Keith Miller more than I had ever wanted anything—his stubby hands, his white teeth, his tan—but what I remember best from that week or two was the setting of my obsession, not its object: the sour smelling cafeteria, with its stainless steel vats of pinto beans, its half-pint cartons of milk to remind you of how alone you were. In class, sitting at the back, I could will myself to go deaf and blind and dumb, but the cafeteria echoed and everyone bumped into everyone else, laughing and jostling trays. It was impossible not to feel every pinprick of my own flesh. I remember the windows all open to the heat, the explosion of flesh—girls in short skirts, boys in tee-shirts—the sudden smell of summer, that terrible combination of exhaust fumes and sweat and tar. Keith Miller was hardly ever in the cafeteria anymore; he must have taken to skipping lunch, hiding behind the gym for a smoke.

Lisa told me that was just the way guys were and then she decided to give Charlie Romero another chance. Soon after, Becky, who'd been consoling me on the phone every night for hours, finally lost patience. She said she didn't know why Keith had lost interest in me, but he had, it was over, and I just had to give it up.

My vision cleared a little then. I woke up the next morning and did not weep; I ate a piece of toast. I remember that afternoon seeing Lisa in a thin, tight shirt and hot pants, leaning up against Charlie Romero outside the gym and then Becky, walking ahead of me across the playing fields towards Exposition, the tendrils of hair that escaped from her ponytail dark with sweat. I was still sad and my throat still ached, but I had made it through an entire day without crying. Still, the sight of Becky, with her strong, slender shoulders, her boyish stride, broke my heart because she wasn't Keith.

Summer was coming; Becky would be all alone in the heat while I sat in the Alps, writing Keith Miller's name over and over in my diary and Lisa went all the way with Charlie Romero. What would she do, all the hot summer long, with her brothers making a racket, and no air-conditioned home to escape to?

But I didn't care about Becky. I was too sad. The only time I'd been this sad before was when I'd spent the week with my grandmother—*You still crying sugar? Are you? Sugar?* I'd crouched all day in the sand, using my plastic shovel to fill my plastic bucket—a bucket and shovel bought specially for me, and for which I should have been grateful—making sand towers because I could do it without lifting my head and I did not want her to see my wet face and swat the backs of my thighs so that I'd have something to cry about, for Pete's sake. She sat a few feet away from me in her chaise lounge, in a succession of flowered bikinis, gossiping with one or another of her friends about my fat, awful mother. She told each one that my mother had trapped my father with a baby and I tried to figure out what that meant, but nothing came to me—I was a baby when I cried, that's all I knew.

Years later, when I was in my twenties, I would think of that week in Corpus Christi whenever my heart was broken and console myself that I had survived my grandmother and so could survive anything; but that spring, when I was twelve, it was no consolation.

Though I no longer sat on my mother's lap, though I lied to her and was embarrassed by her, I still clung to her promise, made seven years before when she came to get me from my grandmother's, that I would never be torn from her again. There was no consolation yet in the memory of what I had or hadn't survived.

I did go to the free clinic on campus for my syphilis check. I went to Miss Pollard, who was the health teacher and the school nurse, for a pass. I'd never been to her office before, and it was nice to knock on her door and sit on her orange naugahyde sofa, it was the sort of thing the older girls did when they had cramps. I had to sit forward so that my feet touched the floor, but I didn't mind; I was used to my smallness. Mrs. Pollard was small, too, a small grey cylindrical woman sitting behind her desk, waiting to hear what the trouble was.

"I need a pass for the afternoon," I said. "I need to go to the free clinic to get tested for syphilis."

She stared at me.

I said nothing, waiting for her to fill out one of her pale green forms. I knew that my request did not fall into the same category as needing a sanitary pad, but I couldn't fathom the depth of her dismay.

"Molly Moore," she said at last, and to my horror, I saw that her eyes were damp.

"Yes, ma'am."

"Molly Moore," she repeated. "I have worried about you all spring." She looked down at her desk. "Hanging around those girls. Becky Lopez and Lisa White. You come from a good family." She looked up at me again and suddenly her eyes were dry, glittering: "You come to school tomorrow—and every day after that—dressed like a young lady, and I will forget we ever had this conversation. You hear?"

"Yes ma'am. Thank you, Miss Pollard," I said, as embarrassed suddenly as if she had made me pull down my pants.

I found Becky in the cafeteria, dragging a fish stick through a film of ketchup.

"What a bitch," I said, sliding into the seat across from her. I could hear Keith, in the cafeteria for once, laughing at something two tables away, and my heart was racing; it seemed to me as if Miss Pollard herself had kept Keith from me, as if it were her prissy, narrow minded criticism that had come between us.

"Who?"

"Miss Pollard," I said, suddenly raising my voice. I had never felt the thrill of rage before and I hoped some teacher would overhear my every word. "She's a fucking bitch." I wanted Keith to hear me, too, to know that I was not just a crybaby.

"Yeah, how come?"

"A fuck-ing bitch," I repeated, loud and slow.

Becky's eyes widened.

"You know what she did?" I spoke as if I were addressing the entire room. "You know what the fucking bitch did?"

"Molly," she whispered. "What the hell damn thing are you trying to do?"

"Said I had to dress like a lady." I had barely noticed that the focus of Miss Pollard's own rage had been my clothes, but now it came back to me, a rallying point, a single, unifying injustice.

"What?"

"She said—" I was almost happy now: we were all implicated in Miss Pollard's criticism; I was not alone. "She said you and Lisa were bad influences on me, and that I'd better dress like a lady."

Becky snorted softly. "Well, fuck her. Just fuck her. What're you going to do?"

"Nothing. There's no damn dress code in this school."

"I can't believe she said we were a bad influence on you," Becky said, but she kept her voice down. "I tell my mom, she'll lodge a damn complaint." She was grinning, and I knew she was relieved; I wasn't keening for Keith Miller anymore.

I told Becky I had a doctor's appointment and after school I walked to the edge of campus, three miles in the opposite direction from home, along roads much busier than Exposition. I'd never mentioned to Becky my concern about Keith's syphilis—she would have thought I was stupid for kissing him if she'd known, and no one but I seemed to have noticed his sore.

The Free Clinic was in an old yellow clapboard house near the corner of 24th and Pearl Street. A small white arrow in front directed people to enter through the back and below the arrow hung a sign: AUSTIN FREE CLINIC, M-F, 9-7, WALK-INS WELCOME. When I had gone with Babette, I had waited in her orange mustang in the gravel parking lot for a long time, watching women in long, colorful skirts or tiny cut-offs and halter tops go in and out the door, laughing with each other. It was a mild day and I was content to sit with the car door open, feeling like I was a part of that small, select group of Texas hippies and entertaining myself by reading the bumper stickers: *Sisterhood is Powerful, Sissy Farenthold for Governor, Nix On Nixon, Keep on Truckin'.*

Today, the sky was pale and burning, the lot nearly empty, and by the time I made it up the wooden stairs to the doorway, I had a heat rash and I smelled worse than I ever had before. I pushed open the screen door into a warm, dim room. Three fans strained to rustle the strips of yellow fly paper that hung from the ceiling and at the front desk a man with long red hair sat watching me.

"Help you?" His hair was thick and wavy and smooth, the way my mother's had once been and his face was half-hidden by a beard and mustache, so that he looked like a Sunday School Jesus, except that Jesus' hair never reached the small of his back.

"I need a syphilis test," I said. "And water, please. Do you have any water?"

He nodded, as if thirsty O'Henry students came to him with venereal diseases everyday. "There's a bathroom over there."

I went and drenched my face and drank from my cupped hands and returned to the desk. The man was still alone, still watching me. "If you'd fill out this form please," he said, sliding one across the desk. "We need the names of your partners."

"My partners?"

"People you've had intimate contact with." His voice was so mild, so untroubled, that I wanted him to go on and on.

"I can't do that," I said.

"We don't use your name. It's just, if you test positive, so we can alert people that they might have V.D."

"But I can't," I repeated. "I don't know who my partners are."

He nodded again, apparently familiar with this dilemma.

"I mean," I began, stopping myself. I wasn't sure what constituted a partner, where you drew the line.

"It's a public health issue," he said gently. "We can't require you to do it, but it would help."

But did I have to call everyone at the party? Tell them all they might have syphilis? "How about, if I test positive, I promise to tell everyone I've—had contact with." I couldn't say kiss. I had the sinking feeling I didn't need to be tested, that I was wasting everyone's time.

"That would be all right," he said. "But the form is still better, if you change your mind." He came around the front of the desk and I stared at the frayed hem of his bellbottoms, his long, slender toes in his flip flops. I wondered if he thought I was pretty, if he'd noticed that we had the same color hair. He took me into a small dark room with a couple of chairs and a screen and a reel-to-reel and then he twisted his smooth, long hair out of the way and set up the projector. "Someone will be in to draw your blood in a little while, but first we'd like you to watch a movie."

I barely remember clenching my fist for the nurse, my own velvety blood filling the vial—she must have turned the light on, and I would have blinked, startled by the row of fluorescent tubes—but I remember the movie: the sad blind men with their oozing sores and elephantine limbs, as awful as anything my parents had ever told me about D-day, because VD was serious, it wasn't a game, a thing for twelve-year-olds to play at.

Who did I think I was, inconveniencing the free clinic this way? My eyes stung and it wasn't because I felt so sorry for the people in the movie, I was just ashamed of having made the nurse and the red-haired man tend to me. Even if I did have VD, it was my own fault; it wasn't like I hadn't been taught all about VD in school.

Afterwards, in the blinding heat of the parking lot, I wanted Babette to show up and take me home, I wanted it so much that I turned around and sat right down on the wooden steps of the building as if she might. I thought of the times I'd kept her company when she was tripping and she told me that I was magic. Once she said I gave off sparks. She said tiny creatures lived in my hair, my ears, my mouth, and if I shook my head they would all come swimming out, because I was phos-phorescent, that's what I was; I was a goldfish—that small, that slippery—and everywhere I went little planktons of light leapt from my skin.

I sat there for a long time, waiting hopelessly for her. Now and then a woman walked past me up or down the steps, quietly preoccupied, her shoulders curved, her head bent forward. I scooted my legs to the side, my face turned away, so no one would see how young I was and send me home.

At last there was only one brown station wagon left in the gravel lot. The light had shifted downwards, though the heat had not let up. I was still waiting.

The red-haired man appeared in the doorway. "Ride forget you?" he asked.

I nodded.

"Where do you live?"

"Tarrytown," I said, and he looked surprised, as if a kid from Tarrytown shouldn't be using public funds, but then he smiled.

"I can go that way," he said. "Come on." He kept smiling while I thanked him, first for the offer, and then for moving a box of papers off the front passenger seat. He had terrible teeth, as crooked as I have ever seen, but I loved his smile: I could tell by it that he wasn't actually mad at me for coming to the clinic. Not mad at all. He put the car into gear and then he smiled at me again, like we were already friends. "Okay?" he asked, and I nodded, resisting the urge to thank him a third time—Lisa said I thanked people too much, that it got on your nerves.

But riding in the front seat of a car with a stranger was like being on a date, which meant we should talk about *something* and the only subject that occurred to me was my gratitude. "It's so hot," I said, finally, but he just said yeah, and all you could add to that was that it was nice not to have to walk in that heat and that would have been just like saying thank you again.

He knew I wasn't a prude or an innocent; we could be on a date. I didn't want him to kiss me, but I wanted him to tell me that he liked me, with my red hair and my willingness to get VD. It would be okay if he put his arm around me, if he held me while we rode through the dusk-filled streets and he told me that in a few years he hoped—

But he asked what street I lived on. He held the steering wheel with one finger, his left arm resting in the window, and the sound of his voice startled me so much that I said, "Oh, here, right here is fine," and when he pulled up to the curb, I jumped out of the car so quickly I forgot to say thank you when I should have.

Then it was over, like a ten minute 'flu. Once more I loved only Keith.

I was just three blocks from home but I wished I could wait for the sun to go down completely, for night to fall and the temperature to go down into the 80's before I took another step. I dragged my feet and when I got home, my mother's pale green Plymouth was in the driveway, and I could see her at the kitchen table, as motionless as stone.

"Where have you *bean*?" she asked, and I realized it was later than I thought. There was a plate of food on the kitchen table, waiting for me.

"I'm sorry," I said.

"Where *where* you?"

"I got lost."

"Lost? For four hours?"

"I wanted to try walking home a new way."

"I telephoned to Mrs. Lopez, and Becky said to her you had a doctor's appointment."

"Oh," I said. "Becky and I had a fight. I wanted to be by myself."

"So you fabricate a lie?"

When my mother was excited, she spoke in the present tense.

"You fabricate a lie, and when you are lost, you do not ask to use a telephone, you—you *wander* for four hours? You should telephone to Daddy or to Mrs. Newell."

"I was by the lake," I said, as if my having stumbled upon a piece of natural beauty might compensate for her anxiety.

"I was worried to death. I was preparing to telephone to the police. If ever you are lost, telephone to someone right away."

Telephone to thoo polees, I thought, wanting to get as far away as possible from her. But I must eat my supper, I must sit with her all night while she watched me, not saying a word.

"I have given food to Buttercup," she said, icily.

"Oh," I said. "Oh, thanks. I should go say hi to him."

"Eat your supper," she said, and my eyes welled up with tears, but I made my way through a plate of liver and onions, which, in truth, I did not hate as much as I might have. What I hated was my mother, for turning to stone. I wanted her to come back, for it to be the old days again, when all we had to do was sit on the porch swing, listening to the dry scuttle of the squirrels in the live oak branches.

At last, when I had eaten everything on my plate, she pushed herself up from the table and said she was going to bed.

It was dark outside now and in the faint glow that hung all night over the city, I could see Buttercup, asleep on the deck. I went outside to join him—the air was no longer unbearable, though it was still muggy—and he began to whine with pleasure, but I hushed him.

"Come," I whispered, and I lay on my back on the scratchy grass and looked up at the salmon-colored sky with its weak stars while he licked my face. The ground smelled almost sweet. After awhile, he lay down beside me and I put my arms around him. For a moment, I didn't hate my mother anymore; I didn't even miss Keith or Babette. I breathed in his rank breath, stroked the surprising coolness of his fur, the velvet of his belly. I began to roll, the way I had done when I was much smaller, down the slight incline to the edge of the yard. He jumped up and stood over me, nudging me with his cool nose, and when we had reached the edge of the yard, we ran back up to the house and I rolled again. Over and over I rolled—I couldn't roll fast because the hill was so slight, but I didn't mind; I'd always loved the dry, hard grass and the dusty smell of the trees, and Buttercup's warm breath in my face. He tried to hump me when I stood up and I pushed him off, laughing, but I could feel his small, wet penis brush against my leg and when I lay down again he lay with me and I held him close, my heart pounding suddenly in the dark and his head in my neck, nuzzling, his penis still outside and wet, his body shaking a little and my own breath ragged, sore, and then, suddenly, he nipped the side of my neck—the pain was so sharp, so unexpected, I reached up and brought my fist down on his back. I did it twice, each time as hard as I could.

I'd done it before, when I was smaller. He had nipped the inside of my thigh one time and without thinking I had punched his back. He had run away from me, his belly low to the ground, his tail between his legs, whimpering, and I had run after him, crying, begging him to forgive me. This time, when he let me touch him again, I was quiet. My heart was still thudding and I could feel the tight, sticky part of my leg where his penis had brushed against it.

We sat for a long time, my face against his neck, and then at last, he rose, shook himself off and started back towards the house; he stopped, facing me, his head cocked to one side. He had forgiven me, or forgotten—is that possible?—and so at last I rose too and crossed the dark lawn to him. I bent down to rub my face against his one last time, to kiss his muzzle, and then I went back through the sliding glass door.

For years it was my desire as much as my fist that made me ashamed, as if I'd molested a much younger child. But now I'm not sure. Between a dog and a twelve-year-old girl, the scales seem balanced enough.

S chool ended and without a shred of hope, I asked my father if I could stay with him that summer. My mother and I were flying to Geneva the next day; I'd gone to her bedroom to ask her for something and found them both in there. It's the only time I remember seeing them both in their room at the same time, and I was as startled as if I'd found them naked, holding onto each other. He sat on his bed, fully clothed, trimming his cuticles, and she stood on the far side of the room, in a bra and half-slip and one sock, looking through her drawers for something.

"Oh!" I said. "Oh! I'm sorry."

"Well," my father said. "What is it?"

A safety pin? A needle and thread? The sight of him at home in his bedroom, in the middle of the workday—I didn't actually think of sex, his presence was startling enough—had made me forget everything. I thought I should leave, but I didn't want to. I wanted to sit next to him on the bed and watch him tend his hands. His hair was still completely black and though I'd seen a bottle of Grecian Formula when Lisa was teaching me how to kiss, it had not lessened my admiration. I still saw his black hair as an accomplishment, a sign of youth and strength.

"Can I stay here this summer?" I expected no response at all, but I wanted to say the words out loud.

My father frowned and for a moment I wondered if he was considering it.

"Of course not," he said.

I tried again anyway. "I was thinking, you know, that if I stayed home it would save money, and then, next summer, Becky—Becky Lopez, you know—could come with us."

"Good God," my father said, his voice at once soft and absolute. "Must you pepper all your phrases with 'you know'?"

"Enree," my mother said, turning at last from her chest of drawers. "It is not a bad idea. We could give to Becky a wonderful experience."

"Who in the world is Becky Lopez?"

"The daughter of Susan Lopez. The woman—"

"Ah," my father said. "I see. She's your friend, then?" He looked at me. "I expect you can learn a great deal from her." He looked back over towards my mother. "But I would be reluctant to whisk her off to Europe. It smacks of condescension and, even supposing the trip provided her a rare opportunity to expand her mind—evidence for which I have not seen among our own children—at the end of the summer she would be back where she started. She would feel what you consider the bars of her existence all the more keenly. My suspicion is that, with a mother like hers, her existence is not as impoverished or constrained as we imagine it to be. And I would caution you both that fantasies of another's misery are often wishful."

My mother shrugged a little and turned back to her chest of drawers.

I stared at my father, who had turned his attention back to his cuticles. I didn't agree with him—Becky and I would have fun together in the Alps—but I had never expected him to say yes; I hadn't even meant to ask for anything. I just liked having a conversation with him.

"Thanks," I said. "You know, for considering it."

He shook his head. "You're even worse than your siblings. 'You know!' I thought you had more sense than that."

I think of that summer now as the last time I was with my mother; I didn't actually leave her until I went away to college, but it was never the same afterwards.

I loved flying across the North Atlantic. I loved the Whisper Jumbo Jets and the slender air hostesses in their pretty uniforms, I loved the tiny salt and pepper shakers you got in those days, like something from a story book picnic, and the tiny doll-house dessert—I thought the food was great—but most of all I loved the freedom of it, the neither here-nor-thereness of the long, disorienting flight across the ocean. Strangers slept side by side, their elbows bumping accidentally, shoes slipping off, mouths agape, and the night consisted only of dusk and dawn. I was scared of a summer alone with my mother and my great uncle, of the Alps without Babette, but the flight was like a slumber party, and the rose-gold mountains beneath us as we approached Geneva a kind of Shangri-la.

We took the bus across the Swiss-French border and I slept on my mother's shoulder; I slept in the dusty, diesel-smelling backseat of my grandfather's Citroen, and then, at last, I slept in a stone room off the stone kitchen of his chalet. I slept for eighteen hours and I awoke to the sound of cow-bells and water rushing down the melting peaks into a trough outside my window.

No sound at all came from within the chalet. I looked quietly through the kitchen, the living room—cold, dark rooms built to keep out the winter snow—and then I climbed the stairs to what had once been the hay loft, where the other bedrooms were. My mother's room was empty, and I heard my great uncle groan and saw, through his half-open door, my mother sticking a needle and syringe into his sagging, naked bottom.

I stood perfectly still, waiting. My mother withdrew the needle, pulled down his night shirt, pulled up the blanket, turned out the light; then she saw me and motioned me back downstairs. He was very sick, she explained. He should never have driven down to the village to meet us, he wouldn't be able to leave his bed anymore and I must amuse myself as well as I could, for she would need to tend to him all summer.

My mother whispered to me in French, and in French she was so competent, and so much more commanding than in English. I must hike down to the village and get eggs, bread, cheese, milk, fruit and ham.

"Okay," I whispered back, in English.

"Molly," she said, and suddenly she smiled. "*Achète aussi des patisseries, pour nous deux.*" Buy pastries, for the two of us.

"Okay," I repeated. Pastries were my mother's one indulgence. Everything else she ate—all those quantities of potatoes and bread and organ meats and wilted vegetables that had made her so fat—were a moral obligation, but pastries were a pleasure.

Outside the chalet the air was so bright and clear I couldn't see at first—the chalet sat alone in a meadow—and then I made my way past the grazing cows, side stepping their fresh pies, to the woods, where a mossy path led steeply down through the darkness and out again into the open air of the village. I had played in those woods, moving between the brilliant light and the mossy shadows a thousand times with Babette and it was always as if we had entered another universe altogether—it was impossible to imagine the heat or the crankiness of our life in Texas—it still felt like another universe, without Babette, but now that universe seemed to be inside me, and me alone, as if, instead of coming to France, France had seeped into my skin, suddenly lonely and ice-capped and forlorn. It was still beautiful, but I didn't want it.

I bought a pack of Gauloises along with the groceries at the little store next to the church—the grocer said, *alors, vous êtes arrivés*—so, you've arrived—but made no other comment and at the patisserie the patissier's wife asked after my mother; and then, for the rest of the day, I spoke to no one. I hiked back up to the chalet, heard my mother rustling in my great uncle's room, unpacked the groceries and went out in the woods to smoke. I smoked until my lungs ached, until my throat was so raw it might have bled.

Every morning I hiked down to the village for provisions and every afternoon I smoked till dusk. Sometimes I helped my mother a little— I made tea for my uncle and brought it to him where he lay, propped up against a mound of pillows, his port-wine stain sunken and shriveled now below his cheekbone like a tiny pool of blood. He had always been a quiet man, puttering in the vegetable garden outside the kitchen door all day and putting up with us only for the sake of his brother, my mother's father. He lived in Paris most of the year and had no friends in the village; he was just a summer resident, as solitary and unmoored as the rest of us. I don't know why he came to the Alps that summer, as sick as he was, with a son in Paris whose wife could have looked after him as well as my mother did; he loved the mountains, but confined to his bed he couldn't see much of them, so he must have loved my mother. She had stayed with him and his wife after the war, while my father was finishing law school; she would have been a kind of daughter to him.

A cup of tea, a bowl of broth, a glass of water—those were my offerings, handed to my mother who handed them to him, and though I didn't like to see him or smell his room, the sight of my mother consoled me and I wanted to stay near her, but she tilted her head after I'd made my delivery, indicating that I should go.

Sometimes I even began to look forward to the sight of my mother—her long, faded braid, her round hips—the way, at school, I'd looked forward to the sight of Keith Miller. There were no tears to fight back, no waves of nausea to withstand once I saw her, but the looking forward was almost the same, a tightness in my chest, an eagerness, and in the evening, after she'd given her uncle his last shot and we had eaten a supper of bread and cheese, and she brought out the box of pastries, I drank in her voice, her slightly sour warmth as if I were an infant.

But though I still had those moments when her company was all I wanted, mostly I was alone and bored and focused on my cigarettes. I wrote to Becky everyday and scratched Keith Miller's name into every tree and piece of slate I could; but obsession and loneliness had numbed me and all I really thought about was the way the cigarettes were packed so tightly in two neat rows and how tricky it was to get the first one out and how sometimes it seemed as if a cigarette would never end and I wanted it to; I wanted to smoke it down far enough so that I could light a new one off the end of the old. That was my favorite part of smoking.

When it rained, I smoked in the granary. In the Alps it can rain for three weeks straight without a moment's let up. If it just rained, I slid my way down to the village for provisions and scrambled back up through the mud; but if the rain fell into fog it was too dangerous for me to go alone and then we ate powdered soups and canned vegetables and in the cold damp granary I permitted myself only one cigarette every two hours and spent the rest of the time with my knees drawn up to my chin, telling myself stories. A story, rather, and even I was sick of it, but I couldn't think of any other: Keith realized what a mistake he'd made, he couldn't wait for eighth grade to start, he would apologize, he would ask me out on my first date.

And then one day, when the sun was shining at last, we had a visitor. Andy Newell showed up at our chalet. He was breathless and pink-cheeked from the hike up and he stood outside our door, dirty brown curls down to his shoulders, a nylon pack hanging off one strong, thick arm and such a smile filling his narrow face that his eyes were barely visible.

He and Ted had planned to travel around Europe together that summer, but Ted was stationed in Germany—he'd never gone to Vietnam—and Andy had been left to discover Europe on his own. He'd gone to Harvard, but he'd never been out of the US and he was no good with languages. After a miserable week in Paris, he'd taken a train straight for the Alps. All he wanted, he said, was to understand what people were saying.

"We are so glad," my mother said, speaking English for the first time all summer. "So glad, we are so glad!"

"God, it's good to see you guys," Andy said.

Everything that was old and dark about that summer lifted then, and the world felt bright and clean and American again; I was going to get to spend time with Andy Newell, whose love for Ted absolved the whole world of its loneliness.

I cleaned out the granary for Andy to sleep in and then I led him halfway up the mountain to a meadow where Babette and I always picked blueberries. I hadn't gone there all summer and the bushes were so thick with fruit you couldn't walk through them without staining yourself; Andy said we should go back to the chalet for pails and he would make us a pie.

I ran ahead of him, proud to show him that I could run barefoot on the rocky paths and that I knew all the special places. Suddenly he laughed and I heard in his laugh such amusement that I stopped short: did he think he was babysitting me? I wanted to be his friend, like everyone else. I had told him how bored I'd been all summer, how much I missed Becky and Lisa, but how would he know from that that I meant bored in a grown up way, that my friends and I did grown up things?

I fell in beside him and was quiet for awhile and then, back at the chalet, found two pails quietly and efficiently to show that I understood the gravity of my uncle's condition, the gravity of life in general. I didn't speak again until we were back in the blueberry meadow, picking as conscientiously as if we were being paid for it.

"You know," I said at last. "It's pretty here and all, but I miss just hanging out and having a few beers with my friends."

He paused in his blueberry picking. "You drink?"

"Well, yeah," I shrugged. "You know, I look young for my age, but I'll be thirteen in the fall."

"I guess you will be," he said. "I hadn't realized."

"Yeah," I went on. "I'll probably look like I'm nine till I'm twenty, though. It's the curse of the Moore's."

"Is it?" he asked.

"Yeah." I shrugged again.

"Well, I wouldn't worry about it. Anyway—nine? You look a little older than that, I'd say."

"You think?" I kept shrugging; then I sighed. "Yeah, well, it's just weird, you know. Leaving everything at home so unresolved."

"Unresolved?" he asked, raising his eyebrows the way older people did when I used a word they didn't expect.

"Yeah, like this guy I was seeing. I just don't know what's going to happen with him."

"A boyfriend?"

"Yeah, Keith." The sound of his name stopped me; I'd written it over and over, but to say it made my skin feel tight. "Anyway," I said, afraid suddenly that my exaggeration would be found out. "It just gets really boring here. I wouldn't mind it for a little while, but the whole damn summer's just too much."

Andy was silent for a long while and I was too embarrassed to look over at him. Obviously I didn't have a real boyfriend; I should just have told him about drinking. That was believable, because it was true, but lying was stupid. Andy would know; he was people's boyfriend, he would be able to tell when someone was making it up. I stopped putting blueberries into the pail and squatted quietly, eating them by the handful to console myself.

"I have an idea," he said finally. "Why don't you come with me for a while? Break up the boredom a little. Get your mind off things till you can get home and resolve them."

"Really?" He hadn't realized a single thing.

"Sure," he said. "You know your way around more than I do. It would be a help, actually."

I didn't know my way around Europe at all—the village and the chalet were all I knew—but there was no need to correct him.

"Come on," he said. "Let's finish up with these blueberries. You're not so good at putting them in the pail, are you?"

I was a little miffed by that, but too happy to complain.

My mother said no to Andy's offer. She admired the blueberries, but shook her head emphatically. "You are kind to offer, but you have waited a long time to make this trip, Andy. It is a pity Ted couldn't go with you—," *Eet ees a peety Ted coodent go*— "but you can still have a good trip."

"I don't mind, Mrs. Moore. Molly's no trouble."

"I know that Molly is no trouble." She smiled over at me. "Molly is an easy child, but I do not want you to spend your vacation babysitting."

I glared back at her, my face burning.

"*Ça va s'arranger*," she murmured, putting her arm around me. "Come, Molly. Shall we enjoy Andy while he is here? Do you really know how to make up a pie?"

My eyes filled with tears.

"The truth is, Mrs. Moore—" Andy blushed. "Molly's French would more than compensate for her age. I wasn't kidding about my language skills—they're pretty much nil."

"Well, it is nothing to be ashamed of—but you will be traveling outside of France, no?"

"Not really. Just Switzerland, and then back into France, up through the Alsace and Belgium, and into Holland, where I think everybody speaks English." He and Ted had talked about Italy, Greece, Yugoslavia.

My mother thought for a while. She still had her arm around me and I knew she was about to give in, but I hated her.

"I can't stand it here," I said, shrinking away from her touch.

"Molly?" She looked down at me, flinching. I had never been mean to her before, and for a moment she looked as bewildered as a child.

"Well," she said, finally, her voice empty and thin. "All right." She turned to go back inside the chalet, murmuring to herself: "*Il faudra*— we will need, you will need—*things*," and then she vanished into the darkness of the house.

I was still mad—madder, because I'd hurt her—and I thought that if Andy said anything about how I ought to have been nicer to her, I'd cancel the trip in a huff and just stick to my cigarettes; but he didn't.

"Want to make a pie?" he offered. "It's easy." He grinned, as if nothing at all had happened. "That's why they say easy as pie."

We left the next day for a ten-day tour of the Alsace, Switzerland and Holland and it was a tour from which, until we got to Amsterdam, I remember almost nothing except the pride I took in traveling like a teenager: there was a wealthy town in Switzerland where I needed to go to the bathroom, and we walked around, unable to find our way out of the residential district, joking about how I could knock on the door of some big house and ask to use theirs; and an old hotel in Belgium where the proprietor yelled at me for taking a shower after ten; but other than that I mostly remember the trains: the tiny red one that clung to the side of the mountain as it carried us out of the Alps, and the large black ones with their individual compartments in which Andy and I, when we could, always took the two window seats facing each other. I remember the sudden open countryside at the window when we came out of the mountains—the squares of different shades of green, the poplar trees, the stone villages—and the way Andy turned to me whenever someone entered our compartment and spoke to us. It didn't matter whether the person spoke French or Swahili, Andy had enormous faith in my powers of comprehension. Once, out of habit, he turned to me when an Irishman asked us a question and, to spare Andy any embarrassment, I pretended that we only spoke French.

He taught me how to play poker and rummy and he talked to me about his plans for graduate school. Unable to imagine what political science might be, I pictured political campaign buttons—Nixon Now, McGovern/Eagleton '72—suspended in a mobile like the seventh grade models of Our Solar System. Sometimes he told me funny things that had happened in my family before I was born, stories I'd never heard before. He told about pranks he and Ted used to play on the twins when they were small and the twins were left in charge: locking the girls out of the house, rigging the bathroom door so that it wouldn't close, collecting worms to offer to their dolls; the list went on and on, and as he told me these stories, he shook his head, as if to say, someone should have tanned our hides.

I loved his stories, the way my family appeared so regular. Claire and Pat were still Claire and Yvonne and Ted was just a prankster, Babette too little to mention. All of them were younger than I. I told him my own, more sophisticated stories of mischief: my week alone with Becky and Lisa, Tony Romero's gifts of beer and cigarettes. He shook his head at my stories, too: "I underestimated you, Molly."

And then suddenly, I don't remember where we were, his grin turned ugly. He leaned forward as if we'd been having an argument: "Ted's an idiot," he announced.

"What?"

"Joining the Navy. What a fucking idiot. I knew he was stupid, but I didn't know he was that stupid."

"What?"

"The fucking goddamned Navy."

I couldn't breathe. The compartment had no air and I couldn't breathe or speak. Andy kept talking over the noise of the open window, but I couldn't draw a breath. Please, I thought. Please, please, please, because I didn't know what to do, I didn't know how to start breathing again. My eyes filled with tears and then it was all right, I could breathe again, but I hated Andy. I hated his fucking guts. I should never have left my mother. I should have stayed right where I was, eating éclairs with her every night.

"Here," she would say, patting the space beside her on the wooden bench. She held out the box of pastries before taking anything for herself and then she lifted an éclair to her mouth and paused for a moment, as if she were taking communion. We ate in silence, as if all that mattered in the world were the glazes, the fillings, the possibility of having a second or a third or even a fourth pastry, if we wanted. "*Merci*, Molly," my mother would say when we were done. "*T'es bien gentille.*" You're so nice.

I missed my mother the way I had when I was five, on the Gulf of Mexico, but I held my eyes open, because I wasn't going to give Andy the satisfaction of seeing me cry.

"You know why he joined the Navy?" Andy said. "To be part of a goddamned group. It's pathetic."

I wanted to jump off the train, but I held myself perfectly still, I didn't blink once.

What he needed was a girlfriend, Andy said. But he always fucked things up. Did I know how Ted would call and beg when a girl wouldn't go out with him?

I glared right at him. Wasn't I always in the house, hearing what all of them did? Then I stared out the window, as if I didn't care at all.

We entered a tunnel and it was too loud for Andy to speak. The train roared through the mountain like water and my face appeared in the window, pale and small, like a doll's head, with a doll's uncloseable eyes.

The tunnel curved to the left and we burst out into daylight again and Andy was quiet, his legs reaching over to my side of the aisle, his gaze blank.

After a while he leaned forward, shrugging. "I just don't want to lose him, fuck. He's my best friend."

What? Now I was breathing too much, gulping in air, I couldn't stop.

"Oh shit," Andy said. "I shouldn't have said anything. Hey, Molly. It's going to be okay. He's going to be fine. He'll get a desk job. He'll be fine. They wouldn't send a guy like him into combat."

Of course Ted wasn't going to die. I just wanted him to have one friend, and he did. A best friend. I don't know what Andy saw in Ted, but I didn't care. He loved him and he didn't want to lose him and that was all that mattered. I wiped my eyes and nose on my sleeve and I smiled at Andy. I was traveling around Europe on a Eurail Pass, just as Babette might have done. Andy and Ted were still friends and I was as good as a twenty-year-old, sitting there in that sooty train.

If I have only the scantest memory of what we saw in Switzerland or the Alsace, I remember Amsterdam well—the sidewalks thronged with girls with jutting hipbones and see-through blouses, the bare feet, the smell of hashish, the music floating out into the street. I remember a girl with long black hair spinning in place, singing *what a drag it is getting old*, and children much younger than I, running in and out of the crowd, dressed in fringed leather and gypsy scarves like their parents.

How long were we there? A week, a weekend? I say that I remember it well, but all my memory is of a single evening. The hostels were full and the only vacancy we found was a tiny room with damp wall paper and a twin sized bed. As chastely as children at a slumber party we had, to save money, shared beds before, but Andy looked at this little mattress with dismay.

"Well," he said. "Let's walk around. Maybe we'll just stay up all night."

"I'm sorry," I said.

"Sorry?"

"If you hadn't invited me, you'd have that bed to yourself."

He laughed. "Or I'd have Ted in there, sticking me with his elbows. Come on, Molly. You worry too much, you and Ted both."

We wandered for hours along the canals, and for hours, though it was night time, the air was still light, the children still darted in and out between their parents' legs. It seemed the most thrilling thing in the world, to walk around a city that way, long after bedtime. There were so many people laughing and so many bars with their doors open onto the sidewalk. Inside the bars, where men smoked hash cigarettes as if they were tobacco, the light was yellow and warm—little pools of butter spilling out into the violet air. I could have wandered that way for days, with the cool murky water of the canal by my side and all the older girls passing by, their hips rolling slightly inside their jeans, as rhythmically as the water lapping its banks.

Andy didn't say much while we walked and though I didn't think of it at the time, he may have been wishing he were on his own by then. Everyone did speak English, and it would have been fun for a college graduate, however timid a traveler, to lose himself in that generous, city-wide party. But if he was tired of me, he didn't let on. He matched his pace to mine, and seemed indifferent to the possibilities all around us.

I entertained myself with a fantasy of moving to Amsterdam with

Becky when we were seventeen. We could dance in the middle of the street and we would never have to walk down Exposition again. I imagined myself in a crowd, laughing with a boyfriend I hadn't even met yet.

Below me, the water turned red. I wondered a little what had happened: it looked like blood, though clear and light as rubies, like the time I'd tried to shave my legs with a naked razor blade. I wondered where the blood was coming from, but I wasn't scared, just curious. And then a sound startled me—Andy coughed, or said my name—and, glancing up, I saw the red lights in the houses and the huge plate glass windows behind which sat the city's prostitutes.

They sat half naked, on benches or stools or on the floor itself, gazing out at no one while the passersby stared in. House after house had its downstairs storefront window, its woman sitting alone. I don't remember them in their entirety, only a bleached mustache, an elbow, a hand on a thigh, a scarf slipping away from a patch of pubic hair. The variety of breasts—the long skinny ones and the small, firm ones, the ones as big as watermelons, and all the different colors and shapes of nipples—embarrassed me, as if such variation were the result of a mistake. But what made my heart race was the flatness of each woman's eyes, as if it meant nothing to her to be gaped at. I wanted the prostitutes to notice me, to see that I was different from the other onlookers, that I respected them. Once, at the Houston Zoo with my grandmother, I'd watched a mother gorilla idly pulling at her fly-covered nipples and I'd told my grandmother we shouldn't look; but then, as now, I couldn't tear my eyes away. I thought of my father, and his deep respect for prostitutes, and I wanted them all to know about it, that I was Judge Moore's daughter.

Then a prostitute appeared before me who looked so much like my own mother that I stopped dead before her. She was a blonde, but as pale as my mother, with the same wrinkled cleavage. She sat on a faded velvet bench and wore a pink kimono open to the waist; behind her the wall was covered with paper cut outs of couples having sex in every possible position, couples whose bodies were much younger and thinner than hers. I stared at her, waiting for her to look down, to smile at me, but she held herself so still, her belly rippled with the effort of holding it in, that she might not even have been breathing.

Andy wandered off to look at other prostitutes and a man opened the door next to me and went in, but my prostitute still didn't move, she didn't even seem to notice that she had a customer. I didn't realize she was just the window display, I was so intent on meeting her gaze; I might have broken down and tapped on the glass if she hadn't suddenly—to ease a stiffness in her neck?—tilted her head and caught sight of me. She hesitated a moment and then such fury came into her eyes I thought she'd get out of her seat and come half naked into the street to slap me. My whole face stung. She glared at me, shooing me away with her hand; but Andy, when I caught up with him, put his arm around me and laughed. "It's okay," he said. "She thinks you're just a kid. Let's get out of here."

We walked down a side street, out of the red light district and back into the light of ordinary lamps, the black water of the canals sparkling colorlessly now at our feet. After a while we came to our hotel and climbed the dusty stairs to the top floor. I couldn't stop thinking of my prostitute and how I'd angered her, and my eyes burned with shame— I knew there was a kindness in her fury, and that only made it worse—but Andy, following me up the narrow staircase to our room, nudged me and told me to lighten up, and I nodded, okay.

He unlocked the door to our room—it was still tiny, the bed still intended for one—and laughed, shrugging. "Well, here we are."

I went down the hall to the bathroom, to pee and brush my teeth and change into my nightgown—thinking that my mother had been right, I was ruining Andy's vacation, but when I returned, he was sitting on the edge of the bed, grinning.

"Tell me a story," he said. "Tell me again about the week you spent alone with your friends." And suddenly I grinned too, because that was a good story, a tale of triumph of youth over old age, of sweet, unpunished crime. I climbed onto the bed and sat cross-legged, describing the whole week from the beginning and adding in details I'd not mentioned before: how I imitated my mother's accent when I called the school, how his mother had made three sandwiches for us. He laughed then, saying what a sot his mother was, the last adult you'd leave in charge of things. I didn't like his laughing at her and I decided then that she had known what we were up to, and that she chose to let it slide, but I didn't say anything. I told him about the spin the bottle game and how Mike Taylor and I had gone to fourth base.

"Fourth base?" he asked.

First base, I explained, was French kissing, second was feeling up, third was finger fucking, fourth was fucking, fifth was oral sex. His eyes widened, but he said nothing, and then I told him that I was worried about what had happened with Mike Taylor, because I knew, from *Everything You Always Wanted to Know About Sex*, that a person's body was supposed to go out of control.

"I'm sure there's nothing wrong with you," he said.

"Really?"

"Sure. Mike probably didn't know what he was doing."

"What do you mean?"

"You have to be stimulated. Otherwise it doesn't work."

"Oh," I said, as surprised as I'd been to learn I was a dog.

"Here," he said. "I'll show you."

"Really?" His offer seemed as great a kindness as the whole trip had been. He lifted my nightgown and pulled down my underwear and put his hand between my legs—my pubic hair was still downy, a lighter red even than the hair on my head—and my teeth began to chatter, but I wasn't afraid he would hurt me: I was trembling as I would have trembled if I'd robbed a convenience store. All my past transgressions, I knew, had only been misdemeanors; this was something different. I held my mouth open so my chattering would make no sound, and I wondered a little if trembling might count—if that was really what the books had been describing—but I knew it wasn't. All I could feel was my own shaking, and a faint dry pinching between my legs.

It never occurred to me to touch Andy; I thought he was conducting an experiment and, mixed in with the fear of committing a crime was such sadness at discovering that, in fact, something was wrong with me, for no part of me went wild. Then I remembered the panting and groaning, so I panted and groaned, but Andy, propped up on the narrow bed beside me, showed no sign of having heard. I gave up and was quiet again, lying sideways in his shadow, motionless except for my chattering teeth.

After a long while he leaned over me and put his hand on my breast—"you have really nice breasts," he said—and opened his mouth to kiss me and I thought, *oh, it's not an experiment, it's sex*, and I wondered if at last I had a boyfriend.

I don't know how it ended. I know that he never took his clothes off—I never touched him—but how we ever fell asleep in that small bed, I can't imagine. I'm sure we didn't hold each other—and so, what then? Did I lie in the crack between the bed and the wall, a skinny girl in a flowered night gown, dejected because I'd felt so little?

We returned to the Alps the next day and had window seats the whole way, so that the orderly squares of dark green and light green and yellow, the poplar trees and the stone villages flowed over us again. I liked the train, with its hard leather seats and the sooty smell of the compartment and all the people in the corridor, resting their arms on the railings and putting their faces to the wind, as if we were on a ship. We ate a picnic of Dutch pastries and Dutch cheese and our crumbs were everywhere in the compartment, the little trash bin overflowing with our juice bottles and candy wrappers and the waxed paper that had held our cheese and pastries. Once, when I got up to go to the bath-room—rocking and steadying myself against the grimy walls, the water gushing out suddenly and unexpectedly and then refusing to come on at all when I stepped on the little pedal, and everywhere warnings in four languages, *verboten, pericoloso, attention, danger*—I stared at myself in the mirror—or tried to stare, despite the rocking—so that I could assess myself objectively and determine how I might improve myself, but I saw only what all twelve-year-old girls see: the hopeless flaws, the misproportions. No girl knows that her clumsiness is lovely, that her whole task, if she has one, is to be as raw and shifting as the light in spring.

Alone again in the compartment with Andy, I raised the question of love. I didn't want to have had loveless sex, I said.

"No, of course not," Andy said. "Of course not." He pushed a curl back behind his ear and then he smiled and gently shook my knee. "You worry too much. Everything's okay. No loveless sex. I'm glad I got to know you better—you're a great kid."

It seemed the nicest thing an adult had ever said to me—that he was glad he'd gotten to know me better—and though I didn't like the kid part or the faint amusement in his voice when he said no loveless sex, for a moment I was happy.

"You're too young to fuck," he went on, and I didn't mind that he was harping on my age. I was even grateful, glimpsing that what had always seemed insulting—the idea that I was too young for some activity—might be consideration.

"Thanks," I said, and he smiled again, his wide, easy smile.

"It's a good thing we're leaving Amsterdam," he added suddenly.

"Why?"

He shrugged. "It doesn't seem like people like kids there. I might go back later, on my own. But you know, it ain't Six Flags."

I froze, the way I had when he'd said Ted was an idiot. I'd never been to an amusement park in my life. What did it mean, then, that he was glad he'd gotten to know me, that we had not had loveless sex, if he could brush me off so easily?

But just before we got to St. Gervais and changed to the small red train full of mountain climbers with their ropes and crampons, he pulled the curtains to our compartment and kissed me, a long, grown up kiss full of tongue. "No worries now, okay?" he said, when he had finished. "Be happy." And I nodded, "Okay."

We hadn't told my mother which train we'd be coming on, so we hiked up from the station to the chalet when we arrived. It was a blinding, clear day, the sky so rich a blue it seemed like glass, and my mother was not with my great uncle, but dozing out front in a lawn chair, her heavy arms at her sides, her fingers trailing the lupine. She opened her eyes as we approached, and for a moment she seemed not to recognize us. Then she pushed herself up into the brilliant Alpine sun and kissed us both. We must be starved, she said. "*Dis-moi—,*" She turned to go into the chalet. "Tell me Molly, now that you've seen a bit of the world, what do you think?"

I didn't see Andy again for many years. Mrs. Newell died and he and Ted weren't friends after the war. I can no longer picture what he looked like when he was young, but I know this: he was young; he wasn't much more than a kid himself, trying to find his way around Europe on his own.

My prostitute, though, my prostitute behind her sheet of glass—I see her as clearly as if I'd never left Amsterdam. For years, I wanted to climb into her cage and sit on her lap, to rest my head on her breasts and have her stroke my forehead; but now I am as old as she. I still imagine her in her pink kimono, on her velvet bench, but her hair has gone white, her stomach is relaxed; she can breathe easily now. We do not speak, or greet each other, but she pats the bench beside her, and we sit together, gazing at the passersby.

My teeth were like glass, like pearls, like that old show tune. I stood before the mirror, sliding my tongue across my straight slick teeth and saw that I was no longer a dog. I was fifteen, almost sixteen, and besides straight teeth, I had thick, glossy hair. It fell in waves down my back now, the way my mother's had once done, the way the man at the free clinic's had. I would never be like the buttery blonde girls who walked with Keith Miller down the halls of Austin High—I was still freckled and skinny—but I wasn't ugly.

I went out to the kitchen and slid open the doors for Buttercup to come in—he wasn't allowed, but I liked to dance with him—and for the first time since eighth grade, when I had moved into Babette's room and appropriated the rest of her belongings, I put the soundtrack to *Hair* on the record player and listened to the song about the sixteen-year-old virgin without my throat seizing up. I thought that song was all mockery. *Can you believe it? Sixteen years old and still a virgin!* It was 1975 and the thing to do was to fuck as many people as possible. That was cool. To be thirteen years old and fucking somebody. Not to be inhibited, a prude, some awful relic from the fifties. Most people in

Texas—even in Austin—weren't that cool yet, but most people didn't have Babette in their blood, Babette living out in California, where people fucked in the streets. I hadn't kissed anyone in three years, not since Andy Newell, not since I'd gotten braces, but now, with perfect teeth, with a month still to go before I turned sixteen, I had hope.

Becky said the boys we knew were idiots. That's why I was still a virgin. She reassured me for hours, pattering on easily, lightly. She'd lost her virginity at fourteen, fooling around with her brother's friends, but Becky could do anything: with no apparent effort, she got straight A's; when we had to run laps for PE, she still ran as fast as the track stars, though she never went out for the team anymore. That was just the way she was, like the way she could drink three beers in a row and still act normal.

But my smooth, white smile was better than any reassurance. When I went back to school on Monday, everyone would be amazed. Even my mother, picking me up at the orthodontist's not two hours earlier, had said I was beautiful. She never commented on anyone's looks, but today she had, and on the way back to the house she had stopped at the store and asked me what I wanted—caramel, chewing gum, an apple?

"Oh, Mama," I said, gazing at her round, mottled forearms as she held the steering wheel, even with the car turned off. "Nothing, thanks. I'm fine. I'm just happy."

She smiled at me then, wisps of damp grey hair stuck to her forehead. "That is all I want, Molly. For all of you to be happy." She turned the car back on, dropped me off at home, and went on with her day.

I turned the volume on high and, lifting Buttercup to a standing position, danced with him awhile before I danced by myself. I belted out all the lyrics and spun and shook and dipped and jumped till I was soaked. *Why do these words sound so nasty*, I wailed, sweat dripping off my forehead. *Join the holy orgy kama sutra everyone*, I raised my glistening arms to the ceiling.

Afterwards I lay on the floor while Buttercup licked my face and the black light made my tee-shirt glow in the dusk of a storm that had been hovering all day over Austin, waiting to break.

I hadn't asked Babette if I could have her room. She was an actress now, performing in a midnight theater in San Francisco, and she only called when she needed money. The house could have burned down for all she cared and it would have been rude to ask her permission, as if I begrudged her her indifference. Sometimes, late at night, she called just to talk to me and she told me how much she missed me, that I was her baby and she never should have left me. I didn't know she was drunk, but I knew she didn't mean the things she said; she just needed to talk the way, when she was younger, she needed to brush my hair.

I couldn't wait for school tomorrow, for everyone to see me.

That night, when my father came home, he came straight to see my teeth. "Well," he said. "They look fine. Just fine." He'd had a tangled bite himself when he was young and I was the only one of his children who had inherited his teeth and suffered like him through years of gum-shredding orthodontia. He'd never had to wear a head and neck brace the way I had, but, still, we'd shared bad teeth. "Hurts like hell," he'd said one day. He always used his Texas voice to speak of pain. "Christ, I remember that. Poor Molly." My braces never hurt, but I nodded anyway, wanting him to say it again. Poor Molly.

Molly.

"Your teeth feel nice and smooth now, don't they?"

I nodded again, beaming.

When I got to my first period class on Monday, it was like the *Wizard of Oz* bursting into color. By the end of the week, three different boys had told me that I seemed like a really interesting person, and they wished they knew me better. After ten days, the count was up to four.

The first, Mark Swift, invited me to see *Jaws* and when he took me home I invited him in and told him my mother was asleep and my father wouldn't be home for hours, did he want some pot or anything?

His eyes widened and he said, "Can we smoke in your room?"

"Yeah," I said. He had a long brown ponytail and straight, even features and his father was a professor at UT.

Before I even got the pot out of my desk drawer, he kissed me. We kissed with the strenuous concentration of thumb wrestlers, and then he put his hand on my breast and I worried that my father would get home before we were done, so I pulled my tee shirt off and started unzipping my jeans.

"Wow," he said, and his gaze rested on my pubic hair. "A red burst of flame," he went on, because he was the editor of the school literary journal.

I lay down and waited for him to undress, but before he did he cupped his hand over my pubic hair and held it there and my chest grew light: I had never thought anything about him except that he was good looking, but now I thought we might be falling in love. Then he took his hand away and undressed and climbed on top of me and into me and it was uncomfortable, but hardly a bolt of pain—it was hardly much of anything at all.

He didn't call a second time, and neither did the other three, each of whom made a gesture—brushing my hair out of my face, stroking my palm at the movies, kissing the top of my ear—that I mistook for love, but I can't say I was heartbroken by their loss of interest. I was humiliated, but that's not the same thing. Having them inside me never felt like much more than riding a bicycle on a gravel road.

Other boys approached me after the first four, but now I became pickier, spurning the ones who weren't handsome enough and holding my prettiness close to me, as if it were an actual virtue, which only equally virtuous boys were worthy of. Those boys and I weren't the best, best-looking students at Austin High—we weren't homecoming royalty—and that, too, I made into a virtue, like upper middle class people who criticize the truly rich.

Lisa wanted a detailed account of every date I went on. She was still together with Charlie Romero and felt everything—every instant of their relationship, every instant of her own being—as vividly as if she were on drugs.

If she had a cold sore, she talked about it all day, and during lunch, which she had at the same time as Becky and me, but not Charlie, she could whisper to us for thirty minutes straight about some new thing Charlie had done to her, like sucking her toes. I thought her passion was a sign of depth and I despaired of ever being like her. She had decided to marry Charlie after high school and though she dressed in hundred dollar blouses and skin tight leather bell bottoms stolen from high-end boutiques, she never flirted with anyone else.

But everything was equally weighted in her heart: the cold sore and Charlie's fidelity, the surprise of his tongue and the importance of a decent wardrobe. She reprimanded me for my fashion choices—ripped jeans and tee-shirts—as if all my future happiness hung in the balance. "You can't wear that again, Molly. Jesus Christ, girl. It looks like you don't care. Guys want you to care."

In my experience, they didn't, but my experience was thin compared to hers.

Every time a boy failed to call me back, she adjusted my look. She loaned me a pair of earrings, or fixed my hair during lunch. Finally, towards the middle of our junior year, when the total number of boys I had slept with was up to eight, and none had stuck around for longer than a month, she decided to overhaul me completely. None of those eight were going to be impressed if I showed up with a new hair color or a new outfit, but Lisa wasn't interested in them; what she wanted for me was another Charlie.

Lisa had no patience with any of the boys I'd slept with, boys I'd known since seventh grade: the college-bound, AP-taking presidents of clubs and societies. But what she didn't quite understand was that, although they didn't stick around, they didn't make fun of me, either. I wasn't like the fat, lonely girls who gave them blow jobs and whom they never kissed. I was tough and smart—a bad girl from way back before their first wet dream—and if I wasn't girlfriend material, I was still respected, still, in my own way, cool.

If I tried, I could remember them better: which college each one attended, who loved which band and who studied what language, who I slept with three times and who four. I could reconstruct their approaches, the shyness of one, the boldness of another—but all the endings were the same, and that's what I remember most—my own fierce clumsiness. *How do you feel about our having slept together?* I could feel the air going out, but I had to do it, I had to ask a boy about his feelings. *Are you glad we slept together? Do you want to be a couple?* I was sure his being inside me had awakened something, or why call it making love?

I imagine they thought about sports when I started talking, that that's why they never made fun of me later: they couldn't remember what I'd said. A few days or weeks after they stopped calling, they smiled at me again, making sly comments as if we'd done some wild,

outrageous thing together—as if they were suddenly bad boys themselves.

Or rather, I suppose, Lisa did understand all that, and didn't care. I was
glad not to be an object of derision, but for Lisa that was no kind of
goal at all. After the eighth boy, she said I needed a brand-new
wardrobe, down to my underwear.

Lisa and Becky and I were sitting in Lisa's kitchen, the rain pounding the windows. Lisa frowned, tapping a cigarette against the edge of
the table. "We're not going to the kids' department, though."

"Shut up," Becky said. "Molly's fine."

"I didn't say she wasn't fine. Guys like small girls. I just want to
find her some sexy clothes. And then I want to find her someone good.
A real boyfriend."

"You think a real boyfriend's gonna give a shit how she dresses?
You are so fucking stupid, sometimes. The problem is not her clothes,
it's the dumbfuck boys in this town."

"They're not all dumbfucks. Anyway, you don't want to come with
us, don't. Maybe you got your own idea about getting her a decent
boyfriend, but I haven't heard anything yet. I'm taking Molly to the
mall."

I liked the way Becky and Lisa argued about what was best for me,
but I felt sick about the prospect of shopping. I still didn't like spending money—throwing it away, as my mother said, and for what?
Things? The way she said things it was as if any object a person might
buy was putrid. Any new object. Anything that came packed with tissue
paper, a receipt, the lingering smell of a department store.

"What the hell," Becky said, finally. "I'll go with y'all."

I looked out at the rain, and imagined hitch-hiking to the mall with
the traffic splashing against us, my free fist clutching a gritty handful
of coins that I was just going to toss away, for nothing.

"Hey Molly," Lisa said, touching my fingers. "It's not an A for effort
kind of thing. You can't get caught."

"Give her a break," Becky said. "She's never been caught at
anything."

Oh, I thought: there would be no receipt, no tissue paper. My chest
clenched abruptly, but it wasn't a fear of the law, or any sense that steal-

ing was a sin. Stealing was much better than shopping: it wasn't wasteful, it was just a sleight of hand, a relocation, like slipping a blouse from one hanger to another. But you had to merit the privilege. You could steal all the shimmery, glittery things you wanted, wear them, horde them, wrap yourself from head to toe in them—but you had to be poor first. It wasn't a matter of need. Who needed a diamond ring, or thigh-high leather boots? It was a matter of worthiness, of having been last and so getting to be first.

Becky stood up. "Y'all coming?"

"Now?" Lisa said.

"Yeah now."

"It's raining dumbshit. You go into a store looking like they dragged you out of the lake, how're you gonna blend in?"

Becky laughed and I laughed, too. We weren't going anywhere. We were just going to sit around Lisa's kitchen table all afternoon, smoking ourselves raw.

The following Sunday, when my father was done with his hour of silence and my mother was not yet back from mass, I went to his study to talk to him. I never did that, just knocked on his door, but I didn't know who else to talk to about Becky, about how to be friends with someone who had so much less than I.

"Who is Becky?" he asked. He had been writing in a thin black composition book when I came in, but now he closed it and looked up.

"The girl I wanted to take to France one summer, whose mother was going to sue—"

"Ah, the Lopez girl." He thought for a few minutes. "You've been friends for some time now, haven't you?"

I nodded and for awhile he was silent, watching me. I looked down at my feet.

"Don't do that," he said, so I met his gaze, but he wasn't talking about where I was looking. "Don't start thinking of her as poor."

"But she is poor."

"It will destroy your friendship."

"I've always known she was poor."

"But you haven't pitied her, you haven't set yourself apart from her."

"It's not pity."

"Isn't it?"

"Her circumstances are harder than mine."

"It would be sad to lose such a friendship."

"But you see inequity everywhere. That's all you do, you and Mama both, you see injustice and you try to do something about it."

"Was there something you wanted to do for Becky?"

I looked away.

"I didn't think so," he said, mildly. "Your description of what I do is inaccurate and clichéd, but that's not what you have come to discuss. You're at an unfortunate age, in which you have begun to be aware of the world, but in a way that is still so partial that it can't do you any good.

"The real task before us—before each of us—is to see that we are in fact equal, that the constitution states this not out of liberal politeness, but because it's true. Few people actually believe in equality, regardless of their politics. Our minds are mostly filled with elaborate systems of hierarchies and divisions in which one man must be pandered to and another one pitied—with generalizations about class and education and all the rest.

"When you wanted to take your friend to France, you may have been eager for her company; but now you're generalizing about her. You're feeling bad because your friend is poor. If you continue to feel bad she will cease to be your friend."

"Mama feels bad," I said. "She generalizes—'the poor orphans'."

My father shook his head. "Whatever your mother says, she's incapable of generalizing. She repeats phrases she has heard, but her entire response to a situation is emotional."

He grew quiet and once again I didn't know where to look. I'd never heard my father talk about my mother unless he was telling the D-day story and I hadn't realized that he still thought about her as someone separate from himself—that he looked at her, noticed her, understood things about her.

"Your mother cannot rid her body of the sensation of cold and hunger and so she sends out clothes and money for food. She doesn't actually think 'the poor orphans'; she simply feels. You say you 'feel' bad, but what you're doing is thinking."

I tried to stop thinking then, to be more like my mother.

"Generalizing is an important intellectual exercise, but it pulls you away from the simple warmth and affection of friendship."

Did he have any friends, I wondered. Had he ever? A group of boys to run around with? I couldn't stand to think that he might be lonely, that for all his strength and beauty, he might have no one to turn to.

"Too great a tendency to generalize," he added softly, "has been my Achilles' heel. I wouldn't wish it on you."

"Oh Daddy!" I said, starting towards him, but he was done talking. I didn't move, afraid to leave him with his loneliness, but he pulled out his notebook again and gestured for me to go.

———

My memory of the mall is of silk. Layers of slippery silk underwear piled high on a low table. Becky walked right up to the skirt rack, unfastened something, dropped it into her bag, and walked out.

Leaning across the jewelry counter, Lisa asked the storekeeper her opinion on some earrings. Such lovely hair, the lady said, and Lisa said, "I was just thinking the same about yours!" Then she turned to me: "Found anything?" and, seeing that I had nothing, set off through the store and filled her arms with clothes before leading me to the dressing room.

"Oh, that's cute," she said, of a peach-colored bra I was fastening. "It's great with your color." Then, in a stage voice, she added, "But it doesn't quite fit, does it?" *Keep it on*, she mouthed, handing me my own clothes to put over it.

I heard her tell the storekeeper that nothing fit, adding that she'd be glad to put everything back, but the lady said no, no, it wasn't necessary, and I walked out in my silk, push up bra: "I'm so sorry I couldn't find anything," I said, trying to make up for all the clothes she'd have to fold.

Becky was sitting on a bench near the fountain, reading a magazine. She spoke without lifting her eyes: "Jesus you all take forever. I've been to three stores already." She continued, softly, "I need to get out of here. I can't just sit here with all this shit in my bag."

"But Molly just got one thing."

"You didn't get anything," I said to Lisa.

"That is not what we're here for. Shit. I guess we gotta go. But next time let's leave Becky at home. She's a fucking klepto." And then we were laughing, racing out of the mall as if all the storekeepers were after us, across the endless parking lot and out onto the highway.

Back in my living room, Becky modeled her new clothes. Her hair, so dark an auburn it was almost brown, was still pulled back in a ponytail, the way it had been in junior high, and her wide, stained smile was unchanged, but her breasts were almost as big as Lisa's. It was always a surprise to see them there, on her slender athletic body, though she herself seemed to take no notice of them.

But I didn't know what to make of her, standing before us in a denim mini skirt and a red angora sweater that clung to her breasts. She seemed naked. She might run a mile in five and a half minutes, ace her tests without studying, drink beer like a man, flick off her virginity like a piece of lint, but she was modest in every sense of the word. I have never known anyone more modest. She neither boasted nor undressed in front of us; nor did she ever mention any of the things other girls talked about as easily as the weather: cramps, leaking, the need to pee. She seemed to me now on display, violated, like a specimen butterfly. She flexed her calf muscles, shifting from side to side.

Lisa laughed. "I know," she said. "I know what's going on."

"What?" Becky asked.

"You're interested, aren't you?"

"Interested in what?"

"Keith Miller."

My throat still closed at the sound of his name. We hadn't mentioned him between us since the end of seventh grade, but I still always knew where he was in the cafeteria, and I could hear his voice, distinct from all the others, in the crowded hallways. He had filled out—I think he played sports—but he was still pretty, and his eyes, more often stoned than not, were even softer than they'd been in junior high.

Once, after an assembly, I dared myself to watch him, slouched in his chair while everyone else stampeded out the doors. He sat with his eyes half-closed, smelling the tips of his fingers and I stood perfectly still, not even breathing.

Bobby Lachaise sauntered up to him and leaned down. "Sniffing that pussy perfume?"

I think that's what Bobby asked, and Keith laughed and rose and the two of them left together, laughing, and it was as if it were my own smell he had been drinking in, I felt that naked.

"You are, aren't you?" Lisa asked, still laughing.

"Shit, I don't know." Becky glanced at me, and I was blood-red.

"Molly?" Lisa asked. "You're not—?"

"Of course not!"

"Well," Lisa said softly. "Shit. That's old news, Molly. You got to get over that. That was nothing. A spin the bottle game, sweetie. Keith has it bad for Becky and it looks like she's interested. Anyway, you got tons of guys."

"I don't care about Keith Miller," I said. "Jesus."

What had happened to going to the mall because I didn't, in fact, have a guy? My heart was pounding and to distract myself I thought of the art teacher, Mr. Keenan. He smiled whenever I came into his room and told me that I reminded him of the Klimt painting of the red-haired woman asleep. Half the girls had crushes on him—he was bearded, and single—but I thought he was a fake. The only thing I had in common with that softly naked Klimt was the color of my hair.

He praised my work, though I had no talent, telling me that although rendering was not my strength, I had a remarkable vision for someone my age. Sometimes, despite my disdain, I flirted with him. I laughed and called him "sir," though he had said we should call him Phil; just last week, he'd kept me after class to discuss my vision, and I had leaned down towards his desk and said, "It's sex, Mr. Keenan. It's not about vision, it's about sex." He flushed, but then he grabbed my wrist and said, "Don't do that, Molly. Don't sell yourself short."

Maybe I could be in love with him—maybe he really did care about me. We could have a secret, dangerous affair, I thought, though I had no interest in him at all.

"Jesus," I said again. "Of course you should go out with Keith."

"Well I don't know," Becky said again, still standing before us, still beautiful in her red angora and her mini-skirt. "Anyway, it doesn't have anything to do with these clothes. I just got them because they were free. I don't see how you can wear this kind of shit, Lisa."

All that evening, I held myself still, waiting for Becky and Lisa to leave; as soon as they were gone, I slid open the glass door and went to lie in the grass with Buttercup. He licked my eyelids. That's what I remember. How delicately his tongue traced that fragile skin. It seems impossible. Why not my nose, my cheeks, my forehead, the way he always did? He must have; he wasn't one to refrain from any particle of salty skin—Charlie Romero didn't have anything on Buttercup—but the part I remember is my eyes, as if he could taste such a richness of tears, only I wasn't crying. I rolled over on my side, cupping his back against my chest. I was just waiting. I wanted Becky and Keith to get it over with. I wanted them to be finished with whatever flirtation, whatever tender, nervous longing they would have to go through before they had sex. It would be okay once they were having sex. Once they were just fucking and they were used to each other's bodies and it wasn't a big deal anymore. But I was holding Buttercup too tight. He pulled away, stood up, nudged me with his nose, as if I should roll down the hill, and so I did, rolling and rolling as I had not done in years.

The next day I stayed in bed all day and my mother came and sat beside me for awhile, gazing curiously at me, though she didn't ask any questions. I was still just waiting, hoping for a sign that they had done it.

In the evening, Lisa called. "You gonna be okay, Molly? I mean about Keith and Becky?"

"Jesus Christ, Lisa."

"Okay, sweetie. Don't get mad. I just didn't realize until last night that you still liked him."

"Lisa."

"Okay. I'll drop the subject."

"Thank you."

"What're you doing tonight?"

"Homework. You?"

"Charlie's coming by. He wanted to go on a double date with Keith and Becky but I said no way. What the fuck would we do? Keith drives a Corvette. I bet he takes his dates to the country club. Poor Becky! But you know it kind of worries me that Charlie thinks we could double date with Keith. He doesn't get it about money at all."

So Keith had fucked Becky. He had lain on top of her, naked, and they had kissed, and she had lifted her naked body, which I had never seen, up to his.

I got up and took a shower and watched the water slake over my own pale skin. After Mark Swift said my pubic hair was like a burst of flame, Johnny Bacon said he'd always *wondered* if redheads were red all over, and Steve Mills said orange pubic hair was kind of weird, wasn't it?

I thought of all those people—rude Steve Mills and handsome Mark Swift, and the Breck girls who had always accompanied Keith Miller down the hall—long-limbed and white-toothed, those girls made no secret of their belief that not just beauty, but money too was a moral virtue—it was one of those girls who had stayed on Keith's fingers all through assembly. The truth was, it made sense, Keith and Becky. I'd known it the instant Lisa said anything, before even, the way sometimes you know right before a glass falls off a table that it's going to break. I even liked Keith better for it—they should all have been after Becky, all the boys at Austin High, but she had the stained teeth and the free lunches and that scared a lot of them away.

The shower was cold by then and I was covered with gooseflesh. I didn't want to look at myself in the mirror when I stepped out, but there I was, so pink I looked as if the skin had been peeled off of me.

Still, Becky loved me as much as she could love any boy, and so whatever thread connected Keith to her connected me, too. I would not be left out.

She called me the next morning to ask if I had done the French homework. That was kind because that was the one subject that was, obviously, easier for me. I gave her the answers and then I asked casually if she'd fucked Keith.

"Yeah, I guess so."

"No good?" My palms were so damp the phone nearly slipped out of my hands.

"No, it's just, it wasn't his fault. We're by the lake and these friends of his come over and start rocking the car, total assholes. And man, Keith was so pissed he was—shit. I was scared he was going to get in a fight."

My breathing slowed down and my heart gave up its racing. We would talk about what assholes other people were, that's what we would do. We wouldn't have to talk about Keith at all.

It helped that you never saw them together, and that she rarely spoke of Keith. Everyone knew they were a couple, and sometimes she mentioned something—a dinner out, a night at the lake—in the same casual, off-hand way she might mention her homework; but she still came to my house every afternoon. Lisa went home with Charlie—soon after our trip to the mall, Charlie broke his shoulder playing football, and Lisa became even more devoted to him—but every day at the end of school, Becky hitch-hiked home with me from Austin High.

Where once we had spent all our time in a sweet, nicotine-filled daze, we now had a bottle of wine, too. There were always jugs of Gallo in the kitchen—hundreds of well-aged bottles had shattered in my mother's cellar on D-day and, though she drank sparingly, she couldn't bring herself to replace the loss with anything better than Gallo. Becky said we might as well be drinking vinegar, but if my mother had bought better wine, she might have counted the bottles, too.

I only needed one glass to feel drunk and then I'd lie down in the grass, with Buttercup beside me, and tell Becky things I'd never told anyone before. She stayed up on the picnic table, listening to me, laughing every now and then with that slow, rich laugh. She'd take her hair out of her ponytail and shake her head back and forth, chuckling, and then tie her hair up again. That's what I remember, that gesture, and the low tones of her laugh, the kindness of it, as if she were saying I'd have killed the bitch, give me your grandmother's address and I'll go kill her now.

She told me stories now, too: how her brother used to pay her a quarter to smell his farts and how, when she was little, she thought she and her brother were the only people in the world who ever farted. She was ashamed of the foul odors that escaped them both, but she saved the quarters anyway, thinking she'd buy a bike until, when she had ten dollars, he stole the money and gave it to a teenager to buy a fifty cent pack of cigarettes and told her he'd split the pack with her if she didn't tell.

"Fuck," I said, and we both laughed.

We would talk until the light faded from the sky and the street lamps came on all across the city so that it was never truly dark, only cold sometimes in the middle of the winter so that we had to sit close together on the picnic table; but mostly I remember lying in the warm grass, not really drunk but softened, listening to her laugh above me and seeing the sweep of her hair in the corner of my eye. We said we disapproved of Lisa's absence—of any girl who would throw over her girl friends for a guy—but we were happy enough alone together and when I look back on our friendship I think of junior and senior year, when Becky was in love with Keith, as our own kind of romance. I loved the ease of her company and the prospect, soon, of freedom—we would be done with school before long—and I imagined us, poised together on the edge of the world, about to leap off of it as a single entity.

Every now and then I slept with someone—usually one of the eight I'd already slept with—but it never amounted to any more than it had before.

One hot afternoon, inhaling deeply on a hash pipe, she told me she was a Buddhist. The pollen hung in golden buds off every tree and we were sitting cross-legged on the picnic table. "I like it that they just say outright that all life is suffering."

I waited, hoping she'd go on and maybe tell me that things weren't going so well between her and Keith; but she said nothing.

"Don't they all kind of say that?" I asked, finally. I might not be the reader Becky was, but I had picked up a few things along the way.

"Yeah, but how they say it, what they do with it, that's what matters. Buddhists tell you what you can do to avoid suffering, but they don't make a big thing about *fault*. If you give up your attachments, you won't suffer—if you don't, you will. It's just matter of fact, it's not some complicated thing about blame and forgiveness."

"Okay," I said. "But here's what I don't get: why Buddhists think we come to earth in the first place. I mean why we become, you know, matter. If we start as pure spirit and end as pure spirit—if we're one with God before we're born and one with God after we die—like assuming you get through all your incarnations—why the big interruption? Why have this material existence where you've got to fuck up all the time and hurt people and get hurt and have zits and, you know, fart—even though you get money for farting, or anyway for smelling farts—I mean why? Why can't we be pure spirit all the time? Are we supposed to be proving something? Why would pure spirit need to prove something to itself?"

Becky shrugged. "You don't get to know that till you die."

"Okay," I said, my brain quickly tired. "I hate religion anyway. Religions. All of them. They just want to tell you what to do. You've got to be quiet, or you've got to hit your chest three times and say Lord I am not worthy, or you've got to sit cross-legged and wait for the light. Got to jump in the water or just let it sprinkle you. The stupid fucks. How do they know? Maybe God wants us to learn how to walk on our hands. Maybe that's the whole point of existence and He's just up there waiting, letting us have wars and Republicans and leprosy and every bad thing until we figure it out—only the lepers'll be screwed no matter what, since they don't have hands."

"You are so fucking stoned."

"What I am is starved," I said, to change the subject from leprosy, because I had just proved my own point, hadn't I? As soon as you opened your mouth—as soon as you just breathed—you started hurting people. You set yourself apart from them—lepers, anyone—and after awhile, for the pleasure of getting a laugh, you were making fun of them, and then—why stop there?—you were hating them, wishing them dead. I was stoned, but it was true, wasn't it?

I went in the house and brought back a box of pop tarts to share with Becky and Buttercup. Feeding Buttercup was a good thing, I was certain of that. He licked my hand, his warm, grainy tongue absolving me as it always had.

I ate until I was sick and my mind was no longer racing and then, when even the sugar had begun to wear off, Becky said, out of the blue, "Your dad's cool."

"Yeah," I said. "He is cool."

"I mean he's like the perfect dad: pays the bills, never home, and like this really good guy on top of it."

"He is a good guy," I said, though it embarrassed me to admit it, since she had no real father at all. I felt as if Gandhi were my father, or Mozart—someone so extraordinary that no one else could compete, a man whose greatness implied great things about me—and I wanted

Becky to have him, too. "You're the only one of my friends he ever talks about. You're probably the only one whose name he knows."

"Shit, Molly. I'm your only friend."

"Lisa's my friend."

"Lisa's nobody's fucking friend. She's a goddamned Republican, she's so married."

"She still loves us."

"Yeah well. So what has he ever said about me?" It's the only time I can remember her asking what someone thought of her.

"Lots of stuff. Shit, even when we were little, he talked about you. My mom and I wanted to take you to France and my dad said we were being patronizing. That it sounded like we wanted to save you from something, and you didn't need saving."

"He was right." She laughed. "I don't want to be saved from poverty."

"You don't?"

"Fuck yes, I do. I want to go to a fancy college where they'll pay for everything, even my fucking deodorant. Miss Di Constanzo says the Ivy Leagues do that if you're poor enough. I want to go to an Ivy League college and wear deodorant on my goddamned eyebrows and never come back here, never set foot in a poor neighborhood again. I want to be richer than God."

"I want to be more famous than God."

"That's because you're already rich. How're you going to be famous?"

I shrugged. What I actually wanted, despite my lack of talent, was to be an artist. I wanted it to turn out that Mr. Keenan had been right all along—that I was desirable and visionary. "I'll start a new religion."

"Like what? The slut hand-walkers?"

"Something like," I said. "I have this feeling my mom'll be home soon."

"I have no fucking idea what time it is. Except I'm not even a little bit stoned anymore, are you?"

My mother came home then. I always knew when she was about to pull into the driveway, though how I knew I can't say: sometimes it was seven or eight and sometimes it was as late as nine. She had a real job with Save the Children now, the people who took out ads in magazines telling you that for just a few dollars a month you could save a child—or you could turn the page. She stepped into the back yard, standing for a moment behind the porch swing.

"Ello Beckee."

"Hey Mrs. Moore."

"You have eaten, you both?"

"We're all set," I said. "Thanks."

It was the same conversation every evening, and I sensed that she wanted to say something more—or maybe not say anything, just sit with us—but I didn't know how to encourage her to speak and I couldn't invite her to join us. She didn't embarrass me anymore, though now, her pre-war clothes having finally disintegrated, she wore polyester muu-muus; I just felt sorry for her. Her loneliness terrified me, and I saw her as the oldest woman in the world. I loved her, but it seemed a vestigial love, a memory of childhood.

"I will eat my supper then."

"Okay, Mama," I said. "See ya."

After a moment Becky said, "You know, I always wanted to adopt one of those kids."

"But you turned the page?"

"Fuck you," she laughed. "We couldn't afford it."

I blushed in the dark.

"You know what my mom did? She got me sea monkeys instead. Her idea of the bargain version, I guess—for a one-time, dollar-fifty fee, you get the same sense of responsibility. I was thinking I'd write my college application essay about that."

"Oh fuck," I said. "I don't know what to write about."

"Molly. I'm being funny. You're supposed to laugh in a sick kind of way, you're not supposed to say oh fuck what am I gonna write about."

"But I don't know what to write about."

"Write about me, write about your poor friend who came so far."

"Come on," I said. "Let's look at brochures."

We slid open the door, nodding at my mother who sat at the kitchen table with her plate of old meat and vegetables and her glass of Gallo, watching *Little House on the Prairie*. She never went to France anymore. My great-uncle died and that was the end of the Alps, the pastries, the long flight across the ocean. I joined my mother less and less these days because Becky hardly went home at all anymore. Keith would pick her up from my house late—honking lightly from the road—or else she'd stay over. Sometimes, if my father was home, he offered to drive her back to her house. He'd knock on my door and ask her if she had a ride and if she didn't, he'd nod and say, "I can take you." I could see that he was tired, but there was no question of my taking a car after dark; my mother's car was covered with dents since I'd learned how to drive, and anyway my father liked Becky—he respected her the way he'd only ever respected Andy Newell—smart, good kids who'd turned out so much better than his own.

"Thank you, Judge Moore," she always said, and when I teased her for being so formal with him—she, who refused to address a single teacher as sir or ma'am—she said she knew how to be polite, most adults just didn't deserve that kind of effort.

In my room, we lay on the floor with the college brochures spread out around us. The photographs of old buildings and students bowed over their books were as beautiful to me as anything I'd ever seen. Everyone was telling Becky to apply to the Ivy Leagues, but for me it was a secret, a thing only Becky knew. Becky said I ought to do it, she said there was no way I wouldn't get in, and when I suggested Berkeley or Stanford— we could live with Babette, I said—she shook her head. I'd never told her much about Babette, but Becky had definite ideas about college. "You got to cut all ties, Molly. You wouldn't go to Rice, after all. Or Heidelberg." I laughed then, agreeing: the twins were in Houston, with babies, and Ted was still stationed in Germany with a wife no one had ever met, but no one was in New England. It was snowy and clear and full of possibility; the only trace of my family was a memory of my father as a young man; I imagined that somewhere among those ivied buildings his breath still lingered.

Keith came for Becky late, around eleven, and I took my homework out to the kitchen table. My mother was long gone to bed, but my father was there, eating vanilla ice cream from the carton.

I spread out my books and papers and after awhile I could feel my father's eyes on me.

"What I like about you, Molly—" His tie hung neatly over the back of his chair, his shirt sleeves were carefully folded back, the hairs on his arms were still perfectly black—"is that you're not boy crazy like your sisters. You don't have a clear sense of purpose, but you're a diligent student and you're not silly the way so many girls are. Well," he laughed slightly. "You'll forgive the generalization, I hope. In any case, you might actually make something of your life. Your friendship with Becky has been good for you. She's awfully bright. You ought to follow her example and apply to the Ivy Leagues. You're not as bright as she, but you might still be admitted. And it would be a good environment for you. Harvard in particular, but any of the Ivy Leagues."

"Thanks, Daddy," I said, and my heart started pounding. I liked the way he ate his ice cream, straight out of the carton with such carefully formed spoonfuls that the top was always perfectly flat. Every morning he rose before anyone else and ran laps around the National Guard Camp on the other side of Exposition. He had come to love running at a Quaker summer camp in New England where he'd been sent as a boy and until he got sick, he ran every day of his life in the thin-soled, arch-less high tops that were the sports shoes of his generation. The counselors at that boys' camp taught him to swim naked in the freezing water and to sleep naked as well, as a matter of hygiene. He had told us these things at supper one night; I had no actual evidence of how he slept or swam, but I associated all these things—the meticulous consumption of ice cream straight from the carton, the bracing nudity, the early morning runs—with manliness and strength. To watch him now, scraping the frozen ice-cream into his foggy spoon, the tendons standing out on his wrist, gave me the same kind of pleasure that someone else might have had from watching her father at a sporting event. His black hair waved back from his head, his clear blue eyes focused simply on his food.

I heard his praise as a thing unmitigated. "Thanks, Daddy," I repeated. "I hadn't thought about Harvard."

"Well, you should," he said, closing the carton at last. "Of course you'll have to buckle down this semester, that's understood."

"Sure," I said. "Daddy? I really appreciate this. Thank you."

He nodded. "The important thing is to stay on track. That's what so many girls seem incapable of." He pushed himself up from the table.

"Becky's a rare exception," he added, putting the ice cream back in the freezer. "Awfully pretty, too, but it hasn't made her stupid."

"Thanks, Daddy."

He sighed, turning towards his bedroom. "Okay."

"I love you, Daddy."

"All right," he said, glancing back at me. "Now good night."

I didn't mind annoying him a little. It was much better than worrying that he might not know I loved him.

Becky and I did apply to Harvard and Princeton and Yale and I got into Harvard and Becky got into all three; but she didn't go to any of them. She got pregnant and she wouldn't have an abortion and Keith broke up with her.

She stopped coming over as much, and if I wanted to see her, I had to go to her house and sit with her at her crowded kitchen table where there was neither the shade of the live oaks nor the chill of the air conditioner.

"But why?" I asked her. "Why would you give everything up?"

She laughed, a soft, quick laugh, no more than a sigh. "It's that I don't want to give anything up."

"Do you think it's wrong? To have an abortion?"

"I don't know," she shrugged. "I just don't want one."

Lisa was sitting with us, subdued in a way that I had never seen her. "She doesn't want to give up Keith's baby," she explained. "It's about Keith."

"But Keith's an asshole," I said.

"Not really," Becky said, and her eyes turned red and I realized then that their relationship had not been simply a matter of her accommodating him, as I had somehow imagined it. She loved him.

"Do you think he'll come around?" I asked quietly, afraid of hurting her.

She shrugged.

"Oh, Becky," I whispered. "I don't think—I mean, what if he doesn't? Then you'd be stuck."

"I'd still have our baby."

"But you wouldn't have any money."

"I can go to college later. I can go to UT. I don't have to go to the fucking Ivy League."

I stared down at my hands.

"All you people talk about having a baby like it's cancer or something."

"Us people?"

"You and Keith. All you fucking rich people."

You couldn't take what she said personally. She was out of her mind with grief, with whatever hormonal waves were washing through her, with her sudden desire for a baby. She had metamorphosed into another girl altogether—solitary, hidden—and I wanted to give up the Ivy League, too, stay in Austin and wait till she was ready to go to college.

I was leaving her apartment, heading out towards the street to hitch a ride home, when Keith Miller pulled up in his Corvette and opened the passenger side door.

"What are you doing here?" I asked.

He shrugged. "Sometimes I just drive around."

"Why don't you go up and see her?"

He shook his head and stared down at his knees. "I can't. Can I talk to you? Can I drive you home or something?"

I got into his car, the leather too thick and soft, I thought, and the floor littered with old soda bottles, candy wrappers, a broken pipe. He needed a shave—scraggly patches of stubble stood out on his chin—and his hair was a little greasy, but he was still beautiful, with his thick eyelashes and his high cheekbones.

"I don't know what to do," he said.

I was silent and he idled the engine awhile and then pulled into traffic.

After awhile I asked him why he had broken up with her.

"Well, Jesus." His voice rose, as if he might cry. "My life is totally fucked up. I'm flunking out. Even before Becky—I just hate this shit. I don't want to go to college. I don't want to do the whole stupid rat race."

"You're flunking out?"

"I'm just sick of it. I can't sit through those classes anymore, can't read the goddamn books, can't keep track of when the fucking exams are."

Becky had never said anything about Keith fucking up. She had said so little to me about their relationship, but I had always assumed that at least part of what they did together was their homework. I figured on the evenings they spent together, they drove around, had sex, and then went back to his house and did their homework. Or maybe they did their homework first. I had no idea what actual couples did, but Keith and Becky and I had always been top students, and for me that required three hours a night of studying. Becky never studied much, but she read quietly while I did.

"You know what I want to do?" he said. "I want to play ball."

"Right now?"

He looked at me. "No, Molly. In life. I want to be a ball player. You're a little weird, you know. Becky always said you were, but I didn't get it. You're like on a different plane."

"Becky said I was weird?"

"Not in a bad way. Like interesting. Cute."

"Becky talks about me?"

He looked over at me again. "Well, yeah. Aren't you like her best friend? And I'm her boyfriend—was, fuck—I'm sure you hear plenty about me."

"No," I said. "Becky has hardly ever said a word about you."

He pulled over sharply and stopped the car. "Becky doesn't talk about me?"

"Not really. I mean now—I know you broke up with her about the baby. But no—we don't really, she doesn't really talk about you."

"Fuck," he said, so softly I could barely hear him.

"It's not necessarily a bad thing."

He shrugged. "When my sisters like guys they can't shut up about them. I just thought girls—"

"Becky's different."

"What the fuck is wrong with her? We can't have a goddamned baby. We've got to go to college. When my father heard she got into all the Ivy Leagues he told my mother to invite her over for supper. They haven't wanted to have anything to do with her before and now they like think she'd be okay for a daughter-in-law."

"I thought you wanted to play ball."

"Yeah, but I can't. I've got to go to college and Becky's got to go and that's how we've got to do it."

"But you're flunking out."

"Well I'm going to pull myself together. How fucking hard is that?" His eyes were red-rimmed, the way Becky's had been when I said he was an asshole and for the first time I understood that their relationship was out of my depths, that they knew each other in a way that I knew no one.

He cried for awhile, his head against the steering wheel and then, for the moment at least, he did pull himself together; he started the car back up and drove me home. I started to get out, but in the same barely audible voice he had used earlier he asked me to wait.

"I'm sorry I was kind of a jerk to you when we were kids."

I turned away, though in the dark he could not have seen my face, and forced a laugh. "Jesus," I said, and forced a second laugh.

"You want to get high?"

"Okay," I said, though I didn't particularly; but I was grateful for the change of subject and for an excuse to spend more time with him.

There was a Presbyterian church one block over and we drove over to it and sat in the parking lot and smoked from a small wooden pipe.

With Becky, getting stoned made me philosophical, but with anyone else it made me aware of the shape of my hands, the texture of my skin, the insignificance of my feet. My arms looked bony and the car was too small for the swollen leather seats, my tongue too dry and heavy. I wanted to stop being stoned the minute I got stoned and I hoped that if I sat very still it would wear off and Keith wouldn't notice that anything was wrong. My chest was sore.

"You're really beautiful, you know."

"What?"

"Jesus, don't jump like that, Molly. I was just saying. I wonder how come you don't have a boyfriend?"

My mouth was too dry to speak.

"You ought to have a boyfriend."

I nodded.

"You don't talk much, do you?"

"No."

He laughed. "You are kind of weird."

"Okay," I said, though it tore my throat to speak.

He leaned over then and kissed me and I did not resist him, thinking I might never have another chance to be kissed by a boy I loved, trying to record every sensation of his lips, his tongue, his teeth, thinking, *and then their mouths parted, and their tongues found each other.* I was afraid he'd change his mind or decide a kiss was all he wanted and anyway I wanted him to know that he could have anything with me, that I was not any kind of prude, and so I put his hand inside my bra and started messing with his belt buckle.

"Fuck," he said, pulling away. "I can't believe what we're doing."

"It's okay," I said. "Nothing happened." I wanted him to kiss me again, but he just sat, breathing loudly, and then he started up the car and took me home again, and when I opened the car door he didn't tell me to wait.

That was the night I dreamt about the hounds, the metal hallway, my mother leading me to the dogs' cage. In the morning I didn't laugh right away about a gun showing up in my dream; I just thought I deserved to die, that I was beyond redemption, and I was sick the whole way to school. I was sure Becky would know I had kissed Keith, and would already be lost to me.

But she was waiting for me on the school steps, the way she always did, and except for the fact that pregnancy had made her face doughy and that she looked perpetually sad, it could have been any morning at all.

"Hey," she said, and my eyes stung.

"Hey," I said back, gazing at her feet.

"I don't know what I'm doing here," she said. "I even did my goddamned Othello paper, like it still matters what kind of grades I get."

But at lunch she disappeared with Keith, and didn't come back for the rest of the day. I went to her apartment after school, and they were both there, sitting at the kitchen table with a couple of beers between them. Her legs were stretched across his lap, and her head was bent, nuzzling into his shoulder. When she looked up, her face froze.

I stared back at her, my eyes burning, but neither of us could think of a thing to say. I don't know how long we were still, watching each other recede further and further into the distance. I knew we wouldn't be friends again; her reconciliation with Keith wouldn't last, but even then she wouldn't want to have anything to do with me. She had been purely kind to me for five years and the one time she was down, I kicked her. Anyway, I thought, her life would move beyond me. She would have her child and find a way to go to college; she would make something of herself, accomplish great things. She wouldn't need to look back and dwell on the fair weather friends of her youth.

I looked down finally and she said, softly, "You really are a slut, aren't you?"

I didn't speak to Becky again for years. Not until she had suffered past the point of words. Only then could I talk to her.

But earlier—when we were still in high school, that last month before the end of the year, when I saw her every day and she didn't turn away from me—from anyone—but gazed blindly ahead; when twice I went to the bathroom and heard her vomiting in the stall and stood there with my heart pounding before I turned around and left—why didn't I apologize?

Kissing Keith, fumbling with his belt, was desperate and quick; but avoiding Becky took time. I told myself she didn't love me anymore, had never loved me, that my presence would only irritate her. I imagined that the rift between us was her doing—that I would never have turned away from her.

I spoke to Lisa only once. She came up to me in the lunchroom (I sat alone now, pretending to do my homework) and said they never should have been friends with me, that I was a back-stabbing bitch. "I'm sorry," I said. But she was already walking away. Lisa's face is a blur to me now, but not Becky's. Becky's is as clear as the Dutch prostitute's. Her stained teeth, her bright dark eyes.

The end of the year came and I didn't attend graduation. I worked at Holiday House, flipping burgers and lowering baskets of fries into the spattering oil; I worked there all summer and then I went to Harvard, as my father had done, as Andy Newell had.

The pins and needles I'd felt before starting junior high were nothing compared to what I felt about going off to Harvard. Now I was being anointed. I tried to say Harvard as blandly as possible, to paralyze my own facial muscles, as if I'd never even heard of the sin of pride. *You?* My father had said when I was accepted. *You got into Harvard?* And I giggled, thrilled to be pleasing him, to have surprised him after all.

All summer, when anyone asked where I was going in the fall, I answered quietly, my eyes lowered, as if to speak of my plans were to say, "I am brilliant. A breed apart."

I flunked out sophomore year, but my breath still lightens when I can work my alma mater into a conversation.

My father took two days off from work and took me to Cambridge. All day every day we were together. We went to Elsie's Lunch and ate hot bacon sandwiches dripping with mayonnaise, we walked together along the Charles, he sang snatches of Harvard rally songs as we went from building to building, re-visiting his old haunts. I knew the songs were stupid, but I didn't mind. "What you will find here," my father told me, "is a singular pursuit of *truth*. In every discipline. Of course you will meet people—snobbish types—who are merely seeking to get ahead, but most of the professors, most of the students, are engaged in a pursuit of truth unrivaled anywhere else in the country. This is a remarkable place, Molly. Such a concentration of brilliance, such pure devotion to the life of the mind."

But when I looked out my dorm window, I could have wept to see so many eager, clean, no-doubt virgins. Where were the truants, the shop-lifters, the sluts? I was as repelled by my classmates' sense of superiority as I was buoyed by my father's.

On our first night together, my roommate, Amanda, alumna of an all girls' school, told me that the great thing about girls' schools was that there was no pressure to have sex. I was already too homesick to speak—how was it possible not to want sex? Even Ted had wanted it—what other way was there to burn off the shame of childhood?

And yet, still, the hours I spent with my father, when he took me all around the Yard, showing me the secret courtyard and the basement passageways, when he walked me up to Radcliffe and down to the river Houses—those hours were as thrilling to me as the dream in which you suddenly realize that you can fly.

The day my father went back to Texas, we went down to the river so my father could have one last look. It was a blue, breezy day and the crew boats were on the water, the boys bending forward and pulling back like a chorus line.

"You'll be lonely of course," my father said. "But it shall pass."

"Will you take care of Buttercup?" I asked, terrified suddenly of his leaving, of being so far away from home, even though it meant that I, too, was special, the best.

"Well naturally," my father said, smiling a little.

"He's just so old," I said, and my eyes welled up with tears. And then my father, who had never done more than pat me on the back now and then, reached down and traced his finger lightly on the scar at my temple, where I had hit the picnic table ten years before. I reached my own hand up and traced where his had been.

How distant college seems now, more distant even than childhood: the cold smell of the stairwells, the din of the Freshman Union, the buzzing silence of the libraries. I could have been at my grandmother's in Corpus Christi, I hated it all so much. Every night my room filled up with Amanda's friends, giddy, humorless girls who pored over the course catalog as if it were a love letter, an illuminated manuscript. Drunk boys banged on the doors, and I would have liked them, except that they had so clearly never been drunk before. They were delirious with new-found freedom—it was all they talked about, besides what it said about them that they were at Harvard—and I thought, this is freedom? At home, untended, I had been free.

Every week I went to the Freshman Dean's office and asked for permission to move off campus. The dean—a scrubbed, boyish man who wore ties the colors of the rich girls' purses at Barton Junior High—told me again and again how important it was for me to bond with my peers. Finally he told me to stop bothering him. He had more important things to tend to, he said, glancing down at a stack of papers. My face burned: I was trying to stay out of his way. I was trying to stay out of everyone's way.

Every week I called home, too. My mother passed the phone to my father. "Ah," he'd say. "I was hoping it would be you." He'd ask about the foliage, whether I'd gone down to watch the boats on the Charles, how I was doing in my courses. He had told me to take as many literature classes as possible—he had majored in English—and I did; I liked reading novels and poetry. I might even have been happy that first semester at Harvard, if, like Ted, I could have taken all my classes by correspondence.

But even more important than the boat races or the colors of the leaves—more important, it seemed, than my classes—were the glass flowers. My father spoke of them as if they were one of the Seven Wonders of the World, his voice wistful, a little thin: "You must go and see them as soon as possible, Molly."

"I will, Daddy. I've been so busy, but I really want to." The Museum of Natural History, where the flowers were kept, had been closed when he brought me to Harvard. "I'm dying to go," I said. "I will, soon. I love you, Daddy."

"Okay, then. Goodbye."

I don't like museums, the endless stopping and staring, the back of my neck sore and my face arranged to look thoughtful. I'm afraid I won't feel what everyone else does and the hushed voices give me a headache, but that isn't why, week after week, I failed to visit the glass flowers. It was the first time I'd ever failed to do what he suggested, and I think, now, that was the point: though I couldn't admit to refusing him, I meant to. It's such a small thing, but, still, it's something.

Becky would have gone. She would have wanted to, the way she wanted to read every book she could get her hands on. What I wanted was to call her, tell her about Amanda and the dumb, innocent, drunken boys in the hallways; I imagined her with a high, taut belly walking around the Yard, always a little to the side and behind me, watching what I did. She seemed to have jumped over the constraints of school into adulthood, into doing exactly what she wanted when she wanted. I pictured her with the wry smile she reserved for everyone we looked down on at Austin High, observing me as I made my way to the Freshman Union, my book bag tearing into my shoulders and not a soul to greet me from the steps of any building. I was as awkward as I'd been at the beginning of seventh grade, sitting by myself at a long table, picking at the kind of school food Becky need never smell again.

By October, I was ready to drop out. I only needed to tell my father; then I could leave. I started to one day, the phone trembling in my hand while I dialed, but the sound of his voice stopped me cold. I couldn't think of anything to say, and then I started talking about the leaves.

I would have had to talk to the Freshman Dean, anyway, and I could hardly look at him. He showed up now and then at the Union, lunch tray in hand, beaming all around, and when he glanced in my direction, I could barely swallow my food—no one but my grandmother had ever suggested I was in the way. I couldn't show up at his office again, even to say I was leaving.

But by November, I had fallen in love and I didn't think of dropping out again until I was a sophomore. Sometimes that story, my first love, seems like everything to me, the story of my whole life; it's not, of course, but there's no story for me without Joseph. He never knew my father or Becky, or Becky's baby, but there he is, in the middle of everything—a pool of rain in the grass, and, in it, all the drowned world, seeming so much lovelier than it is.

Once, in a dentist's waiting room, I read an article about con artists. According to the author, a con artist knows just how to reel his victims in, he has a sixth sense of it—and it's true that Joseph knew what I craved the moment he saw me, that he lied to me as he lied to everyone—but if you know a con artist is lying and you pretend not to know, so that you're lying, too; and if that con artist never takes a cent from you, is the love between you false? That waiting room article said the con grows: the artist starts small and by the time he's middle-aged, he might have to kill someone just to keep his lies intact. All right. But before a lie has swallowed a man's heart, is there no room in it for love?

I met Joseph one afternoon in Mug 'n Muffin. I was sitting at a table with two oversized chocolate chip muffins in front of me, too homesick to eat.

He appeared beside my table, smiling. "One of those for me?" He spoke with a heavy southern accent and I would have been embarrassed for him, had he not been beautiful and wearing a leather jacket. He had my father's coloring—the olive skin and the blue eyes and the black hair—but he looked so different from my father, so much wilder, with his hair in ringlets and his nose flat, a little crooked, that I didn't see it right away. One of his shoulders was bigger than the other, as if he were shrugging—a tilt, I later learned, that came from hoisting ladders all day long. But I couldn't have said that day or the next what color his eyes were or how his nose was shaped—all I noticed at first was the jacket and the accent and the way he stood. A general impression of beauty, of being alone with him in that loud, dingy, margarine-smelling restaurant.

Joe stood, waiting for me to offer him a muffin, and I laughed and held one up to him.

He sat down and said, "Name's Joseph. Joe Price. I don't really want to take your muffin."

"It's okay," I said. "Have one."

"I'd sure hate for you to go hungry."

"It's okay," I said. "Joseph." Already, the sound of his name made my skin ache. "I'd like for you to have one."

"You're sweet," he said, accepting the muffin from my hand without touching my fingers. "You didn't tell me your name."

"Molly. Molly Moore."

"That's pretty."

"It's Marie, actually," I said, pronouncing Marie with a French accent, though I never did that normally.

"That's pretty, how you said that."

"My mother's French," I said. "But everyone calls me Molly."

I asked him where he was from and when he said North Carolina, I was relieved that he hadn't named a worse state—Alabama or Mississippi or even Texas—and then I asked him if he liked Massachusetts and he lifted the one shoulder even higher: "It's a job— I run a roofing company up here."

"Really?" I said, so happy that he was not a Harvard student. I did want him to be smart, though, and devoted to the life of the mind, and some uncertainty must have crossed my face, because he added, "Just for awhile. Till I get enough money together for law school."

"Really? My father's a judge." I spoke as if the law were an unusual, esoteric field, as if I were amazed to find someone besides my father who was interested in it. And he was poor, I thought, happily—he must be, if he had to take time off to scrape money together for school. "These are pretty awful, really," I said, indicating the muffins.

"Taste good to me."

"Oh, I don't know," I said bashfully, as if I'd baked them myself.

He ate his down to the last crumb, his eyes on mine with every bite. "I ought to get on back to work," he said.

"You can have this one, too," I offered.

"You go on and eat it," he said. "Looks like you could use some padding—winter comes around, you're going to need all the padding you can get. Where you from exactly?"

I blushed; I had never thought of myself as having any kind of accent. "Texas," I said. "You could tell?'

"You got a soft voice. Ain't a crime." He smiled and I didn't know if ain't was meant as a private joke between us, two southerners, or if that was the way he talked. Then he laughed, a laugh of pure delight: "I guessed because you're friendly." He rose from the table, pausing for a moment beside me and I thought I should stand up, too, and let him kiss me, but he turned to go. "I'll see you later, Molly."

But when, I wanted to ask. That evening? The next day? How would I know?

I went to the Mug 'n Muffin twice a day after that, lugging my books and papers and three or four sweaters, because my coat, a hand-me-down from a Barton Hills housewife, was a single layer of thin velvet that did nothing to keep out the cold.

I was afraid Joe wouldn't come and every day I grew more frantic, sitting at a small table, trying to read while the doors blew open, letting in waves of street music, car horns, jack hammers—a girl would come in, red-cheeked and hungry, or a man in a grease-stained jacket. It was never Joe.

After awhile, embarrassed at the thought of being found in the Mug 'n Muffin, so obviously waiting for him, I began to loiter in the nearby stores, thinking he might walk past. For three days, I pretended to read the foreign newspapers at the Kiosk; and then, sure he wasn't coming, I gave up, found a payphone and dialed Becky's number. I had no idea what I was going to say, I just wanted to talk to her, but she didn't answer and after twenty rings, I hung up, went to Nini's Corner and stole a Butterfinger.

Emboldened—or desperate for distraction—I asked the clerk for one of the plastic-wrapped porn magazines behind the counter. I imagined Becky beside me, grinning, the two of us shocking all the other customers with our purchase. Becky wouldn't care about the actual magazine, but I loved pictures of naked women. In high school, Becky and I had filched a stack of her brother's *Playboys*—afterwards, she said they were stupid, but I loved imagining what it was like for the models to be so exposed, with a photographer so near. They seemed nothing like the prostitutes I'd seen on display—nothing like any prostitutes I could imagine, those tough women so admired by my father, but like the most vulnerable of girls, just needing to be seen. Buying that *Hustler* felt like the first true thing I'd done since I'd come to Cambridge.

And then, as suddenly as I had doubted Joseph, I knew he'd find me. He wouldn't like my shoplifting or my interest in porn; he wouldn't want to know that I had ever slept with anyone else. I don't know how I knew that—I'd never met a boy before who didn't like my badness— but I knew, as I knew that when he found me, he would invite me to supper. It would be a real all-evening date, the kind I had never gone on; he would hold doors for me, he wouldn't touch me right away.

I realized all this as I stood in the cold sunshine under the clerk's suspicious gaze, and though I returned the magazine, unopened, held up my candy bar and left a quarter on the counter—though it suddenly meant nothing to me to give up all my badness—I felt queasy, too. What did it mean for a young man to have an old man's manners? Only my father held doors for women. Door-holding was like crew-cuts and bouffants—a right-wing affect, unless you were old, and then it was dignified. Joe might be a Republican, I thought, horrified.

I doubted he was going to law school, but that didn't altogether bother me. I was touched that he might have lied to impress me; that, without ever having laid eyes on me, he knew just what lie to tell me. As if it were a deeper truth, his knowing so instantly what I needed to hear.

A week after I'd met him he called to me as I was crossing Mass. Ave. I turned around and walked back towards the sidewalk I'd just left. He was standing in his leather jacket, smiling at me. "Want to grab some lunch?"

Grab some lunch, I thought, over and over; it was the most beautiful phrase I'd ever heard.

Every day for a month we grabbed lunch, but he never touched me. We went to Pamplona, a basement café where there were only three or four menu items, and where we could sit in a corner behind a pillar all afternoon. We'd study the menu, deciding between soup and a guava jelly sandwich, or both, but whatever we ordered, we barely ate. We took turns paying for those sandwiches and bowls of soup we donated to the trash, but otherwise we were like a couple from the fifties: I didn't swear, he pulled out my chair.

Often we didn't speak at all. He could hold my gaze for hours and I'd forget the rest of him then—the ringlets and the boxer's nose—my whole being focused on the gold-flecked blue of his eyes, the sad slope of his eyebrows.

When we spoke, I saw his tilting shoulder again and the strong tendons of his neck, and I couldn't believe we had never touched each other, not even a hand brushed in passing.

We talked about our families. His were all chain smokers, which he hated—he'd left Winston-Salem because he despised the tobacco industry—and I was sad that I wouldn't be able to smoke around him. But I liked his passion about the tobacco industry (though the café was full of smokers) and I liked how kind he was about my siblings. Ted sounded like a good guy, he said, and Babette—he laughed a little, sweetly—she just sounded high strung was all.

We couldn't talk much about anything else. Outside of our families, and the pleasure we took in being together—*It's nice to see you. It's nice to see you, too. Are you free again tomorrow?*—there was nothing we agreed on. He often mentioned the news—bussing or the E.R.A. or apartheid—and I just wanted him to stop. Bussing was awful, he said, kids ought to go to school in their own neighborhoods, with the people they grew up around.

"What are you saying?" I whispered, ashamed to be sitting with him.

"You think I'm prejudiced? My people hate the Klan, one reason I'm waiting on Harvard is I want to see what they do about apartheid." He leaned away from the table, his gaze suddenly flat.

"Do you mean the investments?"

"What else would I mean?"

I gave up, because he was better than I was, because I wasn't putting my degree on hold until Harvard divested from South Africa.

He was never going to Harvard, that much was obvious, but he *would* have waited, I thought, and I loved him for it. He misused words, got the facts wrong about Brown and Roe; if I complained about my homework, he referred dismissively—and incorrectly—to Great Works of Literature. The Canterbear Tales, he might say. What a bore. One minute, pleased that he knew enough about literature to get it wrong, I was moved by the innocence—the bravado!—of his lie, the next I felt a little sick.

But mostly we just looked at each other, day after day, letting our food go to waste.

I knew what my father would say about him, or, rather, what he wouldn't say. My father never referred to people like Joseph—it would have been beneath him to do so. And so I imagined that Joseph and I existed in secret, in a world no one could speak of: a tiny café smelling of espresso and clove cigarettes, where no one had anything else to rush off to, ever. It was a café where no one from work would have looked for Joe, though I didn't think of that until years later, when he was long gone.

Still, I couldn't talk to my father without worrying about Joe. I never so much as hinted at Joe's existence, but even with Babette, who would have loved the story, I said nothing. She would have relished every detail: his jacket, his hair, his plans to go to law school, which I could have presented as fact as easily as he did, but I kept it all to myself.

She called every few days and now I knew she was drunk. Talking to her gave me a stomach ache, but the word alcoholic never crossed my mind. Amanda, who lived in our room much more than I, took her messages. "Sweet Molly!" Babette would cry when I called back, and then, making fun, ask, "How's Hah-vahd?"

"It's okay."

"Oh sweetie," she'd say, her voice suddenly doting: "Do you just love it? I can't picture you with a bunch of college students—tell me that you're having fun. Are you having fun, sweetie?"

"Everyone's pretty straight." I was happy enough now that I'd found Joe, but I didn't want to sound too positive, make her feel bad about skipping out of college and being such a disappointment to our father. If I'd told her the truth, of course, about Joe and his lies, she wouldn't have been jealous, but then I would have had nothing at all.

One day, Joe told me he'd only taken over the running of his company because his boss was *uncompetent*. I cringed and then remembered, suddenly, the lawyers in my father's courtroom. They could barely construct a sentence. Why couldn't Joe be everything he claimed to be? He might mean running the company in a figurative sense. I didn't say anything for awhile, and then I asked him why he had never kissed me.

"I wasn't sure you'd want that."

"Me?"

"You didn't let on."

"Me?" I repeated.

He kissed me then and it was the first time I'd felt anything with a boy, besides the slight pressure of Keith Miller's lips. I wanted to go on feeling, to lean forever over a small table, kissing. It wasn't his deftness, his skill that moved me, it was the bareness of his face. As if touching and being touched were the only truth that existed in the world—whatever you said about anything else, whatever you claimed about what you did or were going to do, was all make believe anyway, so why not just go ahead and pretend you were the King of England? But *this*—the touch of one mouth on another—this was the light of the world. He never closed his eyes, nor I mine, and his expression was so naked, his eyes wide, almost startled—the *Hustler* girls, with their wide-open labia, were nothing by comparison.

I begged him to take me home with him then, but he wouldn't. I had a class that evening, and he didn't want to rush anything, he said.

But the next day, Saturday, he met me outside the Yard in a black pick-up truck and I jumped in, as thrilled to see him at the wheel of his own vehicle as if he'd come in on an airplane. He took me across the river and up a steep, narrow street that looked like France, with its iron railings, its window-box geraniums. We entered a dusty vestibule with a row of mailboxes and a peeling stairwell into which the sun fell dimly from a skylight far above.

"It's on the third floor," he said, motioning for me to go before him, but I couldn't move, thinking of his mangled words, his lies.

"I'm not sure," I said.

"What?"

"I'm just a little nervous is all."

"Then we best not start."

He was on the step below me, looking up. His face was half-hidden in the shadows, as serious as if what we were considering—undressing, having sex—was a thing that would bind us together for the rest of our lives. Couldn't we just have sex for the sake of having sex, the way I'd always done? I stared at his shoulder resting against the wall, the paint flecks rubbing off onto his jacket, and it seemed as if no trivial thing were allowed in that stairwell: the thought of going up sickened me, thrilled me.

"I am sure," I said. "I want to go up."

My heart sank when I saw his apartment. It was a modern one-room, with a single, perfectly made bed, a dinette set, yellow ruffled curtains and a calendar from an insurance agency. There were no books at all. He wasn't cool. Out in the street, he was dark and beautiful and he wore a leather jacket, but in the privacy of his own apartment he wasn't a bit cool; I thought of Keith Miller, how cool he was, and Andy Newell—my father, too—and I was as scared off by Joe's lack of cool as if I'd been a twelve-year-old girl.

"Come here," Joe said, and he helped me out of my coat.

I started unbuttoning my sweater, to get it over with.

"Sh-sh," he said, stopping my hand. He kissed me for a long time before he let me take off any more of our clothes, his kisses slow and unembarrassed, and I couldn't get enough; I forgot all about the prejudices of childhood.

It snowed the whole first week we were together—it was the first snow-fall I'd ever seen—a bitter drizzle that turned grey as soon as it landed, and I only left his apartment to go to class, to get fresh clothes from my room. Amanda glared at me when I came and went, but the only thing she said was that Babette had called three times, very late, and that she had had to tell her that I had moved out, because clearly my sister didn't care whom she disturbed. "Of course," I said. "I'm so sorry. I'll call her from now on."

I passed the Freshman Dean in the Yard one day and smiled right at him.

But once, having breakfast in a diner near his apartment, we met a man who introduced himself to me as Joe's boss. "I thought you were the boss," I said later.

Joe eyed me coldly. "The customer's the boss."

But I'd seen the man's truck through the window, with PUTNAM ROOFING clearly written on the side.

Still, I believed he made everything up to impress me, Judge Moore's daughter, and how could I fault him for that? The fault was mine, for caring about things I shouldn't care about—intelligence, after all, has nothing to do with virtue. Besides, though I was smarter than Joe, he was more beautiful and never lorded it over me. Why should intelligence—a thing as randomly distributed as beauty—matter more? Why should either one matter at all? When he touched me, it was as if my breath, my eyes, my mouth, were proof of God.

But now, when we disagreed—when he said some of those old draft-dodgers should be prosecuted, or spoke of welfare cheats—I wanted to hit him. We stormed out of restaurants, I wept in public, he pinned me against a wall, his face sunk with rage. Afterwards, we'd make love for hours, our skin so sore we could barely touch, but we could not stop touching.

He gave me things no one had ever given me before. Perfume. Silk stockings. Lovely, wasteful things. But once, he gave me flowers, and that was something else entirely—I didn't want a bouquet. Who besides Ted bought flowers? Perfume was sexy, something to rub in the hollow of my thigh, but a bouquet? I had no idea most women loved bouquets; I pictured my mother's watery thanks when Ted brought her armfuls of carnations.

He had double-parked outside a florist's and I was so embarrassed I couldn't look at him.

"Wait here," he said, and I stared down at my hands, the way I used to when Ted sat watching me, waiting for a kind word.

When Joe reappeared he was smiling, his arms full of orchids so darkly crimson they were almost brown. They might be for someone else, I thought, desperately—someone might have died. He handed me the bouquet and slid in behind the steering wheel, but he didn't start up the truck, he just stared at me.

"Are these for me?"

He laughed. "Who else?"

I would not have hurt him for anything. "They're beautiful."

"They look like you," he said, and I almost burst into tears—Of course!—and I thought maybe he was going to law school after all, because didn't you have to be smart to think metaphorically? And even if it wasn't a new or difficult metaphor, still, it meant that buying flowers could be part of lovemaking; it wasn't necessarily just a thing that lonely boys did for their mothers.

I leaned over to kiss him, holding the flowers to the side, and he slipped a hand beneath my shirt, his fingers pressing against my heart. I set the flowers down and took my shirt off with the traffic all around us and the hazards still blinking. "We best get going," he said, but I couldn't stop.

That Sunday, when I called my father, I almost told him about the flowers. He asked if I'd gone to see the glass ones yet.

"No," I said. "But Daddy—do you like orchids?"

"Orchids?"

"Yes."

"Well, I suppose so, but I was asking you about the glass flowers."

"I know, but Daddy, I saw the most beautiful bouquet of crimson orchids. They were almost brown—almost black."

He sighed. "That's all right. I suppose in that brutal cold you wandered into a flower shop to remind yourself of the springtime. That's not a bad idea, actually. I almost wept once in Cambridge, I was so cold."

"I will try to get to the glass flowers this week, I promise."

"Well, it's more important that you take advantage of all that your courses have to offer. You are competing against an awful lot of brilliant students." He sighed again. "It's a real pity Becky couldn't be there."

"Becky?" I said, surprised that my father would even mention her—that he would remember her, now that I was gone and she was no longer at our house in the evening, needing a ride home. "Maybe she'll just start a year late, lots of people do that." I didn't know what else to say.

"Becky?" he echoed. "I should think not. She's determined to keep that child, regardless of the cost. It's a real pity."

"Have you seen her?" I asked, my sternum tightening.

"I've spoken to her mother." I imagined him shrugging. "I offered to connect them with a Catholic adoption agency, but they weren't interested."

"It was nice of you to try, Daddy."

"Well, Becky was a remarkable girl."

Despite my father's assessment, despite my preoccupation with Joe, I was a good student. I don't remember a single thing my professors said, but I remember the nausea I felt before every exam and the sweet tobacco and stone smell of the library, like the courthouse. I remember the yellow lamplight in the middle of the dark day, the rows of bowed heads, and most of all, the thrill I felt when I discovered that so much of literature was about making love. Naturally, I thought, my father didn't read books that way—I think I even felt a little bit superior to him—but it seemed clear enough to me, with Cleopatra going on and on about *a ditch in Egypt*, when she was Egypt, and Blake with all his worms, his *pleasant, trembling fear*, and everything in Faulkner so fecund, not to mention Lawrence. I had discovered a truth no one but the poets themselves, I thought, had ever known: the body, in all its gritty imperfection, was God. Jesus knew it too, of course, but no one else. Jesus, the poets, Joseph and I. Yeats was the best of all. *Love has pitched his mansion in the place of excrement* was the whole truth of the human condition, wasn't it? Joe and I loved each other and lied to each other because *fair and foul are near of kin, and fair needs foul*—because, said Crazy Jane, *nothing can be whole or sole that has not been rent.* Breaking was everything. To *be* broken—and then to come out into another world altogether, Blake said, *translucent, lovely, shining clear...*

But when I went home for Christmas, I wasn't sorry to leave Joe. We hadn't spent a night apart since we'd first made love, and sometimes I nearly cried when I went off to class in the morning; in the evening when he met me after work outside the Yard, my mouth was so dry I could barely talk. I wanted to sleep twelve hours at a stretch, watch a whole day of television, rest awhile from my own hunger.

At the airport, I saw my father before he saw me—the suit, the tie, the thin, straight nose—and it struck me that, as handsome as he was, he wasn't as beautiful as Joe. I felt sorry for him; there was no wildness in my father, no youth. I'd never thought of him as old, the way I thought of my much younger mother, and, suddenly desperate, I called out, "Daddy!" so loud the other passengers turned to look.

"Well, Molly," he said and he blushed a little, but I couldn't help myself. "Daddy!" I cried again, though his hand was already on my shoulder, steering me towards the baggage claim.

In the car, we recovered ourselves. He patted my hand and I leaned back and closed my eyes, breathing in the leather smell of his car, and his own faint eucalyptus scent.

"I suppose you've brought a lot of work home with you," he said. "It's the one thing I disliked about Harvard, the timing of exams. That and the weather," he added. "But I suppose they build character." Then he asked me about my coat, was it warm enough, did it have a good lining?

"It's one Mama got."

"A hand-me-down?" I could hear his mother's dismay in his voice. "No, no, no. We need to get you a proper coat, and gloves. Do you have gloves? Good heavens, we've sent you off to Cambridge without decent clothes. I'm awfully sorry, Molly. You poor thing."

I remembered the exact feel of my braces, the sweetness of our bond.

"It's okay," I said. "It's not that bad, really."

"No, no, no. I should have realized—this was my fault, Molly. Your mother has—she doesn't know. I should have bought you a proper coat when I took you to Cambridge. You can't get a good one in Texas. You need a coat, hat, gloves, a scarf, boots, warm socks—this is terrible, Molly. Terrible. It was inexcusable of me to forget." He smiled a little.

"I suppose I was just so happy to be taking you to Cambridge. The weather's lovely that time of year and the sky has such a wonderfully scrubbed quality to it. It's hard to imagine what's in store, even when you've experienced it."

"That *was* really nice, Daddy."

He was quiet then, his own hands in their elegant leather gloves sliding over the steering wheel as he turned the car onto Exposition. How beautiful the sight of a man holding a steering wheel still is to me. You wouldn't think it would be, but it is.

We didn't have a Christmas tree. My mother hated the glittery waste of American Christmases and my father didn't think about it one way or the other. When we were little we'd had stockings filled with candy and fruit and one wrapped present—a doll, a music box, a necklace—we'd open everything on Christmas Eve, after midnight mass, and my mother would make hot chocolate and a *Bûche de Noël*, which, for all her organ meats, she made as well as any French patissier. The sponge cake was perfectly light, the cream smooth and rich. I loved Christmas Eve, but Christmas day was long and sad, enlivened only by furious scratching fights between Babette and Ted.

After my siblings left home and I stopped going to church, my mother would leave me a Christmas card on the kitchen table, with a five or ten dollar bill and a note saying how much she loved me. I would wake up late and find her in her bedroom, folding underwear or sorting socks. It was always a small chore, something she could put down at a moment's notice; the instant she saw me, her hands froze and in a hushed, eager voice she told me to get my father. We'd sit together at the kitchen table, slicing into the *Bûche de Noël* until it was nearly gone and two or three times my father would say how good it was, that it was even better than the previous year's. I don't remember any other compliments my father paid my mother, and my mother barely acknowledged these: all her attention was on her food, on the rich, creamy, chocolate miracle she herself had created.

But this year they looked up from their plates and said how nice it was to have me home. They each gazed at me for a moment, a gaze as fond as a new parent's, and I said how great it was to be home. I wanted to take my mother's hand and hold it up to my cheek, but my father's presence made me shy.

"Goodness!" my father said. "I'd nearly forgotten." He went to his study and returned with a box wrapped in silver paper in which, between layers of tissue, I found a hat, gloves, and scarf all in creamy cashmere. "We'll order a coat for you before you go," he said, happily. My mother's eyes glazed with tears—jealousy or grief or disapproval, I didn't know which. If anyone ever bought her lovely things, that person was long dead. But suddenly she brushed my hand and murmured that I should try them on. "Nonsense," my father said. "She doesn't need them here." But my mother insisted and so I did. She stared at me, her eyes reddening, while my father finished his cake, and then, in the small, light voice of a young girl admiring an older one, a girl who knows she cannot have what her elders have, she said I was beautiful.

All through junior high and high school, I'd gone to Becky's house Christmas afternoon. Mrs. Lopez bought a game for her children to play every Christmas—Nerf basketball, Sorry!, Twister. She'd play Christmas carols on the radio and set out boxes of grocery store bakery items. Stoned on donuts and sheet cake, the Lopezes would wrestle and laugh through the day's game until Mrs. Lopez sent them outside to shoot hoops so she could cook in peace. When it grew dark we'd go in for turkey and instant stuffing and canned cranberry jelly, which I loved for its trembling, cylindrical beauty, its exact seams. I loved it, but it didn't compare to the cylindrical beauty of a *Bûche de Noël*. The Lopezes had more fun than we did, but I still thought we were a superior breed.

Without the Lopez's to go to, I studied in the afternoon. I was reading *Paradise Lost*, measuring the pages against the clock and hating every minute. Here was something that clearly should have been a sexual metaphor, but wasn't, and I was as bored as I was in science classes.

The twins were due on Boxing Day, husbands and children in tow, and for once I didn't mind. Ted and his wife were still in Germany and Babette always made plans to come home for Christmas and then failed to follow through, but Pat and Claire and their families drove up from Houston every December 26th, filling the house with Texan cheer. I didn't like any of them, but I was glad they were coming.

Pat's Steve was beefy and round-faced and Claire's Dan had thinning, pale-blond hair and a beak nose, but they seemed like twins themselves, always punching each other on the shoulder and talking sports. Next to them, my father seemed much thinner than he was, and my mother became jovial in a way that embarrassed me. She loved those two big, all-American boys bursting onto the scene like G.I. Joes.

Worse, though, were my sisters, parading their children as if they had designed them all on their own. Pat had four-year-old Conroy, brawny as his dad, dressed every Christmas in green plaid shorts and red suspenders; Claire and Dan had the beautiful Ashley and Laura, whom I had never seen in anything but Laura Ashley, and who, at two and three, fought as furiously as their missing aunt and uncle.

I called Babette three times on Christmas day and each time she was more rattled than before. "I hate this motherfucking holiday, what're you doing baby?"

"Studying."

"Fuck."

"Are you going to have dinner with your neighbors?" The first two times I'd called, she was trying to decide whether to go next door for turkey.

"I don't know Moll, I think I'll have a silent night. I wish everyone would have a goddamned silent light, night I mean. A night light."

"You sure you don't want to come home? You still could, you know—I'll bet you could get a flight easily today." I'd heard my mother earlier, urging Babette to come home. It was obvious from my mother's side of the conversation that Babette didn't want to talk to her, so my father got on and listened awhile before he agreed, as he always did, to send more money. But he never suggested that she come home. I was hoping the promise of money would have cheered her up, but if it had, it hadn't lasted. So I did what my mother did; Babette hated my mother's urgings, but she loved mine, the way she'd always loved it when I was small and I followed her to her room.

"You're sweet, baby," she said. "Baby, baby, oh baby baby—what is that song? Shit I can't remember anything. Nah, I'm gonna stay here. Think I'll go out and admire the decorations. Plus I have a tree. You ought to see it, Molly. Lights and everything."

She had told me about the tree before, but I still congratulated her.

"I wish I *could* see it," I said.

"Anyone talk to Ted yet?"

"This morning, he asked if we'd spoken to you."

"Fuck, Ted. He thinks I'm going to get up at the crack of dawn just because it's Christmas? How was he anyway?"

"Okay, I think. He sounded good."

"Fuck that. I got to piss, Molly. Hold on, okay? I want to keep talking to you. I would've come home to see you. Hold on, okay, baby? I'm about to piss myself—"

She never returned and when I tried hanging up and calling her again, the line was busy, of course, but just when I couldn't stand it anymore, when I was about to call the San Francisco police, her phone rang. She didn't pick up, but I knew she was okay, because she had come back from the toilet and put the receiver down.

I wanted the twins to come; I wanted to see what gifts they'd bring and I wanted Steve and Dan to punch me; I wanted one of the little ones to fall asleep in my arms. I didn't want to keep reading, bored and endlessly distracted by the clock, Babette, Joe. By the thought of Becky, not two miles away.

I don't remember much about the twins' actual visit that year—it was like every other, no doubt—but I remember that in the middle of the night, reaching the end of *Paradise Lost*, I burst into tears. I sobbed the way I had at the end of *Old Yeller*, caught off-guard, gulping and choking like a small child. For a stoned kiss, I thought, I'd given up the Lopez's bright kitchen; for a cashmere scarf, I'd abandoned my mother.

After the twins left, I just wanted to get back to Cambridge. I called Joe every day and we barely spoke; we just listened to each other breathe.

But one day we did talk. He told me he'd gotten the results of his LSATs, and that he'd gotten a perfect score. "That's great," I said.

"Well," he said. "It's just a test. You get a good score all's it means is you're good at taking tests."

I liked that he looked at it that way, and that he knew about the LSATs—even though I knew he hadn't taken them, since they weren't offered at that time of year—and then we were silent again and it was as if we hadn't spoken at all, and I could hear him breathing, slow and steady and deep.

When I wasn't studying, I sat out in the yard, with Buttercup's head in my lap. My parents were back at work, the two of them staying at their offices now till ten or later, and I didn't know how to be alone in my house without Becky to keep me company. I knew it was ridiculous not to call her, that to be too ashamed to apologize was as stupid as driving too slowly, but I couldn't do it. I imagined telling Joe about her—I never had—and in my fantasies, he always exonerated me: *You'd never been in love before, you didn't know what you were doing.*

It's true, I'd say. *But still.*

You didn't mean to hurt her.

On and on we discussed my innocence while I stroked Buttercup's old, dull coat. Sometimes he still tried to nose his way into my crotch and I pushed him off gently, laughing; but I was sad, because he was so old, and I didn't believe he could smell much of anything anymore. It was just habit, the memory of an old comfort. If it hadn't been for Joe, I would have let him smell my crotch, I would have let him hump me—what could it cost me?—but now my body was a different thing. I could no more roll around with Buttercup than I could hitchhike out of town and flirt with the first man who picked me up.

I didn't want to flirt, but I did want to leave town. The last two weeks I missed Joe so much my whole body ached, as if I were covered with bruises, and when I left I was so afraid I'd miss my flight or lose my ticket I barely hugged my mother. I didn't go out to the backyard to say goodbye to Buttercup.

W hen I got back to Cambridge, everything was flooded with light. I think it was a clear day, with that washed New England blue everywhere—the sky all scrubbed, as my father said—but I mean our bodies: it seemed to me we gave off streaks of light, as if our skin were phosphorescent, the way Babette had once imagined mine.

If we could barely speak (so many taboo subjects), if all the outer stuff of life (his future plans, my admiration) were pretend, then all that was left was the original, undying, shimmering moment of desire.

But one morning, having gone out for milk and eggs, he came back with a newspaper too.

I looked up at him from the bed. "Why would you get a newspaper?"

"To read?"

"You thought we'd read the paper? Oh, Joe. I hate newspapers."

"You want me to get the *Globe*?"

"It's not the *Herald* I object to. It's newspapers. It's—" I didn't want to have to explain something so obvious, that newspapers were *of the world*; if I said it out loud I'd ruin everything, so I cast about for another reason to hate newspapers: "—the way they *generalize*."

"So?"

"Suppose they generalized about us?"

"Why would they generalize about you and I?"

"They wouldn't, I'm just saying. If you think of how they'd describe us, then you can't believe anything they say, and so why would you buy a newspaper?"

"Lord, Molly. I just want to check the baseball scores."

"The baseball scores?" I didn't even know he liked baseball. "How could you?" I said, weakly. I was still naked, but I was sitting up on the edge of his bed now.

"How could I what?"

"Care about scores when—" I gestured at him finally, at myself. "You have all this."

He sat down beside me, his jacket cold from outside, the bag of groceries still under his arm. "You read."

"Only because I have to. I don't read anything I don't have to."

"Oh Molly," he said, opening my thighs. "I love you, Molly."

Only once did I not want to make love with him. It was the end of January, and my mother wrote to say that Buttercup had died. She had tried to call, but I was never in. That night, when Joe and I made love, he asked what was wrong, but I said nothing. He was mad—he could see that my heart wasn't in it—but I just kept lying, insisting that everything was fine, I was just a little tired, was all. Maybe I was getting sick, I said. A lot of people on campus were sick. I wouldn't tell him the truth, how I had loved Buttercup or how I'd hit him, how I had pushed him away the last time I'd seen him; I wouldn't say, *When Buttercup and I rolled around together, when I was little, such waves of desire washed through me, and I had no idea—*

A dog? He might say. *Shit, Molly.*

And then I would never be able to forgive him.

But that was the only time.

The coat my father promised never came, but on Valentine's Day, Joe was waiting outside the Yard with a chocolate rose and an orange down jacket he had gotten for me at Filene's Basement. "It's bright," he said. "But you can't keep going around in your little velvet thing."

It was as ugly a coat as I'd ever seen, but I would have made love to Joe right there on the slushy sidewalk if he hadn't laughed and told me to get on in the truck, we were going to freeze to death in a minute.

"Now you'll always be able to find me in a crowd," I said, sliding next to him on the seat.

I don't need that coat to be able to find you, Molly Moore," he said, and I could not imagine ever being happier in my life.

In the spring he gave me a silk negligee. I had jumped in the truck when he handed me the bag and this time I said nothing, peeling off my tee-shirt and unfastening my skirt and shimmying the negligee over my shoulders. It was pure white, no bits of lace, no little sewn-on roses. He glanced away from the traffic and smiled.

"We better go to the beach," he said. "You look too nice like that to walk around town."

I hadn't thought we were going to walk around town, but I was glad to go to the beach, to show off my negligee to anyone who happened to be there.

The dunes at Crane's Beach were empty, though, so I took my negligee off and walked naked out into the sand. Joe draped it over his shoulder and he looked like an aviator, with his leather jacket and that scrap of white silk blowing around his face. He'd taken off his shoes and socks and we walked out into the small freezing waves—I should put on his jacket, he said, I was going to catch a cold, but I said no, I liked the air against my body. I felt more naked than I ever had, and his slightest touch—his hand brushing against mine—seemed an intimacy so extreme I could hardly bear it. When, after awhile, we sat at the water's edge, he brushed his fingers across my knee and I jerked, as if I had a chill. He lifted me onto his lap, covering me with his jacket, pressing the palm of his hand against my heart as he would against a wound.

That summer, I stayed in Cambridge.

"Good," my father said. "Very good, Molly. It would be hard to stay focused on your studies if you spent the summer hanging around the house."

I didn't know what he meant—I wasn't planning to study during the summer—but I was glad he was pleased.

I moved out of the dorm, stripping the bed I had barely slept in since the beginning of the year, and rented a tiny apartment between Central Square and the river.

The day I moved in, with only my trunk full of clothes and books, I saw a queen-sized mattress propped on the sidewalk, waiting for the garbage collectors. I dragged it up the stairs to my bedroom, thinking how proud my mother would be of my thrift; I made shelves from boards and cinderblocks, bought two used straight-back chairs and a wobbly table, and hung my negligee on the bedroom wall for decoration. I got a job at a bakery across town in Inman Square where, three times a day, I could make meals from day-old cookies and brownies. In the evening when I came home, trembling from all that sugar, the long blue dusk filled my apartment like water.

Joe was often there, waiting for me at my table, and if he wasn't, I rode my bicycle—a three-speed child-sized bike I'd gotten at a yard sale—across the river to his apartment.

I was so happy that summer, in my own two rooms, which I filled with indestructible philodendrons and china tea sets from thrift shops. I loved getting machine-printed paychecks and I loved the sight of Joe stretched out on my musty smelling mattress. My life was just the way I wanted, and nothing could bother me—not even the middle of the night calls I got from Babette. I'd pull the phone out into the kitchen, so Joe could keep sleeping—Babette still knew nothing of his existence—and then I'd listen to her talk about all the people who had done her wrong and how fucked up the world was. She was always mad at someone—her landlord or a neighbor or some casting director who never called her back.

Once, in the middle of a rant about her utility bill, she said something about our parents, how completely fucked up they were. I barely listened.

"Daddy had sex with those prostitutes, you know."

I rolled my eyes.

"He never should have married a Catholic. A Catholic'll have sex with you, but only because it's God's plan. That's disgusting—having sex because God wants you to."

"Are they going to cut off your utilities?" I asked; what was disgusting was speculating about Mama and Daddy's sex life in the first place.

"They better the fuck not, that's all I can say."

I closed my eyes, and let everything she had to say—gas bills, our parents' sex life—rumble by with all the other late night traffic. You couldn't believe a word she said.

"Plus with her getting so fat and all."

"Daddy doesn't care about that."

"Are you kidding?"

"Listen," I sighed. "How are you going to keep them from shutting off your utilities?"

And then she was off again, explaining how she was going to sue the city, just sue them, and Daddy had better help her out and I wondered how soon I could politely get off the phone, because I was tired and Joe was in the next room, his bare legs tangled in the sheets, like Jesus.

Even when school started up and the cold weather came, I didn't mind. I went to my classes as I had gone to my job at the bakery—punctually—and made my weekly reports to my father about the boats and the weather (we no longer spoke of the glass flowers) but what I thought about all day was the way Joe smelled after he'd been on someone's roof, that mixture of cold air and sweat. I sat in class, imagining his legs preceding me up the stairs to his apartment, the stairwell itself, and at the top, like something out of a fairy tale, a wild promise, the small, grey door to his apartment.

But there were still the mangled words—*forbodement, cautionness*—and the terrible, reactionary views, and because of these I couldn't resist needling him sometimes.

We were sitting on his bed one day with my legs across his lap, the radiator clanging beside us, and I asked him what he thought of marriage. I thought of marriage as a prison, the way Blake did, but it occurred to me that Joe might believe in it, what with the way he held doors for women and his appalling ideas about welfare. I waited for him to answer, heartsick that he might not see how wrong it was to constrain love. I wanted to explain about Blake, about marriage and prostitution being the two equally terrible outcomes of *thou shalt not,* though prostitution was the more honest, and prostitutes more admirable than pious wives. (I exempted my mother, as I exempted my parents' marriage.) "What do you think?" I asked again. "About marriage?"

It was November and already dark by four; a layer of snow shone on the windowsill. The radiator clanged again and still he sat without moving or saying a word. I imagined the argument that would follow and felt tired all through my body. First he would defend the institution of marriage, and then he would say nothing about why, if he believed in marriage, he didn't want to marry me.

I swung my legs off his, but didn't leave the bed. He kept quiet, staring out into the tidy room with the yellow curtains.

"I would love to marry you," he said, finally.

"Oh," I said, and a veil slipped away from the world: this was the true marriage, the holiest of holies—*the soul of sweet delight*, which *can never be defil'd*. Joe had chosen me, brought me into existence, and such an existence it was—"Oh," I said again, and we made love all the rest of that afternoon.

In the morning, I could barely eat, barely look at the shimmering brilliance outside, the beauty of everything: the ragged mailboxes, the girls in my classes with their sleepy made-up faces, the chalky desks in the front row, my Romantic Poetry professor with his small, bright eyes, his drooping pants. *I'm getting married*, I thought, all through the day, and I announced it right and left, when anyone asked how I was in a casual, off-hand way. I had, by then, a few friendly acquaintances at Harvard, whom I had met at Dudley House, in the café for off campus students—a bulimic poet who sometimes ate lunch with me, a crew-cut-wearing politico who called himself Che, a chemistry major who worked in a topless bar—and all their various friends, who knew that I was never available in the evenings or on weekends, but that I was good for a cigarette break or a dirty joke—and every one of them looked at me as if I had said I was joining the Hare Krishnas. I would have felt the need to justify myself before, but not now, not with everything so beautiful and bright, even the piles of slush, the low grey sky.

I didn't think of telling my parents and I didn't think of not telling them; I forgot them altogether.

When I was done with my classes, Joe was waiting for me outside the gate and he opened his leather jacket to me, wrapping up my down one in the heat of his chest.

"I want to wear my negligee as a wedding dress," I said.

"You better," he said, breathing his warm breath into my hair.

But now, of course, our fights grew worse than ever and it was clear I couldn't marry him. What did he expect? That I would change my name and give up my lovely, light-filled apartment and all my books to live in a dingy tract house where he'd want his supper waiting for him every night? Because it was obvious that's how it would be, with his door-opening and his flower-buying; obvious that to become his wife, I'd have to become like him, a Price. I'd have to use his awful invented words, decorate the house in yellow curtains. I didn't say these things, because they were petty and mean, because it would be terrible to tell him I didn't want to marry him, but I screamed at him about other things until my throat was raw—screamed the way Babette did—until the color drained from his face and he stood trembling with rage, telling me to get out, and I burst into tears, because I couldn't lose him, but marriage would kill me. I had never meant to suggest marriage in the first place, but he stood with his drawn face, his trembling voice, telling me to get on out, and I kneeled down, sobbing, my face in my hands, because he had said he didn't believe in community service alternatives to prison, only he had said alternations, and he was telling me to get on out and I was begging him to re-think, because not to believe in rehabilitation, in the possibility of redemption, was its own sin—"You'd just throw away the key, wouldn't you?"

"Go. I said to get out, Molly."

"That's your idea of marriage, too, isn't it?"

"Get out, Molly."

I had started now: "You'd want me home all day in a yellow apron. You'd want me just like your mother."

"Get the hell on out, Molly."

"Please, Joe. I just need to know."

"Know what? You've been hollering at me for an hour."

"Joe—" But it was okay. I had said it: I didn't want to stay home in a yellow apron. It was not okay that he didn't believe in rehabilitation, but I would not have to be like his mother. I loved him, that was all. I didn't want to get married, but I loved him. I sat up, catching my breath. "I love you, Joseph."

"What?"

"I love you. I'm sorry."

"What the hell's going on with you?"

I shook my head. "I just love you."

"Get on out, Molly."

"Okay, I'll go. I just wanted you to know that I loved you."

"Git—"

"Okay." I rose, put on my jacket, my boots. "I love you so much," I said, touching his shoulder before I went out the door and down the cold, narrow hallway. I was free. I wouldn't marry him, but I had told the truth. My limbs were rubbery still, my throat on fire, and it was the middle of the night, snow and rain coming down all sloppily together and dazzling the streetlights—it would be hard to ride my bicycle—but I had told the truth, I had said the one thing that mattered. *What you will find at Harvard, Molly, is a singular devotion to the truth.*

"Molly."

He had followed me down the steps.

"What?" I asked, my heart still. "What is it, Joseph?"

He nodded towards the stairs. "Come on back."

"Joe?"

"Just come on back," he said, softly.

But when he kissed me, I was afraid. My father wouldn't even look at Joe if the two of them crossed paths.

He carried me to the tiny bed, his dark hand stroking my brow, my cheek, and I could barely stay awake.

The next time we fought, I did not say I loved him and he did not follow me out. It was a Monday morning and I made my way through the crowded streets, bicycling slowly, the bright air and the street noises so thin they were like strips of tinsel falling through the air.

He had told me to get out and I had left and I would never see him again and after awhile it would be as if I had never touched him. A car swerved and honked at me, because you could not simply drop your bicycle against a curb and sit down on the sidewalk with your feet out in the busy street.

"You okay miss?" My eyes dried instantly and I rose, climbed on my bicycle and swerved back into traffic. I did not know who had asked after me so solicitously, but it was terrible, only I was sobbing again, never in my life had I sobbed this way, days on end of it and the screaming too as if I'd lost my mind. Not even with my grandmother, not even with Keith Miller had I carried on this way—

I stopped, horrified.

I was on the BU Bridge, the brilliant, cloudless morning flowing past me, my hair whipping behind my ears, my skirt flat to my thighs: I was pregnant. Why else the screaming, the uncontrollable weeping? But all I had to do was go by the University Health Services and pee in a plastic cup; Harvard would do the rest. They would arrange for the abortion, they'd even pay for it.

Only I wasn't, actually, far enough along. I would have to stay pregnant a little while longer, then they could do the abortion. I loathed the smell of the Health Services, the little clusters of vinyl chairs in the waiting room and all the students with book bags at their feet, with 'flus and sprained ankles and hallucinations, with accidental fetuses. I sat back down among the other students, though I was free to go—in two weeks I would be far enough along, but that was a week of mid-terms, so maybe I should wait three?—my only symptom was a soreness in my sternum. I hated the waiting room, but I was so tired and I didn't want to be alone. No one looked at anyone, each patient full of his own private misery. When I got up I would have to go outside, into the bright air, the packed throngs of the Square, and it would be such a long ride back to Joe's, but I had to tell him.

"Oh Molly," he said, and he held my head against his chest, but we were not lovers anymore. I had met him coming down the stairs and at the sight of me he paused and a flash of annoyance crossed his face, so I had said the words as fast as I could, standing at the bottom of the peeling stairwell: *I'mpregnant.*

I could hear his heart and as long as he kept his hand cupped around my head, I was okay. I was just pregnant, like Becky—only she wasn't. All this time I'd thought of her as pregnant, but she wouldn't be anymore, she'd be a mother now and I had no idea if it was a boy or a girl. I had missed it all—she'd had a baby. But I would not. For a moment, standing there, I didn't even think I'd have an abortion. As long as Joe kept holding me, my pregnancy didn't have to be anything more than an ache, a piece of sadness between us.

"Do you want to stay here?"

I kept quiet, breathing in the cool plaster smell of the stairwell, my gaze fixed on the row of mailboxes. I would always love this stairwell, and it seemed to me that the column of dusty light that rose and fell between the glassed in vestibule and the dirty skylight emanated, however weakly, from my own heart.

"And sleep on your floor?" I asked.

He shrugged. "I could sleep on the floor."

"It's all right," I said, turning back towards the door.

"You gonna be okay?"

"I'll be okay. I just wanted you to know."

"I'll call in the morning," he said. "See how you're doing."

We were as polite as strangers caught together in some accident—a stuck elevator, a small flood—and I thought, *this is what love is, what it flames up from and dies back down to: the kindness of strangers.*

At home, I sat with my books spread out around me and stared at the telephone lines beyond my kitchen windows. The hours were infinitely long, silent. Even my classes were quiet, even the construction in Harvard Square. I had decided to wait the extra week for the abortion so I could take my mid-terms—so that I could, after all, stay on track. My chest was always sore, as if the wind threw pebbles against my heart, and the smells carried by the wind—even that frozen, odorless wind—sickened me. Twice a day I ate Cream of Rice; nothing else stayed down. But it was the silence that drove me crazy, the length of those days. Until, into that silence, the phone would ring—a loud, lovely ringing—such a bright colored sound, I could taste it—but it was only a classmate, or Babette.

I let Babette rant—though what if Joe was trying to reach me *right then?*—because I didn't know how to hang up. No matter how soothingly I murmured, she kept right on talking, outraged by everyone except me, she said, I was the only one—until, exhausted, she let out a sigh and announced that she had to go. *Shit, Molly. These calls cost money.*

I didn't call home and my parents didn't call me—except when Buttercup had died, they never placed the calls—but every night, when I couldn't stand it anymore, I called Joe. He was always home and he always asked how I was. I spoke slowly, to make the call last. I'm fine, I was a little dizzy this morning, how are you?

I stopped smoking. I wanted the baby (but it wasn't a baby!) to be comfortable for the little time it had. I took vitamins to supplement the Cream of Rice. And then sometimes, I was unaccountably happy: I wasn't alone. The baby, the spirit, whatever it was, was always with me; it was a part of Joe and a part of me and it lived inside me, and I was amazed that such a thing was possible, that out of our bodies we could create a third, and the third contained all three.

But suppose what I was going to do was a sin? My pregnancy was a part of me the way my ribs were, my heart. If I let that little tissue grow, become a person, then what? Give that person up? The child of my heart? Better to put a stop to the whole thing now, when it was only myself I could injure.

Becky's baby would be almost a year old now. I'd kept right on thinking she was pregnant, and all the while her baby was learning to walk. I thought of Trudy Anderson, climbing into my lap after she peed beside me in her wading pool and rolling her head against my chest to feel what was there. I'd like that—a baby of my own—but I had no idea how I'd raise an actual child. Becky was the only person I knew who was capable of that kind of thing.

Joe called one afternoon and said the day I had scheduled for the abortion wasn't convenient—he was going to take me to the clinic, which was two towns over, and bring me back—could I schedule it a day later? My eyes welled up with tears—it wasn't a dentist's appointment—and I didn't know, either, if I could wait another day to see him: because there was that in my calculations, too, in the marking off of days: that when I had the abortion, I would see him, we would ride together in his truck and it was a half hour ride at least, and I would sit beside him, beside the warmth of his leg. He had said nothing about helping to pay, and he didn't know about Harvard footing the bill; I couldn't stand it that he would have left me to take care of everything alone, and now this—but I didn't say anything. I didn't want to risk losing everything, even his kindness.

When the day came, it was pouring snow. I woke at five, thinking he wouldn't be able to drive in all that snow, that I would never have the abortion, never see him, that nothing would ever happen to me; the windows would always be white and empty, my chest always sore. But he appeared, honking once, lightly, the way Keith Miller did for Becky; I waved and he looked down and blew into his hands while I came towards him.

At the sight of him, I caught my breath: it was not possible that he could hold his hands before his face and not touch me; that I could no longer rest my own hand on his. *But what about the orchids?* I thought suddenly, frantically, as if they might prove something.

I couldn't marry him, but not to touch at all?

"It happened that night," I said. "The night we talked about marriage."

"How do you know?"

"The timing. That's when it had to have happened." It was true, but that wasn't the point. The point was that we had made love that way, that I had been free to touch every inch of his body, and now he sat so formally, both hands on the steering wheel, his body hidden away, as if he had no memory of any day before this day.

At the clinic there was no pain to speak of, just the whir of the machine, and the nicest nurses I ever met. One came with me to hold my hand and the doctor herself was so young and pretty and said that I would be good at having babies, the way I was built and the way I breathed. But afterwards Joe was not in the waiting room. The receptionist said he had come, but I hadn't been ready and so he had gone out but he would be back. I sat in a hard plastic chair and stared at Jimmy Carter and Anwar Sadat on the cover of a three year old Newsweek. Why did they call it Camp David, I wondered, imagining a summer camp for young boys, Dave, Davey and Little D. The magazine opened to an ad for termite control: an anguished woman stood before a house which, though it looked perfectly fine, with its gabled windows and little portico, was already ruined. All it would take one day was a gust of wind and the house would turn to dust. But the woman's hair was nicely waved, she did not have a cotton pad between her legs. And Joe would never come. I hadn't eaten anything before the abortion and I was starving now.

Through the windows of the waiting room I could see the snow blanketing the parking lot; over and over the sky emptied itself, but it would never be enough, in a thousand years the snow would still be falling. This is what my life had come to, I thought, what it had all been building towards: these orange plastic chairs and the outdated magazines, the *Time* and *Newsweek* and *House Beautiful* and even *Family Circle*, and the other girls sitting glumly in the chairs across from me. How young the other girls looked (there were three of them) with their sleepy faces, their hair all messed up. They looked young and glum, no expression on their faces, as if they were angry, as if they had been hurt beyond recall and it was only nine in the morning. They had all had to come out so early to this lovely suburban clinic with the sky pouring down and the kind women holding our hands and the young beautiful doctor. Off in the distance I could hear the beeping of a snow plow, like a train leaving, but we would never leave, any of us, we would stay forever among the orange plastic chairs, the cheerful magazines, sitting on our cotton pads.

But he had come. The door burst open and there was Joe. He was the most beautiful man in the world. He paused just inside the door, shaking off his jacket and looking around, his face a little blank, the way faces are when they have not yet found what they are looking for. But of course it only took a second and I was standing in front of him, with my box of pads and my instructions from the clinic, and I was all done, so there was nothing to do but put on my jacket and go.

"You okay?" he asked, when we were in his truck, settled in our drenched coats with the heater on high and the headlights making yellow circles before us.

"It didn't hurt," I said.

"So you okay?"

I nodded. "I'm hungry. Could we stop somewhere and get something?" In my apartment, there were only boxes of Cream of Rice, but I wanted real food now, eggs and toast and orange juice. And if we went somewhere, that would be more time we had together. We would sit across from each other in a diner; we would have to wait for our food and take the time to eat it. We would be sitting together, across a little table, and neither of us would jump up and leave.

We went to a little place where you got your own food at the counter and there were no eggs, only pastries. He bought nothing, not even a cup of coffee. He had said, "This okay?" turning into a parking space outside the café—we were already back in Cambridge, it would only take a few minutes to get home—and what could I say? That I wanted to go somewhere nicer, Pamplona, or even just the Mug 'n Muffin, where we could sit together quietly?

He said nothing while I ate, as he had said nothing in the truck, squinting into the driving snow. He did not rush me, sitting across from me and watching me eat as he might have watched a child: looking at my hands, my mouth, so that it was as if we were both fixated on my bear claw, as if we had some deep fascination with the pastry itself, the nuts and the sugar and the butter, until I was done. I pressed a nut into my fingertip and put it into my mouth.

"Ready?" he said, already standing.

"I'll just throw this away," I said.

"I'll get it," he said, collecting the paper plate and the napkin and the empty orange juice carton. His voice was soft and low, full of the solicitousness he would show any woman who had stopped off in a café to eat a bite after an abortion.

"Will you come up with me?" I asked when we reached my apartment.

"If you need help—"

"It doesn't hurt," I said quickly; I didn't want to lie to him.

"Then I ought to get on."

"Please come up."

"I ought to get on," he said again. He waited, the truck idling, until he saw that I was inside.

I turned on the lamps, and stood in the middle of my kitchen, surveying the scene: the philodendrons on a shelf above the sink, the four tea cups hanging from their hooks. Five china plates rested on another shelf, next to a blue glass jar full of silverware. By the window was my little round rickety table and beyond that, the door to the bedroom, the mattress on the floor and, on the wall, the white negligee. I turned on the lamps in the bedroom so that the whole apartment was warm and golden. The snow kept falling, but I'd hung yards of cheap white silk in the bedroom windows, and I couldn't see it anymore.

I took a shower and went to bed, exhausted suddenly as I had never been before, as if that vacuum, that whirring machine the pretty doctor held in her pretty hand had sucked the very marrow from my bones. But in the afternoon, when I awoke, I was myself again. I felt better. Okay, even. I thought briefly of calling my mother, just to say hi. Something inside me had stopped: the frantic reminder that I had lost *Joe*. I knew I had lost Joe, but it wasn't pounding against me every two seconds. The apartment no longer smelled bad the way it had when I was pregnant, and I could have dropped to my knees, I was so thankful not to be pregnant anymore.

It was two or three o'clock and the snow had stopped. I got dressed and went to the corner store and bought tomatoes, avocadoes, lemons, bagels, cream cheese, a chocolate bar, cigarettes and some women's magazines. I felt as if I were floating up the snowy street, floating through the narrow aisles of the store, floating back down to my apartment, as if all of Cambridge were far below me, and from that distance, my life seemed only good. Even with the abortion, the breakup. Hadn't everything turned out for the best? I couldn't marry Joe or have a baby, but still I had had a baby inside me, still I had been loved as no one is ever loved in this life.

The whole rest of that afternoon, as I puttered around my apartment, eating snacks and reading about miracle diets and triple-decker desserts, I felt a kind of peace I'd never felt before. I kept thinking about people who have had near-death experiences and how afterwards—after they've seen the tunnel and the light—they're not afraid of anything. *A near-life experience. That's what I've had.*

I thought of my mother again, how she had no real home—no place in this world—and I felt a sudden urge to call and comfort her. The light had faded from the windows and the truth is I wasn't feeling so great anymore. My chest hurt and I was cramping a little. I was scared that it was going to start up again, the emptiness closing in and missing Joe in that awful flu-like way.

I dialed my parents' number, thinking I'd tell my mother some small story—describe the terrible looking éclairs at the bakery Joe had taken me to, laugh with her about how badly Americans made French pastries, ask her how her day was.

What came over me then? She answered the phone and I said, "Mama, it's me, Molly. I had an abortion this morning." As if I'd won a prize. And then I burst into tears. I didn't say anything about Joe, I just kept crying and she didn't say a word, waiting for me to quiet down. I had never cried that way in front of her in my life. Every single person in her family had been blown to bits—at the very least, I expected a reprimand for crying so loudly. But she didn't reprimand me. She told me her own story. I closed my eyes and tried to think of Joe, how he had loved me, but my mother would not shut up. She spoke on and on in that dead, dull voice she used when she was mad. It was time for me to learn the truth. She didn't say that, but I knew that's what she was thinking. I hadn't learned what I was supposed to from the D-day story; she would have to tell me even more: she'd gotten pregnant before she was married, too.

Oh, Mama, I thought. *This has nothing to do with marriage or not-marriage.*

She'd had the baby, they didn't have the luxury of abortion then, and she'd given it away.

Please stop, I thought. *Please stop, Mama.*

Not that she would have had an abortion, anyway. She was so happy to be pregnant, even at sixteen, with the war still raging all around, because she had lost everyone. Everyone wanted to have babies, to re-populate the country, and she went to live with Oncle Jacques and Tante Françoise in Paris; yes, she said, she was happy to be pregnant, even at sixteen, even though she was an orphaned Catholic girl without a husband. Girl-mothers were a thing never to be mentioned, as shameful as shit—she used those very words, *shame-fool as sheet*—but my mother was just happy.

The baby was a girl, Simone, and she learned to crawl and climb onto things. My mother said this as if it were a major accomplishment, as if all infants didn't eventually learn to crawl.

"When she is two, when she begin to run, I go to find your father. I leave Simone with Oncle Jacques and Tante Françoise and I go to find your father."

Now I had begun to sweat and I thought I might be sick.

"I find your father at Harvard and he propose to me. He will come to me when he is finish studying and he will marry me."

I bit down as hard as I could, to fight the nausea. I didn't know if this was a side effect of the abortion; they hadn't said anything about post-partum nausea at the clinic.

"He come to me."

Her English was all shot to hell, but still inflectionless, still dull and driving and with some awful moral I could not make out yet. I was soaked through with sweat from the effort of not throwing up, but the nausea had left me now, as suddenly as it had come.

"I do not say to him about Simone—" She was speeding up now, but still with no audible emotion, as if she'd memorized all her words, had recited them a thousand times in a thousand confessionals: "Tante Françoise is ashamed of me, but Oncle Jacques he is not and I think your father will be like him."

She trapped him with a baby, that's what she did, the big fat cow.

"Daddy say to me Simone will be happier adopted, then she is a war orphan, not a bastard. He is still wanting to marry me and Tante Françoise she is fed up with me and so I give Simone to a Home. That's all."

"Mama," I said. "I'm so sorry."

"She smell like milk," she began, but caught herself, her grammar restored: "If you had known the war, you would understand."

I don't remember how we hung up, what I said, how I let her go. All I remember is sitting on the edge of the tub, with the bathroom door locked, crying. I don't know why I didn't just stay and cry in my bed, or why the bathroom door was locked.

What other comfort is there between women than to say, *yes, me, too, I have done that, too?* But I didn't want the comfort of one woman to another. I would have nothing to do with her, admit to no similarity. *To have an abortion or give up a newborn for adoption, that's one thing—but a two-year-old? A child who knew you, called you by name, nuzzled her milky head in the crook of your arm?*

I thought of the dreams I'd had when I was small, of my mother killing Ted, and how afterwards I'd tell myself over and over that it was only a dream, it didn't mean anything, but maybe it did, I thought now, maybe my mother did not love us the way a normal mother should.

How was it possible that my parents, unconventional as they were—my father with his deep respect for prostitutes, my mother with her total lack of interest in being presentable for the Joneses, much less keeping up with them—could take that most conventional of routes, the child hushed up and given away so the young bride can appear virginal, the young groom blessed?

It was obvious my father had called the shots—my mother was a teenager with nowhere to go—but I didn't care. I blamed her anyway, for all the ways she had suffered that kept her from being the mother I craved. I could no more fault my father for a lack of tenderness than I would have faulted God.

Much, much later, after midnight, I walked down the narrow, snow-banked sidewalks to the river, and listened to the cold slap of the water against the banks, my stomach clenching and unclenching with the waves. Now I understood what my mother had been trying to tell me: I was so fortunate, in every way so blessed—no war, no hunger, so many stores—and I just threw everything away, even my own baby, which I hadn't had to do because she would have helped me as Tante Françoise had never helped her.

She might not think abortion is murder, I thought. *But it's wasteful, and waste is a mortal sin.*

No, I wanted to say. *Abandonment is the mortal sin. Giving your two-year-old away.* I felt as if I'd been waiting all my life for this moment, this proof of my mother's flawed heart.

I think of my sister often. I always imagine a happy life for her. A happy, richly materialistic life. Louis Vuitton bags, Chanel dresses, little escargot appetizers. An apartment in Paris, in the sixteenth arrondissement. Her politics are completely right wing, but she is such a happy person that she can not help loving other people, and when we meet, she is charmed by my shabbiness.

But at first I couldn't picture Simone. I couldn't picture anything beyond the moment when she realized my mother was gone, a scene I re-played a thousand times, with myself as Simone, watching my mother disappear, her long, red, beautiful braid swinging against her back. All she had to do was turn around, but she wouldn't, she kept moving farther and farther away, into a life with other children—a life of endless leftovers and begging for clothes—it would never be enough. No matter how many clothes she collected, how many casseroles she re-heated, she would never see Simone again, and there was no comfort to be had, anywhere.

For days—weeks?—I spoke to no one. I left my apartment only to buy food, I didn't answer the phone. I knew it wouldn't be Joe now.

Still, I got up, got dressed, did the dishes, swept the floor, so it isn't true, what so many people believe, that I flunked out of Harvard because I had a nervous breakdown. I flunked out of Harvard because I didn't go to my final exams, because I was trying to decide what to do next.

For years, I didn't really know why. A broken heart, my crazed, post-partum hormones, a desire to punish my parents? Or maybe the simple combination of events, everything happening at once. In any case, I left. I called the off-campus House Master and told him I had cheated to get into Harvard, that I had just had an abortion, and that the only thing I had learned since I matriculated was that sex is God. I didn't like talking that way. It was what I had done in high school, before I knew Joe, before I knew that sex really was God, but I wanted to make a clean break. I didn't want anyone trying to counsel me back into the fold. That poor House Master was off the phone before I caught my breath, and he never called back, never pestered me at all about Harvard's generous leaves of absence.

For days after I told Harvard I was leaving, I talked to myself, sitting at my kitchen table with the ashes of my cigarettes growing as long as fingers. I pictured Joe sitting across from me, his hands on the table between us: I decided he no longer objected to cigarette smoke. He'd say how much he missed me, that it was terrible not being able to touch each other. I was the best person he had ever known and he should have offered to pay for the abortion. He should never have told me so many lies. *Hush,* I'd say. *There's nothing to apologize for.* He'd start to lean towards me. *What is it, Molly? What's wrong?*

My mother, I'd say though I could never go on.

Oh, Molly.

I did my side of the conversation aloud, and then I just sat, lighting one cigarette off the end of another, inventing his answers. *It's fine to smoke, don't worry.*

Sometimes I thought of Babette's drunken claims about my father, and I was tempted to call and tell her just how wrong she was. Daddy wasn't depraved, he was *brutal*—wasn't Simone the proof of that? I still didn't blame him the way I blamed my mother—I would have thought it was a weakness for a father to care too much about his children— but I was sad to discover that he cared so much about appearances, that he was his mother's son after all.

And then one day, I got up from the table. I could feel my own body, with the young, healthy blood coursing through it, all that strength and possibility and the urge to get up, to go outside and breathe the fresh air. To be so resilient was a sin—but I couldn't help myself. I washed my hair and left the apartment with the windows open. The sun was shining and the snow was melting everywhere. Piles of blackened slush glistened in the sunlight, grey water ran in the gutters, dog shit that had been frozen for weeks had begun to thaw; it was a beautiful day, the sky an impossible shade of blue and birds singing everywhere, as if winter were finally over. I was wearing my velvet coat, unbuttoned, and all I had under it was a lacy, transparent shirt, a flimsy skirt.

I walked over to Harvard, though I had no business there, and on the steps of Dudley House, I saw a boy I knew, a friend of the topless chemistry major.

"Hey Molly," he said, licking a hand-rolled cigarette. "How's it going?"

"Pretty good," I said, and I smiled at him, holding his gaze. He had curly dark hair, dark eyes. He didn't look anything like Joe—this boy was soft and bear-like—but the way the light shone in his hair was the same. I knew then that I'd have other lovers, and I was ashamed. I wouldn't cry everyday for the rest of my life; I'd see my mother again and she would offer me a pastry; she'd talk to me in her deep, rich voice and I'd lean up against her, the way I had when I was small.

"Pretty good," I repeated.

I still had no desire to call the House Master back and tell him I'd changed my mind. I remember thinking that I was free, that even though I wasn't sitting at my table, talking to myself—even though I was getting better—everything happening together had given me the *right*—I could do what I wanted. And there was a pleasure in that, a kind of pride.

I went back home and called my father and told him I had failed my exams and dropped out of school. I hadn't spoken to him since before the abortion and I figured he knew something was up. I offered no apology, because, after all, he had made my mother give Simone away, he'd made me give up Joe—

"All of your exams?" he asked, mildly.

He had no idea we hadn't spoken for weeks.

My heart contracted: he wasn't sorry for anything, and because he wasn't, I thought I had misjudged him.

"All of them," I said, chastened.

"Well," he said and he was quiet for such a long time that I wondered if he had gone back to whatever reading I'd interrupted with my call. I didn't know whether I should say something, so I just waited for him to hang up—the receiver must have slipped off his ear—and then I began to shake. Everything seemed to loosen around me—the walls, my clothes, my very skin—he had been so happy when I was accepted, singing his Harvard songs and not giving a thought to his work. Then the shakes left me and I just felt heavy and cold. I curled up under my blanket, the receiver weighing against my ear.

"Will you be able to get by?" he asked, so suddenly that I started, and then I realized that he wasn't going to say anything about the lost tuition.

"Oh," I stammered. "Yes. Yes, I'll get by. Daddy, I'm sorry. I am so—"

"Well," he said again, cutting off my apology, and there was real kindness in his voice.

Even now, with all that has happened since, I remember the sound of his voice when I dropped out of college, how gentle it was, how empty of recrimination. What did it matter if he was kind out of indifference?

A few days after I called him I went down to the corner Laundromat with a box of tacks and a notice offering my services as a housecleaner. I thought I'd become an artist, supporting myself with menial jobs as I struggled my way out of obscurity. I could take up abstract painting, as Mr. Keenan had once suggested, though when I pictured the years before me, they never included stacks of canvasses or the smell of paint or my own art on the walls. In my fantasies of the future, my rooms were almost bare: what you'd notice when you first walked in were my silk curtains, billowing slightly, and me, so beautiful I took men's breath away.

But despite my great beauty and the breathlessness of the men who saw me, in these fantasies I had no lovers. Just the child I might have had, like a wisp of something, a play of light, and across the river, Joe, who thought of me all the time.

I posted the notice as visibly as I could, imagining Joe on the other side of the plate glass window, watching me. It was cold again and I was wearing my bright orange jacket. *Housecleaning? What happened to you?*

But an actual man, pulling his laundry out of the dryer, asked if he could hire me. He was tall and blonde, with eyes as round and bright as bluebonnets—and he grinned over at me, stuffing his clothes into a canvas bag without folding them.

"Can't manage it yourself?" I said lightly, hoping he thought I was pretty.

"If you saw my apartment, you would weep."

I smiled at him. "Okay."

"You'll clean it?"

"Or weep," I said. "Name your pleasure."

His raised his eyebrows. "Well. Ten dollars an hour. I don't know if I can afford that."

"I'm really good." I just wanted to flirt with him a little, to encourage him to think I was pretty.

"I'll bet you are," he said. "I just—"

I shrugged. "I guess only the Brattle Street matrons will ever find out how good."

He grinned again. "Do the Brattle Street matrons hang around laundromats, reading the notices?"

"Shit." I laughed. "You're right."

"Post a notice at the Blacksmith House, or the Formaggio over on Huron Avenue," he offered. "One of those places."

"I'm such an idiot."

He smiled. "A little idiocy can be a good thing. I wouldn't have met you on Huron Ave."

I smiled back at him, but now my throat was hurting. I only wanted to flirt a little; I didn't want it to lead anywhere. But if I pulled back, he'd feel stung. He wouldn't like me then, he wouldn't even think I was pretty anymore, if he ever had. "I owe you," I said, still smiling, my hand pressed up against my throat.

"A housecleaning?"

"A cleaning, a weeping, whatever you like."

"My name's Rich," he said.

"Molly," I said. It hurt for the air to pass through my windpipe.

"And that's your number?"

I nodded.

"Want to get a cup of coffee, Molly?"

"We could just go to your apartment," I said. If we were going to go to bed together, I didn't want to wait; I didn't want to try to make small talk, wondering all the while if he still liked me, still thought I was pretty. "I could see how dirty it really is," I added, to give an impression of coyness.

"This very minute?" he asked, his eyebrows arching again, but I couldn't see any pleasure in his face now.

"Or not." I leaned against the door to push it open, my cheeks burning. I had moved too fast, startled him: he didn't like the pretend-whore game.

"Wait," he said. "Wait. Sure. Why not?" He slipped quickly into his coat and gloves and hoisted his laundry over his shoulder.

The wind was blowing and we walked with our heads down, barely speaking, though he told me that he was a law student—a real one, I knew, and for a moment my heart lifted, and I imagined introducing him to my father. Then I was afraid Joe would see us and know we were about to have sex and he would not be jealous so much as disgusted.

Rich's apartment was tidy but dusty and right off I asked him if he had a good vacuum cleaner. If he didn't like the whore game, I wouldn't play it.

He paused in the midst of his boot-stamping and hand-blowing. "You really came to clean?"

I still had my hat and coat and gloves on and the snow I'd tracked in was all around. I forced a grin. "That's up to you, remember?"

"I'd rather you didn't clean."

It seemed like such a generous thing to say, as if he didn't want me to trouble myself, and I thought of the way Joe took care of me, wrapping me in his coat and buying me my own. I lay my hand on his arm.

"I've never done this," he said. "I mean, just picked up a total stranger."

I froze. He didn't like me at all. "I might be a serial killer," I said, trying to be funny.

"No, I mean—"

"We don't have to." I took my hand off his arm. "I ought to be out posting notices."

"No, I want to," he said, and he smiled again. "It's just strange, that's all." The blue of his eyes was a color you'd paint a baby's room, that clear, that innocent.

"You sure?"

"Yes, I'm sure. Absolutely."

But when we made love, he was so tender I believed he nearly loved me. How was it possible to touch someone that way—his fingers so light on the sides of my ribcage—if there was no affection at all?

I didn't hear from him again, but a woman who'd seen my notice at Formaggio called to have her house cleaned and liked my work so much that she told all her friends and soon I had five customers, one for each day of the week, and enough money to live on. There's no way to speak of my love of cleaning and sound serious. But I did love it in those early years. I was good at it and every week one or another of my employers said how much she wished I were her daughter; it was the perfect job for me. I might have failed my father, but wasn't housecleaning as good in its way as Harvard? A job so humble, so poorly paid, had all the spiritual authority of foot-washing. Sometimes in the morning, when my father left for work, I heard him humming to himself, *'tis a gift to be simple*. If I could not be the best student, I could possess the greatest humility—and that was almost better: thousands of people went to Harvard, after all, but very few people gave everything up to scrub floors.

I was tending the rich, of course, and that was a problem—the rich don't need their feet washed—but I took such satisfaction in restoring order to a woman's home. When I was finished, the good I'd done was there for all to see: the silver was polished, the dead leaves were plucked from the plants and all the goblets shone.

Now and then, one of the women I worked for asked me to have a cup of coffee or tea with her before I cleaned. I always liked that. I had friends—I still saw Che and the others from Harvard, all of whom thought it was really cool that I had dropped out—but there was something about the ritual of coffee or tea with these women that felt like going to a five-star hotel. The way they wanted to please me was like nothing I'd ever known.

It was mostly Kathy and Bunny who wanted to talk. Kathy had a schizophrenic daughter and Bunny's husband never came home at night, and neither had a confidante besides me. Every few weeks, Bunny asked me what I would do in her situation. What did I think of private detectives? And how did I manage to stay so thin and lovely?

Should she go to a spa?

"You're beautiful," I insisted. "You have no idea how beautiful."

Finally, I said, "Divorce him. You've got to. A hundred men would line up at your door."

"No," she said. "I know what I am. Look—" she lowered her voice, as if she were going to show me something dead and rotten, a corpse beneath the floorboards: "Look," she repeated, jiggling the loose flesh beneath her arm. "What's the point in leaving? I won't find anyone else."

"Bunny!" I cried. "Other men aren't like Hank."

She smiled at me: "You're thin."

"Oh, Bunny! Loose flesh is not a pestilence."

"I didn't go to Harvard, Molly. I'm just talking human nature."

"My parents still love each other," I said, and I believed it. "My mother doesn't wear makeup, her hair is grey and she's fat, but my father loves her."

She smiled again. "Should I try that? Let my hair go grey?"

I almost told her then about the summer when I was thirteen or fourteen, when my mother had a hysterectomy. For a long time afterwards, she walked with a slow, shuffling gait, bent over like the oldest of women. One night I heard her cry out from her room, and I ran to her; I knocked and knocked, but she didn't answer.

She just kept crying until at last there was a long silence, and then my father's labored voice through the door: "What the hell is it?"

Even now, eating cake with Bunny, I believed those were cries of passion. I knew they weren't, but I believed, and I would have told Bunny that story—about how some men love women even when they can't stand up straight—except for the possibility that it would have made her feel worse.

Kathy was another story altogether: grey, bristling eyebrows, no husband in sight, all she cared about was her daughter. She was as unadorned as my mother, and I would have done anything for her, but there was little to be done. Finally, when her daughter was in the hospital, refusing to see Kathy, I offered to visit for her. On Saturday mornings, I'd sit awhile in the visitor's lounge, trying to meet Marina's Thorazine-gaze, listening to her talk about the hospital food and when she expected to get out—and then I'd go out to the parking lot and tell Kathy that I thought Marina seemed much better. What was the harm, if it made Kathy happy?

We'd head out for Mclean at dawn, as if the hospital were a thousand miles away, and on the way home, she always insisted that we stop off for a pastry. She focused on her cannoli or her Neapolitan as intently as my mother would have, hunched quietly over her plate; afterwards, laughing at her own ravenousness, she'd say, *I could eat a goddamn horse.* And then: *Tell me something. Anything. Tell me about that boy you met last week.*

But even my other employers, the ones I saw only in passing because I insisted that they not be home hovering around while I cleaned (a rule they accepted because I'd gone to Harvard)—even they said every week how glad they were to see me, how beautiful my work was, how they wished they could adopt me.

It was as if, like Joe, my employers knew everything about me, knew the very words I craved. *You, Molly.*

I did know everything about them. It's impossible to clean beneath the sinks and beds and sofas and remain ignorant. To overlook the vial of cocaine or the collection notice, the list of *things I'd like my husband to do for me.* To ignore, on a shelf behind the baby grand, the daughter's photo turned to the wall.

But knowing their secrets only made me like them better. Even their most insignificant beauty secrets—all those exotic fading creams —softened me when one or another of them revealed some bit of pure ugliness: Sharon asking me to keep an eye on the Jamaican yard man lest he try to steal—what? The silver frame in which her daughter faced the wall? Sharon was awful, but how could I hate a woman so embarrassed by a tiny patch of eczema?

I knew it was wrong to pour over their jars and tubes and scraps of paper, but I couldn't resist. I'd been spying on people my whole life: Ted calling girls on the phone, Babette popping the foil backing of her pills, and through it all, my mother's sad refrain, *you weel not stop?*

What's hard to believe is that for so long I guessed nothing about my father. The clues were obvious—his prostitutes; his vanity; his disgust with any girl who craved a boy; his indifference to my mother, my siblings, me—evidence tossed around as casually as in any house I ever cleaned—and I saw nothing.

I was too busy being young and answerable to no one. I loved my freedom, the way, when I was small, I loved flying in a Whisper Jumbo Jet across the ocean: the ease of strangers resting on each other's shoulders, the pretty hostesses in pill box hats, the boundless sense of possibility.

In the years after I dropped out of college, I slept with more men than I can remember. I met them in bookstores, cafés, parks, on the trolley, at the movies. My old friends at Harvard introduced me to their friends who, in turn, introduced me to theirs. It was mostly friendly. Even the one night stands. I'd run into a one night stand years later and he'd grin slyly at me, just like those boys in high school, and say we ought to get together sometime. I might laugh and say, "Why wait?" as if all I cared about in the world was a good time. To delay even a single evening seemed risky—suppose this man was the one I'd been longing for, and suppose he slipped away?

Those lovers come back to me now in fragments: the long legs of a man swinging over the bookstore counter he tended, so that he could kiss me while the line behind me grew and grew; the slender fingers of a pianist, lifting my skirt from behind as we stood on a balcony watching a St. Patrick's Day parade; the twitching feet of a police officer who slept as fitfully as a dog.

A man who kissed like a hummingbird tried for months to teach me to play poker and when it was clear I'd never get it, said it was no use, we were no good for each other.

He couldn't be with someone who was so obvious about everything, and besides, he said, I smiled too much.

Sometimes it was like that, a bad taste at the end, a flash of something mean or stubborn. Sometimes it was worse—doors slamming, a raised fist—but with nearly every man, until things ended, I was happy. I loved a man's coarse skin, his unguarded breath, his hands on the small of my back. I loved the sweetness of the early revelations—where we were from and who our parents were. Most of all, I loved the absolution given with every first kiss. No matter what you've done, a new love is a new world, with a new, clean slate.

My lovers were young and old, fat, thin, rich, poor—I ended up in bed with almost every man I had more than a five minute conversation with. I didn't know how to talk to men in any neutral, matter-of-fact way. My questions were too personal, or I blushed, or laughed too freely, or leaned forward and touched their forearms without realizing it. It seemed unconscionable to reject a man out of hand—Why would I? Just because his shoulders were too soft or he spoke with a lisp? What kinds of reasons were those? When some men told me about the insults they'd received along the way—the women who had told them they were too quick or too small—I was as indignant as I'd been with Bunny. *What did she know? First of all, you're great, and second of all, sex isn't about technique.* Then I'd preach awhile, even to men I'd only known an hour, about how the only thing that ever mattered was love.

There were, of course, men who didn't need my reassurances, much less my preaching. Nice-looking, self-confident men for whose benefit I plucked and shaved and bought silk underwear even if I was late on the rent. But the ones I remember the most fondly are the ones no one else would have, men who wouldn't have cared if I'd worn my mother's torn white cotton panties, as long as I was kind.

I had a lover once, a fat and dissolute man named Isaac who couldn't bring himself to touch any part of me below my ribcage, but craved me all the time, my lips, my breasts, my hands on his body. He bought me chocolates and flowers and jewelry and wanted me more, he said, than he'd ever wanted anything; he'd climb into bed beside me where I lay in a pair of silk pajama bottoms and I could feel his desire lighting beneath my skin, a thing I could never get enough of, and I thought, this is it, with a little patience, kindness, this will grow, it will turn into love. I'll start to feel everything again, the way I did with Joe.

Isaac always came against my leg and it made my heart ache, made me want to lay my whole body on top of his until his terror of me dissolved.

But the truth is I was mostly alone—I was the only constant. My clean, barely furnished apartment, with all the books, the plants, and in the afternoon, the light spilling across the floor. The smell of bleach on my hands. The sticky corn muffins from the corner store that I could eat three times a day when I ate by myself. Cigarettes. Those are the things I remember more vividly than any man's breath.

Sometimes I thought, *I am as solitary as a nun.* There were men who questioned my ambition, who couldn't believe I would choose to live the way I did; wasn't it in some way irresponsible, when surely I had gifts, talents, to develop and share with the world? These were mostly men who taught at Harvard or B.U. or Brandeis or Tufts or B.C. or one of the other colleges. What about a nun's ambition? I wanted to ask.

Others couldn't believe I'd ever gone to college—men who hadn't gone themselves, who needed me to be a step below them, maybe. But that's a different story, the funny, different ways men reacted to my college career, as if it had been as defining an event as going off to war. They said Harvard dropout the way you'd say Vietnam Vet.

Joe was better than that. He didn't care what I did about college, I'd think, forgetting that college was all imaginary for Joe.

I admit that sometimes sex wasn't about love. Still, it was, at the very least, a gesture of politeness. There were men whose interest in me I failed to recognize right away. Other men found that even harder to believe than whether I had or hadn't gone to college. *You sleep with everybody, how could you not have seen where things were heading?* Old men, in their seventies, eighties. I never got it. As if my illusions about my father extended to all the men of his generation. Jimmy Stillman, who played piano in a bar I had gone into in hopes of sneaking into the bathroom. He was old and stooped and no one was listening to him, so I sat down and stayed through the last set. I told him he was wonderful, let him buy me drinks, told him my life story, asked him about his. Even when he put his papery hand on mine, I didn't realize. Not until the bar closed and all the chairs but ours were on the table and he leaned toward me, brushed the hair off my face, and whispered, "Your place or mine?" and my heart sank. I never needed a man to be hand-some, but there was something about old men, some disappointment I felt that they were not beyond desire—or rather, beyond desiring *girls*. They should want women their own age, be done with the superficial appeal of youth. But I didn't have the heart to turn him down. In the morning, when he sat at his table, having a bowl of Grape Nuts and a cigarette, I invented a jealous boyfriend. "I should have told you sooner," I said. "I'm so sorry—but I couldn't resist." It made him happy, after all, and what did it cost me?

Now, when I remember those years, with the different men, they seem to me like a single year, with a single lover—a year of such calm, peace; a single day, even, and I alone in its vast and endless hours. But of course that isn't right. Each man was different—there were two or three I could have made a life with, if I hadn't always been thinking of Joe. Kind men, who truly loved me, just as there were those who despised me, though I could never believe it. A man asked me, *How is it you've never been raped, going around like that, dressed like that?* And I laughed, *You can't be raped if you always say yes*, but I was just acting tough. I didn't believe desire could exist without tenderness.

And then, as startling as a gunshot, one of my siblings or my parents would come to visit. I always went to dinner with them, feign-ing delight at their arrival, as if I'd thought of nothing else for months. My father came almost every year on business trips, my mother more rarely, stopping by on her way to Paris, where she went to attend the funerals of childhood friends. When they came I met them at the airport, my palms damp, my heart beating a little too fast, and when they left I just felt sad, because I didn't think I had really shown them how much I loved them.

It was as if Simone had never existed—as if my mother's revelation had changed nothing: I wanted them again the way I always had, worrying about them, imagining my need for love as theirs.

My mother stayed in my apartment—she slept with me in my bed—and though I'd looked forward to the smell of her for days—that faint odor of coffee and sweat—when she was finally in my bed I clung to the outer edge of it, clenching and unclenching my jaw because she snored. In the morning, bleary-eyed, I could not stop fussing over her: had she been comfortable during the night? Should I run to the store for donuts? How much sugar for her coffee? My father didn't irritate me—besides the trip from the airport to Cambridge, we only saw each other over a meal—but I fawned even more over him.

It was different with my siblings—my innocent siblings!—I felt nothing but dread at the prospect of their visits. Pat and Steve came as often as my father, swinging by on their way to take the QE2 to England; Claire came when she had Vassar reunions and wanted to extend her vacation; Ted made a stopover when he retired from the Navy and returned to Austin to take a civilian job with Lockheed—he took me to dinner at a Howard Johnson's and talked non-stop about computers. The wife we'd never met had divorced him and he seemed as raw and sad as ever, going on about languages and applications and storage capacities, none of which I even wanted to understand, though I murmured encouragingly. I hoped no one would see me with him. Though I dated men with no teeth, though Ted was tall and lean and straight, articulate as our father, no one embarrassed me more.

Babette never came, of course, but threatened to every other time she called. "Please come," I'd say. "You should. You need a change of scene. We'd have a blast."

My stomach knotted up when I spoke to any of my siblings. They said how nice it would be to see me, and it was as if I'd been sent back to the first grade, and Mrs. Mann were telling me how much she looked forward to having me in her class again. They seemed like relics of my childhood, reminders of a time when my teeth were crooked and I had not yet discovered sex.

When my father came to town, he stayed in a semi-monastic boarding house on Kirkland Street; it advertised itself as a bed and breakfast though breakfast was only coffee and toast and the beds had nothing in common with the fluffy four-posters of B&B imagination. He always admired my small, spare rooms and I admired him for not taking advantage of being away from my mother to splurge on some two hundred dollar a night suite with turn down service and breakfast banquets featuring fresh berries and clotted cream and homemade scones and smoked salmon and bagels and cream cheese and caviar and sour cream omelets and organic, hand-made sausages and mimosas. I'd had a lover once who had moved to New York and who would come up now and then to see me and we stayed in that hotel and I loved every minute of it. I'd show up at his room in my old velvet coat with nothing on underneath and he'd have already ordered the oysters and champagne and the chocolate-dipped strawberries from room service.

But my father. He came to town, checked into his small room, attended whatever meeting he had to attend, went home. Treating me to a meal was the only non-tax-deductible thing he did.

"It's *so* nice of you to take me to lunch, Daddy. I really appreciate it."

We were eating, as we always did, in the Garden Café or the Garden Coffeeshop, I can never remember the name—an inexpensive, plant-filled restaurant with soups and sandwiches and salads, his old favorite restaurants having vanished finally or gone too far downhill. Once, I'd taken him to a fancier place and though he'd liked it, the waitress had been rude to him and I never wanted to go back. She told my father that the fish was de-boned and when he corrected her grammar, she leaned right into him and said, "What I mean is that the bones have disembarked from the fish." She was right, of course; he had no business correcting a waitress, and it was a stupid move in a college town, but that only made it worse. I had never in my life seen anyone be rude to my father and the fact that she happened to be pretty—wild blonde curls and large breasts—made it worse. I felt that he had been humiliated and then he actually smiled, as if he were charmed by her, and I wanted to put my napkin down and leave, but I just stared at my plate and ordered in the smallest, coldest voice I could, to show that pretty waitress that I wasn't fooled by her, she wasn't anything special, just pretentious, like my father, but he was my father so I'd side with him even if he had started the whole stupid thing, even if *he* thought she was lovely. He kept smiling at her, as if he meant to ask her to sit down, and when, at the end of our meal, she brought the check, he touched her hand and left her a forty percent tip.

But now we were at the Greenhouse Café—was that it?—and all I could think to say to my father was how grateful I was that he was taking me out to lunch, as if I were not his flesh and blood child, as if he had lifted me off the street and were providing me with my first real meal in weeks.

"Well," he said, to change the subject from my boundless gratitude, because who would not? "What do you hear from Becky?"

I blushed. "Not much, you know. Our lives are so different."

He sighed. "That little girl keeps her busy, I suppose."

I put my fork down, ashamed—but to write now—*I heard your baby was a girl, I'm sorry about Keith Miller, I'm sorry I've been out of touch*— seemed stupider than staying quiet.

"And you?" my father asked. "You are still content to exist invisibly in this town?"

I blushed again, this time as if I'd received a compliment.

"All these resources at hand, and you want none of them?"

"I go to lectures sometimes," I said. "I take advantage of the bookstores." This was true. I did go to lectures if I happened to be sleeping with a man who was giving one; I spent hours in bookstores.

"But you have no desire to re-enroll?"

"Harvard seems to think I've graduated," I said. "They've started sending me the Harvard Magazine and just last week I got a call requesting a donation."

He laughed then; I don't think I'd ever made him laugh before. "They certainly leave no stone unturned. Do you read the magazine? It has some very interesting articles."

I nodded, though I never did.

He sighed. "So you just want to be a maid? A well-read maid."

"I like it," I said. "I like cleaning."

He shook his head. "Sometimes I think you're a bit like a nun, Molly. Living all alone in your little garret and willingly performing the humblest of tasks. It's an odd choice, but I suppose it's no worse than the choices your siblings have made. Perhaps it's better. You are certainly not dependent on any man. If I were a young man, I should want to marry you."

I thought it was the nicest thing he'd ever said to me, the nicest thing that any man—relative, friend, stranger—could say to a woman. *I should want to marry you, if I could.* And he had said I was like a nun; he knew me better than any living being. Then I grew cold, remembering, after all, Simone. How had I forgiven him so easily, who had tossed away his first born? *He means nun in the conventional sense,* I thought. *He doesn't know shit.* I almost rolled my eyes. But however cold, however furious, my heart was still pounding. I looked down. "I'm so sorry about the tuition, Daddy. I really am. If I could, I'd—"

He shook his head. "Deliberate waste is one thing, Molly. Your mother has always been very clear about that and I agree with her. But spilled milk is another. If by some chance you come into a great deal of money, you can donate it to a worthy cause, but you needn't ever worry about re-paying me."

I looked back up at him. Who was I to judge anyone? I, who lied so much and gave nothing to the world.

And yet, I couldn't fault myself entirely. That evening, in my apartment, as I got myself ready to meet—I can't remember who now—as I shaved my legs and rubbed lotion on my skin, put on a lace, demi-cup bra and perfume on my throat, behind my knees—I couldn't believe that touching a man was *nothing*. If I had charged for it, I could have given up housecleaning, been the kind of fierce girl my father would have been proud of, but I didn't want to charge for it. I wanted to take a man's longing and protect it, hold it in the palm of my hand—to reassure him: you are irresistible.

I thought that was a kind thing to do for someone, whether you loved him or not. Kinder if you didn't. To convince a man that he was all anyone could want. And then, when the time came, to leave in such a way that he never doubted you loved him. I thought he would carry with him forever the belief that he was desirable.

And wasn't he? How did God see us if not as infinitely loveable? Wasn't the truth, then, that we were? And wasn't our task on earth to believe that of one another? All I had to do, I thought, was overlook my own puny vision in which a man was unappealing because he smelled bad or lacked muscle tone and act as if he were the most desirable man in the world, and after awhile, I'd believe it.

I lived that way for fourteen years. For fourteen years I cleaned the same women's houses, tidying up an increasingly desperate array of beauty products. Sharon's daughter had children of her own and her photograph was turned back around. Bunny had a mastectomy and afterwards took up meditation and let her hair turn grey. Marina was in and out of the hospital seven or eight times, but medicine evolved and she moved at last into a group home. On Saturdays, Kathy and I still went driving, but without any particular destination now. We rarely talked about Marina and I suspected that her cobbled group home life had broken Kathy's heart more surely than all her years of delusions.

We talked about books now, and movies—Kathy sometimes watched three movies a day—and every few weeks she asked me what new guys were on the horizon.

I wrote Becky once, but the letter, sent to her mother's address, came back, and I didn't want to ask my father where she lived. Kathy said those old childhood friendships were never what you hope for, best to let them go, and so I did.

Every couple of years, I went home for Christmas. A few times, Babette came too, but of those Christmases all I remember is her fighting with Ted. As the years progressed, none of us ever seemed any older. Once, when the fighting was at its worst, my father rose from his seat, went behind Babette and Ted, took their heads in his hands like two melons and slammed them together. It wasn't really like melons at all; it wasn't *like* anything, just bone striking on bone.

Sometime during those fourteen years, I learned what had become of Joe. I was lying in bed with a ballet dancer—a handsome, cocaine-addicted man who was as promiscuous as I and who used to buy me books of poetry in languages I couldn't read—and out of the blue, he said, "You know that guy you went out with when you were in college, the one you dropped out because of?"

"I didn't drop out because of him."

"Joe Price, right?"

"Yes," I said. "Joe Price. Yes."

"Your heart is racing."

"Yes. What? What is it?"

"I know a woman who went out with him."

I was as covered with sweat as if I'd run ten miles. "What? What is it?"

"I haven't known whether or not to tell you."

"What? Tell me. What is it?"

"He lied to her, in a big way. They were living together and he told her he was in law school and he got her to support him—food, rent, even some tuition—and then she found out he wasn't in law school, he hadn't even gone to college. He'd gotten fired from some roofing job, and he was just loafing around—she never did find out what he did with the tuition money."

I was shaking, but I didn't say anything.

"I'm sorry, Molly. I figured out a while ago who he was, but I wasn't sure if I should tell you. Finally I decided it could only help, to know the truth."

"I already knew he was a liar."

"Then what is it, Molly? What's wrong?"

"What's she like, your friend? Is she pretty?"

"Oh, Molly. Jesus."

But I couldn't stop. "What's she like in bed? Tell me. Tell me exactly."

"Molly, the guy's a con artist."

"Is she like me? Is she small? Does she move the way I do?"

"Molly."

"Tell me goddamnit."

"She's gorgeous." He paused.

"Go on."

"She's tall and athletic, nothing like you. She dances with me, that's how I know her, and she's an incredible dancer. Long dark hair, huge eyes. A total sex fiend, like nobody I've ever met. Okay?"

"Okay," I said. I burrowed into the crack between the mattress and the wall and lay there, as still as I could. The important thing was to make no sound at all, to move nothing, not even my eyes. It had never occurred to me that Joe might have another lover.

And then one day, I was pregnant again. Naturally I didn't know whose it was. There were five possibilities, five men I will never forget, because any one of them might be Zim's father.

Sharon's husband, Mike, would be the worst possibility. He came home unexpectedly one day and found me on my hands and knees scrubbing the kitchen floor. "God you're beautiful," he said and that was that. We fucked all over the kitchen floor where Sharon herself could have found us if I had not so strictly banished my employers from their homes. He and Sharon had an open marriage, but she would as soon have found him with the yard man as with me. I claim nothing about Mike. I didn't try to see him as God sees him. He was handsome and he said God you're beautiful and it went to me like a shot of amphetamines. He wasn't a nice man and there was no dissolving tenderness, just the pounding blood as if desire were an itch like any other, only more urgent, more maddening.

Skinny little Eric Vine would be all right, but he is the least likely of all the possibilities because he was so scrupulous about birth control. He was never very nice to me, but I knew his coldness was only fear.

Stephen Coles would have been all right, too, except for the possible genetic factors in schizophrenia, which seemed to be the only mental illness in those days. Stephen didn't have it himself, but his mother did, and even without it, he was completely crazy, and mostly drunk. Still, he was brilliant, and fun, and he was a friend to me for years.

It's unlikely that it was Phil Williams, since Phil was black, but you'll have that sometimes, a baby who shows only the racial characteristics of one parent.

Leo Ellis was in his sixties, and he would be the best possibility, because he is, like the imaginary father I have created for Zim, dead. But I don't think it's him. He was mostly impotent and anyway he had a wife, who is still living. They hadn't slept together in fifteen years when I met him, sitting outside Pamplona, reading Françoise Sagan. I asked if I could sit with him, since there were no other tables free and then, when he put his book down, I asked him stupidly if he was French, as if, in a town like Cambridge, the ability to read French meant anything at all.

Zim's imaginary father is named Stephen Ellis and he was killed tragically in a motorcycle accident, a detail I added to discourage Zim from ever climbing on one. He was a roofer and his parents were dead and he had no siblings, so he was all alone in the world, but it was stupid to have made him a roofer, when I could have made him a lawyer and Zim never would have thought then of climbing high on top of things and testing his balance.

I was as sick with Zim as I'd been with my first pregnancy, but never overcome with a sense of inexplicable joy. I don't know how I made it through those nine months or the two sleepless years that followed.

I told almost everyone that I had unexpectedly inherited a chunk of money and was moving south. Only Kathy knew that I was pregnant, and that I did not feel I could raise a child in the snow.

"But what will you do? Go back to Texas?"

"Oh no. God, no. Maybe the Keys."

"But you won't know anyone. You need friends."

"You know what I don't want? I don't want a father for this child. I don't want some guy deciding he's the father and getting all involved and suing for rights and telling me what to do."

"Oh, Molly. You're doing a terrible thing. I'm going to miss you."

"I'll miss you, too, Kathy. I really will."

I had no idea. I loved Kathy and I loved Cambridge—I loved my life—but all I could think was that you couldn't push a stroller around when the sidewalks were banked with snow.

I called my mother then and told her everything, almost—I reduced the five men to two, but that was shock enough and for ten minutes the phone line was silent while I wondered what story of her own she was going to tell me. I could have told her there was only one man, who didn't want to be involved, but that wouldn't have been fair, blaming someone who had done nothing wrong. And then at last she said, "Do you want to come home?"

"Oh, Mama. No. I'm sorry."

"That is all right, Molly." Still the O, almost long. *Moly.* "You will need to have money."

The offer surprised me, made my throat catch.

"I will speak to Daddy."

"Thank you, Mama."

"I hope you will be all right. You can always change your mind and come home."

"Thank you, Mama," I repeated, and for a moment I did want to go home, to move back into my old room and raise my child on the porch swing.

They sent me twenty thousand dollars, which was forty times more than I expected—I had thought they would pay my plane fare to whichever southern city I chose—and for a long time, holding that check in my hand, with my father's signature—those slanting, illegible letters I loved—he had not called or included a note with the check, there was no mention between us of what the money was for—I just stood there, as blank and shattered as I had ever felt in my life. What did it mean, this generosity? And what would I do with so much money? It was twice what I earned in a year, a hundred times what I ever had in my checking account—it seemed to me for a moment as if I would never have to work again.

I sat down on the stoop, where I had torn the envelope open, excited by the prospect of a few hundred dollars, and my heart was racing so hard I was afraid it would hurt the baby. And then I thought, *twenty thousand dollars, he has given me twenty thousand dollars*, and I was sure he loved me, and for a moment, forgetting everyone else in the world, I was bathed in light.

"Thank you, Daddy. I had no idea. I can't tell you—"

"Well," he said. "You'll need more than that in the long run. Are you still planning to be a maid?"

"At first, you know, when it's little, I can bring it with me, in a basket."

"Well," he said again, and I knew he was shaking his head. "You're not like anyone else I know, Molly. Except perhaps your mother." There was admiration in his voice, that I wasn't greedy, that in my own way I was like a Quaker, and I was grateful suddenly that he had said nothing about adoption.

"I had supposed your friend Becky was like the two of you. Independent minded and without material desires. It's an awful shame what's become of her."

"Becky?" I asked, thinking *your friend*. He hadn't referred to her as mine in years.

"She has a terrible drinking problem."

"Oh, no, Daddy. I'm sure she doesn't." But I remembered all those bottles of Gallo.

"I became aware of it when she was arrested for assaulting an officer. I had to recuse myself, but in any case it was thrown out—she had simply refused a breathalyzer. Nevertheless, she's a drunk, pure and simple. And I'm afraid that daughter of hers has simply gone wild."

"Becky's daughter?"

"Well. See to it that you manage being without a husband better than she has."

"Of course I will, Daddy. But Daddy—"

"I'm glad we could give you something, Molly."

For a long time I lay clutching that twenty thousand dollar check to my heart. I pictured Becky drunk, listing outside a bar, and I could hardly breathe. *My friend*, whom I had turned away from.

I discovered later how my father had tried for years to inform Becky of the opportunities that still existed for her, the night school and the paralegal training. After the case against her was thrown out, he went over to her apartment and tried again. He caught sight of her daughter there, a sullen pretty girl in combat boots whom he began to notice afterwards standing on a street corner with a group of grotesques—girls hideously and deliberately cut and dyed and stitched together to look like devils. They stood very near the corner where, years before, he had sometimes offered a prostitute much older than Kate, and much more appealingly dressed, a hundred dollars for an hour of her time.

But all I knew then was that Becky was a drunk. She wasn't, in fact. My father was wrong about her, and wrong about Kate, too. Becky liked to drink and Kate was a bad girl like her mother before her, but neither was what my father imagined—a fantasy of ruin from which he alone might save them.

CHAPTER

ELEVEN

The last thing I did before I left Cambridge was visit the glass flowers. It took all of ten minutes, it was such a small exhibit, and I couldn't see why it had moved my father so much. The artistry was impressive—those flowers looked just like slightly faded specimens collected from outdoors—and the magnified stamens, so delicate and swollen, were more explicitly erotic than any novelty book I've ever looked at, but, still, you'd have to really care about botany to get excited about it all. Or glass. For awhile, later, I imagined that my father's interest in the flowers was nothing more than a dirty joke—that that swollen glass excited him—but I don't think anyone's that simple.

I took his twenty thousand dollar gift and went to North Carolina, looking for Joe. I knew he still lived in Boston, but I thought I might find some trace of him—a smell, a gesture, something. Once he'd said he wanted to live in the mountains, so I turned my new seven hundred dollar Toyota (rusty yellow with orange racing stripes) onto the Mass Pike and headed towards Appalachia.

Twenty-two white-knuckled, nauseated hours later—I was still a bad driver and afflicted with all-day morning sickness—I started up a hairpin highway and found myself in a land of small, somber churches, each with its own billboard warning about the afterlife, of used trailer lots and discount strip malls, where no one sounded a bit like Joe. I had come to the worst part of the country, I thought, and then it began to rain so hard I pulled over and sat in the car, crying. But when the rain stopped, I got out to stretch and that's when I smelled it—that rich, damp, galax-smelling breeze I remembered from the Alps, from the days when Babette and I danced to *Proud Mary* in the granary and my mother, back among her own people, was as competent and presentable as anyone. It was the first thing I'd smelled since I'd gotten pregnant that didn't make me sick.

When you get up above the churches and the strip malls, the Blue Ridge look like ocean waves, they are that small, that soft. Zim and I live in a trailer on the edge of our own meadow full of Queen Anne's Lace, and though we can't see our neighbors, we can hear them when the air is right: tobacco farmers, loggers, hippies, their dogs and target practice and parties like the distant murmur of grownup voices when you are small and have gone to bed before anyone else. There's a town ten miles from us, with a grocery store where people just recently stopped smoking in the aisles, their cigarette ashes all velvety beside the crates of iceberg and pale tomatoes. When the owners remodeled and started bringing in arugula and goat cheese, they banned smoking, but that's just a gloss for tourists—hardly anyone here looks down on tobacco. I like that, and I like how people recognize me here, recognize Zim. I like being a landowner.

My trailer is the most beautiful I've ever seen. I knocked down half the interior walls, painted the particle-board white, had the windows enlarged, lay pale tatami mats down on the dark linoleum, and when the sky is clear, the whole place fills with light. But what I like best is how flimsy my trailer is, how temporary, making no claims on its little rectangle of earth. It's like a dollhouse, with cabinets that really open and close, a toilet with actual water that you can flush.

I named Zim when he was three days old. When, still reeling from labor, I called my mother to tell her I had a son, she suggested Jacques, but I said no, picturing an old man. She offered to come out, but I misunderstood: "I do not suppose you want me to come?" she said, and

I thought she didn't want to spend the money. "No, that's all right, Mama. Thanks," I said, and my father, on the other extension, praised my independence.

I didn't even want to leave the hospital. I had forgiven the nurses who told me, all through labor, what a good job I was doing, as if a bad job were an option. I had forgiven them and wanted to stay right where I was, eating mashed potatoes and jell-o for the rest of my life and hearing over and over how healthy my baby was. As long as they told me that, as long as they were right there to take care of him if anything happened, we were okay. The young nurses came and showed me how to bathe Zim and clip his nails, the older ones told me what to do at home for thrush, colic, diarrhea, mastitis. I could hold his whole naked body against my breasts and feel his blood pumping next to mine.

For three days, Zim lay with me and I drifted in and out of consciousness, afraid each time I awoke that he'd be gone—until I saw the blue-grey pools of his eyes, his soft, open mouth, the bars of the hospital bed making a crib for us both.

But finally I had to get up, pack, call a neighbor to pick me up, and I had to name him before I could leave. The state had given me three free hospital days, and I'd used them up: the registrar was waiting in the doorway. She had tiny blue curls, pink nails.

I was so bruised and torn it hurt to stand.

"You can't take it without a name."

"My baby?"

"They don't let you take if off hospital property without a name."

"My baby?" I repeated, stupidly.

"You could give it its daddy's name."

I'd thought all along I was having a girl—Rebecca Simone Moore. There were no boys' names I didn't have associations with, and standing so long was making me dizzy.

"Or you could name it after your own daddy," she said, frowning. "If you don't know its daddy's name."

I stared at her, seeing spots, and then I sat down and flipped open the Bible on the bedside table. After a minute, the spots cleared and I saw a name I'd never seen before. "Zimran."

"Zimran?"

"Zimran Moore," I said, feeling better all over.

The registrar said nothing for a long time. "You going to give it a middle name?" She asked, finally.

"Yes," I said. "Ignatius." I'd never slept with an Ignatius.

"Zimran Ignatius?"

"That way his initials will spell his name."

"Zim," she said and then she smiled. "Well, that's all right."

"It's beautiful," I said, my eyes welling up suddenly because I had succeeded in this, my first official task: he was recorded, legal.

He'll hate his name when he's older, but an unusual name is the least of my maternal sins: I haven't given him a father, I haven't given him anything except poverty and a meadow and my own jumpy love.

And churches. There's one every fifty yards or so, each one outdoing the next in warnings and recriminations. If you get sick or your house burns down, your pastor comes with food and blankets, but I wish they were quieter about it. Every Sunday morning and Wednesday evening, too, the parking lots of all those hundreds of churches are overflowing with endorphins: women dressed to the polyester nines and men who spend the rest of the week throwing their weight around just a little too much, all of them harnessed together in a fervor of desire and surrender. The first thing people ask when they meet you is the name of your church. Sometimes I make one up. St. Joseph's. The Church of the Immaculate Deception. The Charge of the Light Brigade. No one's listening. The Freewill Handwalkers. That's not true, of course: they listen intently, their faces eager, concerned, and I look down, whispering some no-answer, as embarrassed as if I were naked.

Still, I love the mountains, how wood smoke carries through the rain and how, in the spring, the dogwood petals scatter like snow across the grass. I love the galax and all the forbidden flowers—trilliums and lady slippers—the damp summer growth racing up the mountainsides.

I don't remember much of Zim's first year. I was so exhausted, and terrified at every turn that Zim would stop breathing or develop a brain-damaging fever. I lost all interest in sex. When I first arrived in North Carolina, my belly standing out in great contrast to the rest of my undersized body, so that I looked more like eight months pregnant than five, I gazed at the men in the town square—the old ones gossiping at the hardware store and the young ones getting in and out of their trucks; there was a state trooper with a shaved head whose long-limbed stride I loved to study—and I didn't understand why none of them gazed back. I was hurt when I finally caught on, as if these were the very men whose physical imperfections I had once overlooked, and now they'd turned against me. It never occurred to me that they might recoil from the evidence of another man—respect it, even; I'd never belonged to anyone, not even Joe.

I forgot about all that of course after Zim came. I forgot about everything but Zim.

I took him to work with me in a basket, the way I'd planned. (It didn't take long to find chalets and Lincoln-log mansions to clean; the mountains are poor, but full of rich people.) When Zim began to crawl, I left him with Frankie Burdell, who lives at the bottom of our driveway and charges two dollars an hour per child to watch over half a dozen babies. She keeps the TV on all day and thinks everyone besides the thirty members of her congregation is going to Hell, but she loves Zim, and when he was a week old, she left a basket full of food on my doorstep: rolls and sweet tea and chicken and dumplings and mashed sweet potatoes with marshmallows and pound cake that I devoured right inside the doorway with my hands, I was so ravenous.

I've forgotten so much—when he first rolled over, walked!—but I remember that I ate all the time when Zim was nursing. I ate all day and still grew skinnier and skinnier until I was just a stick with dark circles under my eyes and enormous, veiny breasts that clogged up no matter how many hot compresses or cabbage leaves I lay on them. I remember how my whole body would dissolve with love and then, two seconds later, I'd be shaking I was so afraid of something happening to Zim. That was the hardest thing—harder than not sleeping and being poor and forever on the verge of getting sick: how fear kept after me, so that, though I could see that Zim was perfect, trailing all those clouds of glory, I couldn't bask in him. We might both be naked, curled up together, but after I left the safety of the hospital, after fear got a solid hold of me, I couldn't be with him the same way. I saw him—that fuzzy hair, that dreamy, underwater waving of his hands—but I couldn't feel the comfort of his weight against me until, suddenly, I'd notice that my arm was aching, or my back, and I'd have to set him down. If I had known that he would live, I would have laughed all day, danced his naked self from one feeding to the next—but the world was full of danger, and I knew nothing about protection.

Every day as he continued to breathe my terror lessened, but even when he'd made it to a year I was still mostly scared and sleep deprived beyond all reason. I couldn't think straight.

One day, my mother called and said Daddy had been in a car wreck and I figured he was dead, but I could only worry about one person at a time. *When you're dead you can sleep*, I thought, because I couldn't do it; whatever I was supposed to feel about my father's death, I didn't have the strength.

Then she told me the rest: that Daddy had given Becky's daughter a ride—how he'd met Kate at Becky's when he went over there after Becky's arrest, and how he'd seen her afterwards on the street and tried to get her home—the roads were icy and Kate hadn't put on a seatbelt. Kate was dead, but my father was only bruised.

"Mama?" I said. "Mama? I have to go."

Zim was asleep. I crawled in next to him with my clothes on—he slept in my bed still—and lay without moving, just my teeth chattering a little. I felt hot and dry, but great streams of sweat rolled down my sides onto the mattress. All that mattered was that I not think about Becky, or how my father could have failed to tell a fourteen-year-old girl to buckle up. I couldn't consider a single piece of it, not the girl, not my father, not the grieving mother with her small, stained teeth.

For days I didn't think and discovered that that was a better way to raise a child; if I couldn't think, I couldn't worry. I cleaned house better than I ever had before, dripping sweat onto the floors I scrubbed, and I read *Goodnight Moon* with such gusto that Zim laughed and held it up again and again, a story meant to put everyone to sleep. I organized his clothes, washed all our windows, bought a potty, trimmed his wispy orange hair—he looked conveniently like me—and began to teach him French, though he only spoke two words of English, *Mama* and *ball*.

But then Babette, smelling disaster, moved back home; she couldn't leave a single thing alone. She set herself up as our father's defender, though no one was attacking him, and sent me every newspaper article there was about him, her own maniacal opinions scrawled in the margins.

There was an editorial about the folly of trying to help people like Kate Lopez, accompanied by a small, grainy picture of Kate: light-colored hair and a tattoo of a rose on her collarbone.

What were *people like Kate*? Punks, the newspaper said. Street kids. The problem of street kids had become grave in the past few years. Not all of these children were from disadvantaged families, moreover, but all were swept up in a world of drugs, vandalism and small-time prostitution. (What was *small-time* prostitution?) What was needed was a city-wide curfew for teenagers.

Judge Moore's unfortunate offer of a ride was simply a metaphor for the city's failed attempts to control the rise of juvenile delinquency.

My father, dressed in his robes—the standard election year photo—lamented both what was a private family tragedy and a certain editor's recent attempts to view that tragedy metaphorically.

L.K. Linton, of Barton Hills, sent a spitting letter about what Judge Moore was doing with a fourteen-year-old hooker in the first place; Babette wrote in the margin in huge, block letters: *CAN'T HE READ? DADDY WAS JUST TRYING TO GET HER OFF THE STREETS!*

The next day's mail contained a Sunday Magazine profile of selected street people: girls with surgically forked tongues and horns stuck to their foreheads. As luck would have it, the reporter had begun research-ing her article a week before Judge Moore's accident and she had snapped a photo of Kate the day before she died. Lucky indeed, though no doubt the reporter had to put in some long nights in order to take advantage of her good fortune and finish her profile in time.

Kate was tiny, a head or so shorter than the other girls in the photo-graph. She had Becky's smile, Keith Miller's coloring.

No way was Kate a whore, said Monica, a girl with multiply pierced eyebrows, but no horns. *Sure she kidded around, you know, twenty bucks for a hand job, just to see what people would do, but she was joking.*

Monica doesn't know the half, Zadie said. She had no piercings or tattoos and her tongue was whole, her head smooth, but her hair and lips and eyes were blood-red and she was covered in dog collars. *I'm not saying Katie was a whore, I'm just saying.*

But Sparrow, fat and horned and double-tongued, had the last word: *Kate was a virgin. You all don't know anything about us, do you?*

I just think it's awful the way they split their own tongues, Babette wrote, in smaller letters this time. Then she added a P.S.: *This whole thing doesn't look so good for Daddy. It might help if you wrote something to the editor about how you knew the mom—Daddy said you knew her—or I could. Just so it doesn't seem like Daddy was hanging around street kids for no reason.*

He wasn't, I thought.

I felt as if my blood flowed backwards, strong as an undertow. My father had had sex with Kate. He'd raped her. *Daddy had sex with those prostitutes, you know.* How was it that Babette saw nothing now?

I folded the newspaper clipping over and over, until it was as small as the notes girls pass in junior high. Zim was in bed and I sat curled up in the hallway outside our room, with the lights off.

Hadn't he understood the difference between the grown prostitutes he admired and a rebellious kid?

Only that the one was fresher, more irresistible.

Oh, Kate.

I remembered what it was to be young and ignorant of an old man's cravings: I'd been a matter of life and death for the likes of Jimmy Stillman—not me, of course, but my smooth skin, my silky hair.

Twenty dollars for a hand job. You, yes you I'm talking to you. What brutal old man could resist such an invitation, however insincere, however unspoken? Because it wouldn't even need to be spoken. All it would need would be for the girl to be there, breathing.

He had gone to Becky's building after the charges against her were dropped. There, in her clean, bare apartment—Becky would not reveal herself in the flotsam and jetsam of her bathroom and kitchen counters, there would have been no wax or cream or ointment, just a stack of coupons, maybe, and a six-pack—he would have taken off his hat and nodded, the dignified, elderly gentleman, Judge Moore, who had let his hair turn grey at last.

He talked awhile to his daughter's old friend, that brilliant girl who had let all her talents go to waste. He would have lectured Becky about discipline, about pulling oneself up by one's bootstraps and staying on track. *Without perseverance, Becky, no man can achieve greatness.* Sitting there, the well-mannered Quaker at the clean kitchen table—*You sure you wouldn't like a cold beer, Judge?*—he saw her daughter, her beautiful, sandy-haired daughter with a tattoo on her collarbone, but no forked tongue, no horns, because she was just playing, she wasn't really serious about being out on the street.

He recognized her a few months later, standing on the corner. *I'm afraid she's gone completely wild, Molly.*

All I wanted was to sleep. The night was windy and the trailer was trembling slightly; I loved that aluminum shudder. I wanted to fall asleep to that sound forever.

Did he offer Kate a ride home that first time? *I used to give your mother rides when she was your age.*

It was easy to imagine those girls, huddled on the corner, trying to stay warm. The cigarettes, the black-rimmed eyes, the torn fishnet stockings. A cliché maybe, except that for the young, there are no clichés—everything is always happening for the very first time.

A car pulls up to the curb and the window slides down. *Would you like a ride? Kate?* It's an old man, leaning across the passenger seat, wearing leather gloves.

They must have laughed, those smooth-limbed girls in their outlandish costumes. The clichés of the old are another matter—a joke everyone knows.

It's twenty dollars for a hand job, mister.

I don't want—

That's all I've got, mister. You want something else, keep on driving.

I would simply like to talk with you. Of course I shall pay you for your time.

Whatever gets you off. Or maybe now they are laughing too hard to say anything at all.

He wouldn't be deterred: *I have always admired the fierceness of prostitutes.* First the conversation, then the sex.

What got her in the car that night? The cold, or just the fun of an old man's gullibility? The hilarity of riding with a well-dressed man who really believed she was a prostitute. She must have hated listening to him, going on and on about—? Staying on track? I'll bet she stayed on track. *Want a hand job?* Anything to shut him up.

And yet his voice was so rich, so musical. He wasn't a man you could interrupt, not because he would get angry, but because he would simply fail to notice the interruption, the way a person pretends not to notice a rude noise or a bad smell. Only he wasn't pretending, he really didn't notice, his courtesy was that absolute.

You can accomplish anything if you persist. There is a wonderful line of poetry—I don't suppose you read much poetry?—'If the fool would persist in his folly, he would become wise.' Of course, that is about much more than persistence—it suggests a great deal about the nature of folly—but it is also about the transformative power of staying on track.

I don't know if he even read Blake. I just know that he wouldn't be interrupted, and he wouldn't want a three-minute hand job. He would require a bed, a woman's full and naked attention. A girl's. They would have to go to a hotel. A motel. A thirty-dollar dive where he wouldn't be recognized. That would be easy to arrange: he would give her a choice: drive her home to her mother, or put her up in a motel. It would never occur to him that they weren't going to have sex, once she chose the motel over her mother's wrath and they were settled in with the door bolted and the polyester bedspread pulled back.

Her virginity was the only problem. All those nights on the street—you'd have to want your virginity, to hold onto it out there. But a man like that, so athletic, even at seventy-two, so used to being obeyed—he would appreciate the challenge. What did she do, then, to enrage him? After he subdued her, what did she do to make him drive too fast and neglect to make her fasten her seatbelt? He, who always observed the speed limit and kept his hands at ten and two?

She must have kept fighting too long. She was too small to keep him off, but she must have kept fighting even when he was finished; when, bathed in the afterglow of his success, his every cell was buzzing with possibility—that's when she could have gotten loose to scratch his face and claw at him.

He would have lost his temper. That's enough, now. Settle down, Kate.

Settle down you motherfucking bastard? I'll kill you.

She couldn't have been more than four-foot eleven, eighty-five pounds. Clearly it was time to get her home. She had no business there, away from her mother.

It could have happened another way. It could have been a single ride, no conversation, her seatbelt laid across her lap but not buckled, the way kids will sometimes do. But I knew that wasn't it. I might have had the props wrong—there might not have been a motel—but not the charges. And I was right, as it turned out, even about the props. I'd gazed at him my whole life and I could almost see him now.

Or it was a lucky guess—a luck like that reporter's with her Sunday Magazine spread.

I knew the way you know when you have to eat or sleep or defecate. How was it possible, in the end, not to know?

I sat motionless on the floor, the folded square of paper damp in my palm. I didn't move until the morning, when Zim crawled out of bed and burrowed into my lap. "Come on, sweetie. Let's go. Mama's got to go to work." I stood up and swung him onto my hip and made my way to the bathroom.

I couldn't know everything, of course: I never fought a man off, I was always so eager, or, at the very least, polite. I didn't know what it was like to fight, except to get the juices flowing, ratchet everything up a little bit; I didn't know how my father—I stopped: my father was nothing. A gavel, a little libido, nothing more. He might as well have stood on a street corner himself, naked beneath his robe and flashing all the passersby.

And yet he worked so hard, reading late into the night, all that law and history and poetry.

I never called him. I didn't call anyone at home.

I certainly didn't call Becky. I could barely say her name, though I thought about her every day, and Kate, too. Or rather, I didn't think about Kate, she just appeared before me, so tiny, with her single tattoo, her coloring so cheerleader perfect, her teeth so dark and lovely. It made it hard to eat, to sleep, though I was too tired not to sleep, but my sleep was all nightmares now. I wandered the halls of the Austin State School and saw the children lying dead in their cots, and I had killed them all. One morning I dropped my third crystal glass and lost a job.

Sties grew on my eyelids and the chapped skin on my hands bled—but there was Zim, with his soft red hair curling around his ears, his sweet hysterical laughter when I tickled him. When Daddy killed Kate, I was shocked out of all my dull maternal terror—as if I'd been crippled and then the world blew up and I wasn't crippled anymore. I loved him easily, laughed at the very sight of him.

I bought a card for Becky finally, and got her address from my mother. I was so sorry, words could not express, etc. I'm still embarrassed to think of it, but no card at all is worse, isn't it?

One day my mother called to say she was moving back to France. No mention of my father, nothing—just the date of her departure. "In two weeks. I will go in two weeks."

I felt sick again, the way I had when she was gearing up to tell me about Simone. But all she talked about now were her dates.

"In two weeks, on the twenty-first."

A flash of terror lit through me, as if she were telling me some new and awful truth about my father, when, in fact, she was telling me nothing. But why would she leave, if my father were innocent? I didn't want her to confirm what I knew, to so much as hint at it, but she might as well tell the whole story from the very beginning as make that plane reservation.

"I arrive on the twenty-second."

"Okay," I said, to stop her. I was looking out the front window at the brown meadow, the black trees around it, and the tops of the mountains, visible only during the long, raw stretch between November and April. Zim was sitting on my foot. I made an effort to sound cheerful, for his benefit. "That sounds good."

A thin deer bounded across our view and Zim pulled himself up to standing against my leg. "Great," I said. "I'm glad to hear it." I was losing track of what we were talking about, and my mother responded, a little quizzically, "Okay—?" and then I remembered, but all I could do was repeat myself, as she had done, and for awhile the two of us just said the same lines over and over, like characters out of Beckett:

"I will go on the twenty-first."

"Okay."

"On the twenty-second I will arrive."

"Great."

"Okay."

"Great."

"Okay, then."

"Great."

After that Babette started calling three or four times a day. Could I believe how awful Mama was? How fickle? She, Babette, couldn't fucking believe it. Could I? Well, could I? I stopped picking up the phone. I let it ring for days and days and then I just unplugged it.

It didn't occur to me that my mother might try to call again to say goodbye, much less that she would want to visit Zim and me on her way to France.

I went to work—Estelle Bennett, whose wine glasses I'd broken, hired me back, and anyway, I had the other four: Dr. and Mrs. Colton in a six-thousand square foot A-frame, the Turners in Lincoln Logs, the Drs. Browning and Ferris in a pre-assembled Victorian and Roscoe Mitchell in his wheelchair, quietly parked in the living room of his double-wide while his sister, Faye, followed me from room to room, making sure I was doing a good job. I worked, I read to Zim, I covered the tatami mats with elaborate wood-block constructions for him to knock down like dominoes—it made him squeal with laughter every time—I put old Mo-town tapes in the boombox on the kitchen counter while I carried him on my hip and fixed his shameful canned and frozen dinners—noodle soup, frozen waffles, Chef Boyardee. I bathed with him and fell asleep with him—we slept on a foam mattress on the floor of my room—and when the moon was full the last thing I saw before I sank into my nightmares was the meadow, turning silver.

One evening I was coming home from work, Zim fast asleep in his car seat, his little orange head tumbled forward on his chest and my own head barely staying upright, when I saw a girl—I thought it was a girl—at the bottom of our driveway. She was wrapped up in a long woolen coat and a head scarf that covered half her face and she was leaning back against a steamer trunk from the nineteen forties, which should have been a clue, since I had seen that trunk a thousand times before.

But I was so sure it was a girl. My heart started going like a steel hammer in my throat and I could hardly breathe, but I was wide awake now. I slowed the car to a stop several yards away so I wouldn't startle her, but she didn't even look up. A runaway, I thought. How tired she must be. I sat in the car staring at her. I would take her in and put her to bed, but I must move slowly, gently. I didn't want to scare her. My own bed. Zim and I would sleep in the living room. And in the morning, when she awoke, what then? My heart was at it again, like a jackhammer, as if it thought that this was Kate, as if it were the stupidest heart alive. But any young girl—she'd be sullen, naturally, I had to be realistic. They're all sullen. As soon as they begin to shed their baby fat and stand there with their own new breasts, the world turns on them, all scorn and longing—the miracle is that it's only sullenness, that teenaged girls don't kill everyone in sight. It is a miracle. That they still want the world.

She must be hungry. I could offer her something to eat.

Anything, anything at all. A sandwich?

Three please, Mrs. Newell.

Well, what difference did it make if she thought I was an idiot? I could still feed her, as poor drunk Mrs. Newell had fed me.

I turned the car back on and drove as slowly as I could.

"Ma-ma," Zim whispered, his voice as soft as sleep.

"Hey Zimmie. There's a girl in the road, see?"

"Ma-ma."

I stopped the car again and got out and then I saw my mother's face, a thousand tiny wrinkles, her eyes like a raccoon's, they were so dark and sunken. How was that possible? She looked ten—twenty!—years older than she had the last time I'd seen her. It hadn't been that long—a few years—but in all Babette's raving, she had never mentioned our mother was just a handful of bones now.

"Molly," my mother said. Moly.

I kneeled beside her. "Mama?"

"Molly," she said again, taking my hands in hers.

"Why are you here?"

"I want to see you and Zeem before I go to France. I have tried to telephone to you, but there is never an answer and so I have come. In Asheville there is only one taxi and it costs one hundred dollars."

A hundred dollars on a taxi. She was so small, and she had spent money like it was nothing. Confetti. I lifted her up and took her in my arms—as wasted as she was, she smelled the same.

"Come on, Mama. Come meet Zim."

That night, after we had eaten peanut butter and jelly sandwiches and canned corn, after I had bathed Zim and read him my up-tempo version of *Goodnight Moon*, I drew a bath for her.

She lowered herself into the tub, her eyes on my cracked hands and swollen eyelid. "Molly," she said. "Are you sick?"

"No," I said. "Just tired."

"I am tired, too," she said, sliding under, and that was the closest we came to mentioning Kate or my father at all. She told me her plans while she soaped her arms and legs, her skin like wrinkled silk beneath the water. There was a house in Normandy that had belonged to her all these years—a little cottage that had belonged to some cousin and that had remained intact throughout the bombing. Oncle Jean had managed it for her, renting it out until he died, and then another more distant cousin had taken over, so that it was already outfitted with furniture and linens and towels and dishes.

"That's great," I said, as if her life couldn't have turned out better.

She just smiled, a faint, indulgent smile, as mysterious to me as old age itself.

When she had gone to bed—tucked in beside Zim; I would sleep in the living room after all—I made myself a box of instant chocolate pudding and licked the bowl clean. That night, for the first time since Zim was born, he slept straight through, and I slept dreamlessly. In the morning, I felt so rested I was giddy.

It had snowed six inches during the night—I wouldn't have to go to work—and the meadow was a white lake. "Look," I said, lifting Zim up and pushing open the front door—the air so cold and fresh it seemed to rush right past us, though the world was as still and silent as I have ever known it. Through the snow-bowed trees at the edge of the meadow, we could see the mountains, flushed with pink. I stepped out onto the snowy deck in my socks, knelt down so Zim could touch the snow and then I spun his wet-diapery self around, slipping in every direction. I laughed stupidly and my mother, watching from the safety of the tatami mats, laughed too, that young girl laugh she had never outgrown.

The roads were impassable for three days, but my mother had given herself a one-week layover, a fact as shocking as the hundred-dollar taxi—any layover through Asheville would have doubled the cost of the plane ticket. When had she become so thin, so profligate? One night, going through my fridge, she threw out some leftover chicken, Tupperware container and all. The rest of the time, all she wanted to do was lie on the bed and watch Zim crawl from place to place.

I gazed at her sunken face and she gazed at Zim's and that's what I remember most from that week, besides the fear I felt when the snow finally melted and I had to go to work and leave her alone all day in the trailer.

"Well," she said. "Leave Zeem."

"Zim? Leave him?"

"So I am not alone."

"Oh, Mama. He's too much work. I'm just afraid—"

"Of what are you afraid, Molly?"

"If something happens to you while I'm gone."

"Do not be ridiculous. I am alone for the rest of my life." And she smiled her ancient smile at me again, a smile I never saw when she was fat and thrifty.

That night after I put her and Zim to bed, I looked through her steamer trunk. There, all neatly folded, were her meager, patched over clothes, taken in to fit her new small self; her books—a Bible, a Latin hymnal, the fables of La Fontaine—and a shoebox full of photographs of us. The twins, Ted, Babette, me, the grandchildren. I'd sent her some of Zim and here were Ashley, Laura, Conroy. We had all just drifted off separately, unmoored by whatever it is that keeps other families together, however unhappily.

And yet my mother loved us all. She wasn't truly profligate—the taxi, the layover, the thrown-out chicken, what did they mean? Some wild gesture of love, farewell? *I am not the miser you think I am.* We were all she had, stacked in her shoebox.

There were no pictures of Simone—they were too poor after the war for photographs—but there were as many of Ted as of any of us. At two or three, sitting in his pajamas on top of the picnic table. At five, maybe, with Andy Newell, the two of them in matching oversized cowboy hats. His first trip to the barbershop, when he cried and cried to lose his orange hair. More of him, really, than of me—it's always that way with youngest children. I didn't mind. She loved him, and must have loved Simone, too.

Protection is another thing—and patience. She could offer neither of those, only love. But who was I to have blamed her? I, who had never crouched beneath the sudden shadows of B-17s, never lifted stone after stone in search of the people I loved? She'd given up at last, exhausted, and turned to find a soldier staring at her. She was sixteen. The prettiest thing he'd ever seen.

In another life, she might have been the kind of mother a body dreams of, all fat warm nourishment and kindness, but this was no other life.

The day she left was one of those sudden, spring-like days you get a lot of in an Appalachian winter. The sky was bruised and warm, the wind so strong I had to fight to keep the car on the road when I took her to the airport. You could still go with people to the gate then and I held her hand until the last minute, thinking I'd visit her in France. I wouldn't let years at a time go by any more—she was so small and old, though only sixty-seven—how would she manage?

I'd visit her and it would be the way it was when I was small, when the rest of the family was so vague to me it might not have existed, except in dreams.

But I didn't have the money to fly to France. I guessed my mother's cab and layover were the first and only excess she'd ever have permitted herself. She wouldn't take money from my father, she'd live on whatever the French government gave her and there wouldn't be enough for airline tickets.

The others would see her—they had money (even Babette, who still demanded an allowance from our father)—and they'd see each other, all back together in Texas now. It was only I who was unmoored after all. How was that? How had I come loose?

They called her flight and I held on to her, the way Claire and Pat had when they'd left for college.

"Mama!"

"Molly," she said. "I love you, Molly." And then she turned and walked out to the plane, as small and disheveled as a bag lady making her way across the windy tarmac.

CHAPTER

TWELVE

I sometimes wonder what would have become of you if you had been more successful at Harvard, but the older I get, the more convinced I am that no potential is ever fulfilled. Even the great men of antiquity, whose works have lasted thousands of years, had no doubt a greater reach. From time to time it makes me think there might be a god, by which I mean only some eternal repository of unmet potential to which we all ultimately return.

But that is sloppy thinking. What is certain is that I shall never fulfill my own potential. I shall instead, by degrees, slip away from what I have accomplished. This is a bitter thing to face, far more bitter than the lost esteem of my colleagues. (In my youth, I confess, I enjoyed their admiration, but as it was rarely mutual, I should not mind losing it.)

What saddens me most, of course, is to have lost the ability to shape events—and all because of an icy road! Well, Molly, I can't expect you to understand—but pity an old man who has fallen so far in his own eyes. And please write. Letters mean the world to me.

He had retired. He was too old to keep running for office, he said. He'd always been unopposed but now, who knew? The few people who had questioned his being with a fourteen-year-old street girl had hushed, but you never knew what a new, eager opposition might dredge up.

Babette, who had installed herself as our father's housekeeper after Mama left, called me three or four times a week to discuss how he was getting on. She couldn't believe he was retired, she said. It was just awful. *You know why, don't you? Awful, evil people with their awful, evil suspicions. Mama's no better. I know she left him because of the accident, I don't believe she ever even loved him.*

The Harrisons had had a party and hadn't invited Daddy. Could I believe that? At least Andy Newell came by one time—*he* wasn't a total asshole.

"Andy Newell?"

"You don't remember Andy? Shit, Molly, I guess not—you were so little."

"I remember," I began, but she was on to other grievances:

Ted! She'd never forgive him for joining the Navy, that alone had probably cost Daddy five years, it was such a slap in the face. And now he was coming around all the time, like they ought to be having Sunday supper or something.

Well, she sure as hell wasn't going to start cooking for Ted. Daddy was one thing—somebody had to look after him now that Mama had left and she realized I was too busy—though the twins could sure help out more than they did, Houston wasn't exactly the South Pole—but she wasn't going to start cooking for Ted.

Did I know what Daddy liked? Fried chicken and hamburgers. Could I believe it? All those years eating brains and what he really wanted was fried chicken.

"Zim is fussing," I said, every time.

"He sure fusses a lot. Is something wrong with him?"

"He's teething," I said. Or his stomach was upset or he had a little cold. I figured I'd keep him fussing in her imagination until he went off to college, and then I'd invent something else. I could listen to her for about three minutes now, but that was it.

Zim, in fact, was no trouble at all. By the time he was two, he could entertain himself for hours, rolling his truck across the bumpy terrain of the tatami mats or covering page after page with bright streaks of crayon. He slept nine straight hours a night plus an afternoon nap and my skin regained its youthful glow, my body filled out a little. I could see the men in the town square looking at me, but I didn't want any of them now. The thought of being naked with a man repelled me. All the flirtatious games, the small deceptions and the drowning pleasures—I couldn't imagine how I had ever wanted any of it. Sometimes I'd stare right back at a man and imagine all his foibles in bed, and my hatred seemed to lift me up, to make my skin glow even brighter.

There were exceptions. If a man was broken enough, I didn't recoil. I never shrank away from the old sad men with watery eyes and speech impediments who hung around McDonald's or the front of the grocery store. I smiled at those men, though we never spoke to each other. There was never any question of a conversation, now that I had a toddler on my hip. Still, I did not recoil.

But the handsome ones, the young, grinning men in work boots and Carhart jackets, and the older, dignified men, too—it satisfied me to hate them. As if, simply by hating a nice-looking man, I could be Kate's avenger. And avenging her, forget her. So I could live in peace. Go to work, raise my son, watch how the shadows swam across our trailer. Zim wasn't a man yet, and by the time he was, I'd be done with hating. Or something like that. It would work itself out somehow, like our poverty and the question of his paternity, which, obviously, couldn't depend forever on my flimsy motorcycle-daddy story. But I couldn't worry about the future. I just wanted peace.

Only Joe disturbed the calm now and then; I'd dream he was slipping into bed next to me, and I'd awaken with such watery limbs that I'd get up and make biscuits and eggs and grits for Zim. I was all dewy-eyed and provident, who usually just managed a pop tart handed over the back seat of the car.

"What's up, Ma?" he'd say, in his squeaky little voice (and this was a miracle—that I had fed and clothed and loved him and here he was, a boy, walking and talking and with a budding sense of humor—runtish, it's true, but still: two arms, two legs, a mouthful of teeth brushed twice daily).

"Well, I think you ought to eat every now and then, don't you?"

"Is it necessary?" he'd ask, grinning, mimicking a phrase I'd used on the phone.

Then Joe would fade again and we were back to pop tarts. Zim would munch quietly on the way to pre-school or kindergarten or first grade, I'd drop him off, clean house, pick him up again, go home. The routine of our life absorbed me completely. The routine and the small calamities: ear infections, past due notices, car trouble.

It was never really all that peaceful, and I worried about my effect on Zim. Sometimes I thought I was no better than my grandmother, alone and fixated on her only son. Then I'd get scared that Zim would end up like my father and the next day we'd go to the animal shelter. We have five cats now—they sleep with Zim and he teases them with bits of string, so he's not completely alone—but I cannot bring myself to get a dog, which is what he wants. I don't want an animal following me around all the time or running off and getting hit by a car or biting one of Zim's friends or even just rolling in shit and needing to be washed off.

Once, though, I almost gave in. Zim was two, hardly old enough to beg convincingly, but I'd just weaned him and was inclined to say yes to all requests. I didn't, though. I held firm. And then one night I awoke with the realization that I could smoke again—I had no milk to spoil. Every night, after I put Zim to bed, I could step outside and have a cigarette. I was as excited as if I'd walked into a surprise party in my honor. It was spring—blossoming trees scattered through the woods, daffodils rising out of the raw banks—and I went outside to sit on the front steps and drink it all in. A stray dog was standing in the moonlight, staring up at me. She had a long, silver and black coat and the most intelligent eyes I've ever seen on any creature. She was so thin, I never guessed that she was pregnant.

In the morning, Zim christened her Polly, because it rhymed with Molly, and after we fed her for a week—she was more ravenous than any dream-dog—she crawled beneath the trailer and had Jim, Tim, Kim and Sim.

People came to the trailer sometimes: Frankie Burdell, with extra peaches or apples from her trees; the mailman if one of the twins sent a gift for Zim; the meter-reader; Jehovah's Witnesses. At the sight of them Polly growled and bared her teeth and no one could come near the trailer, but we all just laughed and said what a good mother she was. Alone with Zim and me she was completely gentle. Zim picked up her puppies and dropped them, and she dozed on the ground, ignoring him. Sometimes she licked him a little. At night, when I sat outside smoking, she lay her head in my lap, and I talked to her.

Mostly I talked to her about how tired I was, how scared I was of fucking up Zim's life and how sometimes when he looked at me I was sure he hated me, and then how ashamed I was for imagining a thing like that about a two-year-old. It wasn't even anything he did—a scowl or a tantrum or anything, though he did those things, like any two-year-old—it was just the fact that he existed, and was mine. He deserved a better mother, a better situation in life: a house and a father and a sibling and money and a mother who knew how to make casseroles and which kinds of rashes needed immediate attention and which would go away on their own, a tall woman, with big, capable hands and a strong back—not a skinny, nervous mother who could provide no better home than this second hand trailer flimsily perched on a hillside. And I believed that though he was only two, he must know these things and despise me, and that was the worst thing of all, that I somehow kept forgetting what a two-year-old was: trusting and helpless and not in a position to reassure his mother. I told her these things, which I could tell no one else, and she gazed at me the whole time with her grey, intelligent eyes, never looking away, never even thumping her tail or sighing, as if to say—what? That she loved me, that was all, I had saved her life. All mothers worried about one thing or another, the specifics hardly mattered; it was just an instinct, like all the other mother-instincts. Then I would reach down and lift her face to mine and kiss her soft, long muzzle, the white fur beneath her eyes. I never talked to her about my father or anyone else. I just talked on and on about myself and she listened with the infinite patience of all dogs.

When the puppies were no longer welcome at her teats, Zim and I took them in a cardboard box and sat out in front of the grocery store; within an hour we'd given them all away. The next day I took Polly to the vet to get her spayed and a week later, I hired a man to put a dog door in the trailer.

Polly growled at the man the whole time he was sawing and drilling, but I held her close and explained that she had just weaned a litter of puppies and probably still had all those maternal hormones going. She was really a very friendly dog, I said.

"Reckon so," the man said, crouching down and fitting the door to the opening. He had a wide, pink, friendly face and was intent on his job.

Polly flattened her ears, growling louder and snapping her teeth, and then she began to shake and I realized she was scared; I murmured close to her ear, but still she pulled against me, as if the only balm for her fear was to lunge at a stranger.

"She's scared," I announced, laughing a little, embarrassed by her unfriendliness. "That's what it is. And the hormones," I added, though any fool could see this man didn't want to discuss hormones.

"Reckon so," he repeated, and he stood up slowly, favoring one knee. "It'll be twenty dollars."

"Oh," I said, wondering how I could reach around to my back pocket for my check book and hold Polly at the same time. "Could I maybe give it to you through the window of your truck?"

He looked down at Polly with an expression of profound disapproval, but said nothing, and climbed up into his truck. I let Polly go and she jumped after him, her toenails sliding furiously against the shiny surface of his door. "Down, Polly, down!" I cried pointlessly, trying to write a check as fast as I could; when I was done I grabbed Polly by the scruff of her neck and waved the check at the man and called out over Polly's barking and through his closed window that I was sorry and would pay for any scratches. He rolled his window down a half inch, took the check and was gone.

Polly stopped instantly, her eyes softening, and when I let her go, she licked my hand. But she was still shaking.

"It's okay," I said. "Okay, sweetie. He didn't want to hurt you. Or Zim, or me for that matter. He didn't want to hurt anyone. You can't act like that."

But she was a dog, after all. Even when her teats had shrunk back inside her coat, her ears flattened and she shook violently, letting out a long, low growl when anyone but me came up the drive.

And yet at night she slept with me and if Zim awakened, she heard him first and nudged me with her silver muzzle. She'd get over her fear of strangers, I thought. It only needed time.

Only there wasn't enough time in this life. After awhile, the mailman wouldn't come up, no one would read our meter. I didn't want to tie her up, and so at last I gave her away, to a man with a chain-link fence around his house, who wanted a guard dog. I had to trick her into his truck and she cried the whole way down the drive, but what else could I do, with Zim still in diapers and the exhaustion of motherhood still aching along my skin?

I promised Zim we'd visit her, though I knew we wouldn't. At night, sitting out on the stoop with my one or two or sometimes three cigarettes, I tried talking to myself, to keep from thinking about her, but I didn't know what to talk about now. Without her everything I said sounded ridiculous and slightly shameful.

And then another dog came. I thought, will we ever be done with these strays? The new dog was white and fluffy, some lost, expensive, vain pure breed without a collar, and I took her to the shelter, certain she'd be adopted right away.

The white dog jumped calmly in my car, jumped calmly out when we reached the shelter, but when we started up the steps, a dog on the inside started barking as I have never heard a dog bark before or since. I would have turned around, driven away by that wild barking if the door hadn't opened and the manager come out. "Had to see what was going on," she said. "Never heard that dog bark like that before." Her voice was rich and deep and she reeked of cigarette smoke and weighed no more than ninety pounds, her bones all visible beneath her skin. "Come on in," she said. "We got half a dozen puppies in here today. Don't let that one scare you."

Zim, distracted by the playpen full of fat, golden puppies, did not look at the dog long enough to recognize her.

She stopped barking as soon as she saw me, her eyes locked on mine.

"How long have you had this dog?" I asked.

"Bout a week. She come in last Saturday. Fellow brought her in, said he got her for a guard dog, but she wouldn't let him near her. Took him a week to get close enough to throw a leash on her and put her in the back of his truck. Most folks'd shot her, but he said he never could shoot a dog. Never heard her bark like she done today though. She just growls most of the time, bares her teeth—scared to death, poor thing, but I ain't gonna be able to get rid of her, have to put her down—but I'll keep her as long as I got the extra cage."

"She's pretty," I said.

"Sure is. Ain't a bad dog, just scared, but folks don't want to get near her."

She gave the new white dog a biscuit and put a collar on her, and when her back was turned, I put my hand inside Polly's cage. She licked it, whimpering, and I put my head close to hers. "Oh sweetheart," I murmured. "Sweetheart."

She nuzzled me through the bars, waiting for me to unlock the door.

"I love you," I whispered, and she thumped her tail. And then I went over and scooped Zim into my arms, holding him so he'd face away from Polly. "We have to go," I said. "We'll come back another day."

I didn't wait for nightfall to have a smoke. The minute Zim went down for a nap, I went outside and lit up. Sometimes his naps lasted an hour, sometimes five minutes; but I couldn't help myself. I sat on the stoop having cigarette after cigarette, straining for a sound from him. When he woke up, I'd say the meter man had been by, smoking, and that's why I smelled so bad. Or I might blame it on a Jehovah's Witness.

The days progressed, the seasons; Zim lost teeth, he learned to read and write. Once a week or so Kathy and I talked on the phone—once she even flew down and visited me—and I learned to exchange pleasantries with the mothers of Zim's friends. I got off the phone quickly when Babette called, skimmed my father's letters, wrote polite thank you notes to the twins and little vignettes about Zim for my mother—and to Ted, who sent me information about computers, suggesting every few months that I get one—it would be so handy to be able to email each other, and no boy should grow up in a house without the internet—I sent the same reply every time: *Thanks, Ted. This is so helpful.* Every Christmas, Babette and the twins said I should come home, they couldn't believe they had never met Zim, they missed me, and every year I said *next year, I promise.*

Now and then Faye Mitchell abandoned her job as overseer and went to town to get her hair done and hear the news—who was pregnant, who'd gotten a new truck, what truant child had gone to juvenile court—and I was left alone with Roscoe. He really had been hurt on a motorcycle and, confined to his wheelchair, had gone to fat. Faye took care of him in exchange for his share of the sale of their parents' farm, which she spent on small luxuries, like her hair color, and me. But Roscoe was a kind man, forever telling Faye not to follow me around and apologizing to me because she did, and when Faye was out, I sometimes took a break and sat with him. He always offered me a beer, and I always declined. We talked about the weather and he asked me what my boy was up to now. I showed him pictures and he said what a nice looking boy he was, and smart, too. You could tell by looking at him.

"He does well in school," I said, and I always blushed.

Once, when Zim was in the second grade, Roscoe cocked his head. "You ashamed?"

"Of what?"

"A smart boy."

"No, of course not."

"Why're you blushing, then?"

I shrugged, still blushing.

"You're smart, too," he said, his head still cocked. "Folks always make fun of the smart kids. I'd've been smart, I'd've held it over everyone." He laughed softly. "And I wouldn't be sitting here."

"A lot of smart people have motorcycle accidents," I said.

"I don't know about that. Was his dad smart?"

I hesitated, feeling guilty that I'd invented a tragedy Roscoe had really known. "I don't know," I said at last. "I don't know how smart he was."

Roscoe was quiet for awhile. Then he asked, "You miss him?"

"No," I said, too quickly.

"Treat you bad?" He asked, with such gentleness I could hardly stand it.

I shook my head. "I don't know."

"Don't know if he treated you bad?"

"Who he was."

He was quiet then for such a long time, and my face was so hot that I thought I should go back to washing the dishes, but he shook his head. "Don't know about you," he said mildly. "But I miss those days."

I looked straight at him and laughed suddenly and then we were both laughing so hard our eyes were tearing up.

"I never told anyone," I said finally. "About not knowing."

"I'll never tell," he said.

"It was a wild time."

"Sure was," he agreed, as if we'd had the same wild time, and with each other.

I looked at him, thinking what a handsome man he must have been. His eyes were slate blue, his teeth perfect. On a wild impulse I gestured vaguely towards his legs. "Would you like me to—?"

He laughed softly. "You don't want to mess with me, Molly. Get on back to work."

"I could," I said, standing firm.

"Shit, Molly."

"Why not?"

"Because," he sighed. "Even if I was the man I used to be, you wouldn't be with me. I'm a redneck and a high school drop out and I drink more than I should. I don't know what you are, but you're something else."

"You don't end up not knowing who your son's father is if your taste is limited," I said, but I walked away and started running water in the sink. I was embarrassed now, but Faye would be home soon and I ought to finish up.

"Molly," he said.

I turned around and saw that his eyes were red and it wasn't from laughing anymore. "This may be the worst thing a man ever said to you, but I could pay you. I don't mean that the way it sounds."

"Please don't pay me," I said, and I walked back over to him.

Afterwards, cleaning us both off, I thought I should kiss him, something to show that it wasn't pity, that I really liked him, but I didn't like him that way. It wasn't pity, but it wasn't love, either, and I felt like crying because I didn't want to kiss him, I had just wanted to do some small nice thing for him—and then I could hear Faye, pulling into the driveway and I stood up quickly and went back to the sink, scrambling for some excuse for my slow work.

Faye was as little and mean as her brother was big and kind and she burst in, with her newly permed and coppered hair and glared at me, but Roscoe stopped her before she could get started: "Washing machine seized up again. Molly fixed it."

After that, if Faye was out, I finished the cleaning before I did anything to Roscoe, and there was never enough time to worry about kissing or payment or anything else. I figured it was just something I could do, like shoveling someone's walk or carrying his groceries. All those times I'd wanted to feel something with a man and been unable to—it seemed now like a trick, to make myself numb, and I supposed that was the etymology. I didn't sit with him much anymore, but we talked while I dusted or did the dishes, and I always bragged about Zim now, showing Roscoe his report cards and quoting what the teachers said about him.

The nicest thing Roscoe ever did was not to pester me about what I was doing—why I was giving him blow jobs every month or so when there was nothing in it for me. I couldn't have said.

He always thanked me afterwards and I always smiled at him, to let him know he was welcome.

———————

Every few months, I broke down and wrote my father back. I imagined the register of my voice going up, a sudden, high-pitched fawning.

Dear Daddy,
Thanks so much for writing to me. It was so good to hear from you. Zim and I are fine; he's doing well in school and my little cleaning business is thriving. I miss you!
Much love,
Molly

I couldn't help myself. I hated him and yet—suppose I was wrong? Suppose nothing had happened the way I imagined it?

And then one day Babette called, and though I told her that Zim had just cut his lip, she kept right on talking and told me that Daddy had Lymphoma. "It's no surprise," she said. "Everybody knows you get cancer when you're unhappy. I'd like to call up all those people who haven't invited him to their parties and tell them that he's dying."

"Is he dying?' I asked, thinking that if in fact Zim had cut his lip I'd probably forget about it for a few minutes while I absorbed this news.

"Yes! Yes, Molly, there's nothing they can do!" She was screaming now. "I can't believe Mama left him. I just cán't fucking believe it. Over a car wreck! Do you know how many car wrecks I've had? Oh Molly, what are we going to do? You've got to come home now, okay?"

I let her cry for a long time, murmuring in the pauses that of course I would come—I hadn't seen him for ten years—and all the while thinking through the best arguments for not coming. Poverty was no good because one of them would end up sending my plane fare. If I said I couldn't leave Zim, they'd send two plane fares, and no one would believe I couldn't leave a housecleaning job for a few days; they'd tell me I should just move back to Texas if that was the case. I decided that Zim needed surgery and that, of course, we had to do it here because he wouldn't be able to get insurance in Texas with a pre-existing condition. But what condition? What urgent problem I had never mentioned before?

"How soon can you be here, Molly?"

"Tomorrow," I said. "A few days at the latest." I told myself there were things I needed to say to him, but the truth is I just wanted one last time to breathe in his smell.

He was more beautiful to me than ever. His hair was white, his face had grown as lean as a medieval Christ's. He had a trim, white beard, but you could still see the hollows of his cheekbones.

"Daddy," I said.

"Molly." He smiled at me. I don't remember him smiling before. His teeth were yellowish, his smile as friendly and innocent as a boy's.

They'd let him out of the hospital since there was nothing they could do, and he was sitting at his desk in a suit and tie. It was hard to look away from his eyes, to take in the bagginess of his suit. His suits had always fit him perfectly—but old age is poverty: his hands were skeletal and liver spotted; a few of his back teeth were missing.

And yet how luminous he seemed, my father, with his discarded prostitutes, his wild, wild vanity and his cold Quaker rage. What is it that makes one person look like the son of God and another, kinder soul resemble the Gorgon? Maybe if we had a religion where Jesus was drawn with deformities—a club foot or a harelip. Maybe then we wouldn't strive so much for perfection, beauty. We'd love the least of these, get down on our knees and thank God for our clumsiness.

But I couldn't work it out right then, with my breathing so constricted. Should I touch him? I wasn't sure, under the circumstances, what the proper etiquette was.

I leaned over and kissed his cheek and he clapped his hand on my back and began to weep.

"Oh Daddy," I murmured, automatically. I kept my arms around him, bent awkwardly over his old body, and he cried for a good long while. When I could feel that he wanted to speak, I pulled away and sat back on my haunches.

"I'm all shot to hell," he said. "I shan't survive."

He said it as if he were refuting someone—the world!—as if everyone kept telling him that he was fine and he alone could see the truth. He alone was sufficiently brave.

And then I realized that's what he wanted—he wanted people to say *you're not dying*, so that he could keep showing his courage—and I did. I said, "Don't say that, Daddy. You're so strong. If anyone can beat this, you can."

"Nonsense," he said, and he straightened up a little in his chair, his face once more composed.

My voice grew brighter and thinner with each denial and with each pronouncement of the truth, he seemed more like his old and vigorous self.

At last he fell asleep in his chair and without thinking of how he ought to be positioned, I tore out to the backyard and started lighting cigarettes. Babette was running errands—I hadn't seen her yet—and I was alone with the live oaks and the heat—all that dust and humidity and the dead no-color of the air; I had to get out of there fast. He was dying, I'd give him that, but it wasn't going to be this week or the next and I couldn't very well hang around till he did it. I had Zim to think about, thank God.

I didn't move. A taxi had brought me from the airport and when we pulled up in front of the house, I felt that the driver should stay with me, that we should not be parted. That to have entered this world together, we should stay together. On the street side of the house, the air had been yellow, pollen-filled; but now, on the back side, nothing. How was that possible, when there were so many more trees behind the house? Then I realized that it was just a function of time, the sun going down.

The taxi driver had turned around, headed back towards Exposition. He had driven right out of the yellow air and left me standing before the house, which was shabbier than I remembered. For this Becky had left the cheerful chaos of her mother's kitchen? This low-slung ranch-style ugliness?

But now I could hear Babette on the other side of the sliding glass door, talking to herself. She hadn't seen me and, my heart leaping unexpectedly, I almost turned to look at her—but stopped myself: if I made no sudden movements, I had a better chance of smoking undisturbed.

"Molly! Molly, Molly, Molly, Molly. Oh, Molly." She held me tight and then she pulled away to see me better and all her hair was iron-grey, her belly larger and firmer than her breasts, her eyes as filmy as an old woman's. To my surprise she smelled not only like cheap wine, but like menthol cigarettes. I burst into tears and she joined right in with me.

"It's awful, isn't it? Can you believe how thin he is? How old?"

But it wasn't he who broke my heart. For all her drunken calls, it had never occurred to me she was so ravaged. She must have looked bad the last time I saw her—she'd been drinking for years by the time I stopped going home for Christmas—but I hadn't seen it. She'd always looked so good to me, blessed with an ageless beauty like our grandmother's. I remembered the time she had made herself unappealing when Andy Newell was on the verge of falling in love with her, and saw in her ugliness a depth of kindness and self-sacrifice I had never imagined anyone in our family might possess.

"Oh, Babette," I said. And then I laughed a little. "Shall we have a smoke?"

"You smoke?" she asked, disapprovingly, though I'd been smoking when she found me, and when she saw my pack of camel straights she said I was crazy to smoke such a high tar cigarette, didn't I know any better? But we had barely lit up when she said we ought to go check on Daddy.

My father sighed loudly at the sight of Babette. He had woken up since I'd left him, but he was still sitting at his desk and was looking through a small notebook.

"What is it?" he asked, as if, in fact, there were nothing wrong with him, but he had work to do and wasn't to be disturbed.

"We just wanted to see how you were feeling," Babette said.

Our father turned to me and sighed again. "She's after me like this all the time. How're you doing? How are you doing? She means well, but it's exhausting. I'm dying, as a matter of fact."

"Daddy!" Babette cried out, in genuine distress.

"Well, we must face facts," my father said.

"You could be a little nicer," I said, as softly as I could. "After all, this affects all of us. We're all terrified of losing you." This was good, a lie that might help Babette.

"Well," he said. He smiled at me a second time, that same innocent, friendly smile. "You were always the peacemaker, Molly, weren't you? Always smoothing things over."

"And you," I said. "Have always been the strongest man I know. You'll beat this thing, I have no doubt of it."

He might deserve to hear the truth, but I didn't have the heart to tell it to him. That he was dying was nothing—he knew that—but that no one but Babette would miss him, that he was no better than a murderer? Why would you tell a man such things? He didn't know any of it. He must still believe he was his mother's son, unblemished. A man who tipped his hat to every lady, regardless of her race or pocketbook. Such self-delusion was a kind of innocence, and who was I to shatter it, when there was nothing he could do except, perhaps, tear his own eyes out of his head?

Anyway, that's how I figured it. Let him die ignorant of his sins and he'll die innocent. But that wasn't the whole story. The truth is a slippery slope. If I told him that I knew he'd raped Becky's daughter, that he'd as good as killed her, I might tell him while I was at it how much I loved him. Except, of course, I didn't; I hated him, and all day long like a little ping pong in my head love hate love hate love hate.

Babette insisted that we all have supper together while I was there. The twins had come up from Houston for the day, and Babette got a family-sized bucket from KFC.

"Should Daddy be eating all that fatty food?" Claire asked. She looked exactly like Nancy Reagan now, that small and tight; but Pat had let her hair grow out and was wearing a faintly transparent tunic over silk pants; I wondered if, the QE2 notwithstanding, she had a lover.

"Daddy likes fried chicken."

"Well I just wonder is all," Claire said. "They say that for cancer you want to eat healthy."

Our father was resting in the bedroom, Ted hadn't arrived, and the twins, Babette and I were setting the table, as if it were a four person job.

"It doesn't really matter what he eats, does it?" Pat asked, mildly, and then I was sure she was having an affair. I had never known either twin to contradict the other.

"As a matter of fact," Babette said. "It matters a lot. Being happy is what matters, and fried chicken makes Daddy happy. Truly happy people don't get cancer."

"Well," Claire said. "Now that he does have it, I'm just suggesting—"

"Well you don't get to make suggestions, do you? I'm the one taking care of him, I'm the one who left everything to come help out when help was needed, so I don't think I need your suggestions, Claire."

"As I understand it, Babette, it suited you to come back. You didn't have a dependable income."

"Oh, hush," Pat said. "The current situation suits all of us. Daddy does need help."

"I don't know what the hell you mean," Babette said. "Does it suit you that Daddy's sick?"

Pat sighed. I was full of admiration for her honesty, and miffed, too. How had she, Miss Nixon 1972, come to be so clear and straightforward?

"You look good, Molly," she said. "Do you work out?"

I started to answer, but Ted rang the doorbell. He looked as pale and raw as he had as a boy, though he was past fifty. He came into the kitchen and stood behind the place that had always been his, lightly tapping the rim of the chair back.

"How's work?" Babette asked him, her voice suddenly restrained, almost gentle, and I felt that I should have been notified if they were going to be friends. I had worked so hard to soothe her after their fights—just a couple of months ago, she'd been complaining again about him coming to dinner, and I had tried to calm her down—but now it was as if nothing had happened. I was like those old Japanese soldiers, I thought, still hiding out in the Pacific.

Ted nodded. "It's okay."

"You in the mood for some fried chicken?"

"Sure."

"Claire thinks we ought to be eating brown rice and broccoli."

Ted smiled faintly. "Why not cabbage and liver?"

Claire rolled her eyes, but Pat and Babette both laughed, and I felt the way I had when I was small and knew that I could not penetrate their allegiances.

She was my friend, I wanted to say. The girl he killed was my friend's daughter.

It seemed to me, when my father had come to the table and we were all seated before our plates of fried chicken and biscuits and gravy, that no one missed our mother. I had never discussed her departure with the twins or Ted and my father had never acknowledged it at all. Only Babette had ever had anything to say about it and now it was as if our mother had never really belonged to us, as if she had merely shopped and cooked for us for a few years before moving on.

But suddenly my father dropped his fork against his plate. "I can't eat this. Everything makes me sick."

Claire raised her eyebrows triumphantly.

"Are you okay?" Babette asked. "Daddy?"

"No. I'm not okay. I'm going to lie down."

We all rose from the table at once, as if we meant to carry him. He started moaning then, a low, animal sound, and Babette, wide-eyed with terror, put her arm around him. He pushed her off. "I don't need any goddamned help. Your mother ought to be here—" His voice cracked, and now he shrugged as helplessly as a boy. "I don't know why she left me."

But later, after the chicken had been cleared off the table and put in Tupperware in the fridge, after Ted had gone back to the office, Claire had headed back to Houston, and Babette had driven to Whole Foods to buy organic vegetables, he sat in the living room with Pat and me. "Let's talk," he said. "I don't have enough interesting conversation these days." We were quiet for a few minutes, searching for a topic, and then he said, "I pity your children. The world they shall inherit. It's an awful mess."

"It sure is," Pat said, nodding.

"I'll be well rid of it."

"Oh Daddy," I said. "Don't talk that way." I was sick of myself, but I didn't know how to stop.

"There's no point in hiding from the truth," he said, and I thought, *Kate?*

"Still," Pat said. "Things have looked bleak at other points in history, and then—there *has* been progress."

"Well, should such a miracle occur, it won't be thanks to the idiots you voted for."

"We all make mistakes," Pat said.

"Do you mean to say—?"

Pat shook her head. "I've come to hate his little possum face."

My father kept staring at her. "What does Steve think?"

"Well, Steve—"

"Ah," my father said. "So there's a new man in your life."

"Daddy!"

"I wondered about this new look of yours."

"For God's sake, Daddy." She rose, her face white with rage, and turned to me. "I'm sorry we didn't get to visit longer. You do look good, Molly."

"Perhaps I was too hard on her," my father said, after she left. "But I will say it again, Molly. Of all your sisters you were the only one who was never boy crazy."

As it turned out, I was right about my father not dying. I was just making it up, but I was right anyway. When I went out to Austin, the doctors had given my father two to six weeks, tops, but he lived another year. I went out four more times to say good-bye to him—each time, Babette called and told me to come right away. *This is it Molly. This is really it.*

The first three times, I stayed two or three days, leaving Zim with his friend Tyler's family or with Frankie, saw that my father was sick but not yet ready to die, and flew back home. I stayed in my old room in Austin, with Babette on the other side of the wall, and it was as if I hovered an inch above the mattress: I never sank down into it, never slept, never quite touched anything in that house. I shrank from the dingy walls, the baseboards peeling away from the sheetrock, the dirty shag carpeting. I tried to help Babette with the cooking, but she was on a mission to find something Daddy would like to eat, and all I could do was the dishes. Our father scorned her cooking, scorned her, but asked me every day to sit in the living room and talk with him; he had so few opportunities for interesting conversation, he always said. I knew he liked me better now only because I was, like my mother, gone; and I couldn't stand the way he treated Babette—but still, sometimes, it caught me off guard, his desire to keep me near him in the living room, and, wanting to please him, I made my voice higher and thinner than ever so that whatever I said would barely disturb the air into which he talked.

Once, he sighed and said, "She was so pretty, your mother. If you could have seen her—! Of course, she was never at home here, and I suppose she ate for consolation. You never knew her when she was slender, did you? Well, the loveliest girls are soonest ruined—look at your sister, Babette."

"There's nothing wrong with Babette." But it was as if I were dreaming and I could not raise my voice above a whisper.

My father smiled. "You're a good girl, Molly. Always smoothing things over. I'd like to give you a task."

"Of course," I said, in that same thin, dream-choked voice.

"I've kept a diary since I was a boy. When I'm gone—"

"You're not—"

"I'd like you to go through my diaries—there are over one hundred volumes of them—and—edit them, perhaps. But carefully, Molly! Do not over-edit. Perhaps I should ask someone else..."

"I'd be glad to do it, Daddy."

"Well, certainly you have the time. Ideally it's a task for a law student, but they're so awfully busy. And if you were to do it, it would serve a dual purpose. You need something more than housekeeping, Molly. You were always a bright girl and though things didn't work out for you at Harvard, still—this would be a good task for you. I assume you know how to type?"

I nodded.

"Good, then. What I shall want you to do is to read through the diaries very carefully, taking notes, as I'm sure you used to do in your literature classes. Then type them up verbatim—this will force you to read the diaries a second time and you may notice important details you missed the first time.

"When you have finished typing, you'll want to go through with a black marker and cut out many of the most personal items—what I ate on a particular day, for example. The idea is to show how my thinking evolved over the years. I always noted what I was reading, and often wrote down my reactions to what I'd read, but in the interest of honesty, I also noted details that, to someone else, might seem irrelevant—if I had indigestion, for example. Did that alter my reading? In the moment, I might not recognize the effect of a stomach ache on my thinking, and so it was necessary to write everything down. Nevertheless, I realize that an excessive amount of information about my digestion will not interest most readers and that's why it's up to you to edit my diaries. When you have typed up a clean copy, you'll want to contact a publisher..."

I listened to his instructions and was only flattered. It didn't occur to me that a publisher wouldn't be interested in his diaries and though he said nothing now about his reputation, I believed that what he wanted, more than anything, was for me to rehabilitate it. And I was flattered. In the dream, I was the chosen one: Homer, singing the great stories. I was bright enough, my failure at Harvard notwithstanding. And with the shifting logic of a dream, it seemed to me suddenly that his desire for rehabilitation was a kind of repentance; it was the most he could articulate, shy and self-flagellating as he must be, beneath the stern exterior.

A minute later I was disgusted. Who cared about his diaries? He clearly wasn't dying in the next day or two, and I needed to get home.

Babette said didn't it tear me apart to see how thin he was? He doesn't look so bad, I said every time; because the way I imagined him when she called and said *this is it* was in a coma. She was the one who looked worse and worse: she'd taken to wearing an old apron of my mother's, and stray hairs sprouted above her lip; all day she puttered around the kitchen, with a glass of rosé in one hand and a menthol cigarette burning itself out in an ash tray on the counter. She steamed asparagus, sweetpeas, kale; she made sushi, stir-fries, omelettes, mashed potatoes, julienned carrots, hamburgers, miso soup, minestrone, roast chicken, pudding—all of it went down the disposal.

I couldn't stand to think of what would become of her when he did die. What would she do with herself?

And then I would go home again, to Zim. I was mostly home that year—if I add up all my time away, it only totals thirty days—but it seemed to me that I was always in Austin, that I would barely catch my breath and it was time to go out there again, and though it meant that I could sleep late, that I didn't have to clean anyone's house, didn't have to scour the grocery aisles in search of a cheaper can of tuna, or figure out how to hang more blankets in the windows to keep the cold out, the trips exhausted me as if, each time, I were having to learn to stay longer and longer underwater. I needed something to get me through, but I didn't have anything, and I was short-tempered with Zim and then, each time, overcome with a remorse that frightened him more than any punishment. *Don't cry, Mama. Please don't cry.*

But then one day after a sleepover at Tyler's, he raced into my arms and announced that he'd been saved. I started to laugh before I realized he meant it: Tyler's mother had been taking him to church. I felt as if the wind had been knocked out of me, and it wasn't because my son had joined the evangelicals—a person's religious beliefs are his own business, and besides, he was eight—it was because he had found what he needed and I'd had nothing to do with it. I'd arranged everything until now—play dates, doctor's visits, haircuts—and though I worried that he had no siblings, it never occurred to me that he might need Jesus. What else had I overlooked? How many other things that I would never realize until he was grown and it was too late?

"That's great, sweetie," I said. "That's just wonderful."

"Can I go with Tyler to church on Wednesday?" He was still nestled in my arms, not yet restless the way he would be in a few minutes, and I nodded, trying just to focus on his small boy smell of leaf piles and river water. He kept still and I did, too, holding him in Tyler's front yard while Tyler kicked a soccer ball against the trunk of a red bud tree and Tyler's big, blonde, twenty-four-year-old mother hung a row of underwear on the clothesline. I watched all those fluttering bright bikinis and suddenly in the confusion of the windy sunshine and the smell of Zim's head and my own nervous heart, I thought, Zim's fine. I sat in that yard with its year-long, life-sized plastic crèche on the front porch along with a couple of bikes and a toy kitchen, and after awhile I came to believe they were the words of God—*Zim's fine.* I was so relieved I nearly burst out laughing. I might not know what other mothers knew with their strong arms and their casseroles, but I loved Zim, watched over him, and that was only good.

I stayed late at Roscoe's that Wednesday and did the windows. Faye went off to her own church and when I was finished cleaning, I lay my hand on Roscoe's shoulder to let him know I was available if he wanted me. I was hanging around town till Tyler's church let out.

Roscoe laughed a little. "Saved, huh?" He was parked in front of the sliding glass door, wearing a Tar Heel tee-shirt that was tight around his biceps. "I remember when I got saved," he said. "Down in Blue Creek."

"Oh," I said, embarrassed. "Are you still?"

"Well as you know me, you think I might have a little something going on the side with the Holy Rollers? No thank you. Not interested."

"Were you? When you got saved?"

He shook his head. "Just thought if I joined a congregation, I wouldn't be lonely anymore. Shit. I was lonelier than before. Everything about church made me want to cry. Folks all dressed up, like the main thing worrying Jesus is fashion. Like what's wrong with the world the other six days of the week is we don't wear enough pastel."

I laughed, but he was quiet, gazing out at the field of wild onions that was all that was left of his parents' farm. "All I ever felt in church was homesick. Fourteen years old and I could hardly keep from crying."

"Oh," I said and I wondered if I should remind him of my availability; but if I touched him now it would be like we were making love, with his talk of homesickness in the air. My throat felt heavy, and my chest, because I didn't want to make love now any more than I ever had. The longer we sat looking out at his field, the worse I felt, thinking about people being lonely, and then I was mad suddenly, the way I was when Buttercup nipped the inside of my leg—so I put my hand on Roscoe's shoulder to stop it, but he must have sensed how cold I'd grown, or maybe he just didn't want to be all alone on the receiving end anymore, because this time he insisted on paying and this time I accepted. "You've got your boy, Molly. He's going to need more things."

At first I didn't even think about what that money could do for me and Zim, though Roscoe paid me fifty dollars—two twenties and a ten he pulled from his pocket before I started—I was just grateful: Roscoe knew me as well as if he'd come with me all the way from Texas.

Then it was August and Babette called to say Daddy had gone into Hospice, I had to come right away. The mountains were at their dankest and greenest, and I could hear Zim and Tyler playing in the creek. I sat on the stoop with a mosquito whining idly nearby and I said, "Okay. Okay, I'll be there. It'll take me a couple of days to make arrangements for Zim and everything, but I'll be there."

"No, Molly, you have to come right away. He could die today—the Hospice people said it was *imminent*."

"I'll do what I can. Maybe tomorrow."

"You can't wait until tomorrow. There's a hurricane coming—flights will be cancelled. You've got to come right away."

"The nearest airport is two hours away, Babette, and I have to make arrangements for Zim."

"Bring Zim. Doesn't he want to see his grandfather before he—" She burst into tears, such loud, terrified weeping that she forgot what she'd been saying and I didn't have to answer about Zim, didn't have to say that I didn't want him to see his grandfather. I didn't want him to know what his grandfather was like.

But I did fly out that evening, my heart suddenly racing, because Daddy was dying and I still had never said a truthful word to him— Tyler's mother folded Zim back into her family and all the ladies I cleaned for sighed and said, well, you've got to do what you've got to do. Only Roscoe didn't begrudge me. Through the phone lines, I heard the brake on his wheelchair engaging. "You take care of yourself, Molly."

I got to Austin at one in the morning, picked up a rental car and drove straight to the Hospice, the air so soft I kept the windows down.

The Hospice was near an empty lot and a run down school, but to enter the building you walked through a walled courtyard complete with fountain and benches and for a moment, seduced by that balmy air and the sound of the fountain, I forgot my father and imagined myself young again, coming to meet a man. But in the lobby there were the bright lights, the nurses' station, the nurses with their glazed donuts, and my imaginary assignation vanished; I could feel only the buzzing excitement of catastrophe.

"I'm Judge Moore's daughter," I said, at the nurses' station.

An Indian nurse smiled at me, mid-donut. "He's in room nine, down the hall."

"Is he alive?"

"Oh, yes, ma'am. He's sleeping peacefully. Your sister's in there with him now."

"But it's imminent?" I asked.

She consulted her charts, took another bite of her donut, smiled up at me again. "Well, you never can tell. Looks like he had a good supper when he got here."

The room was big and dimly lit, with French doors giving out on the courtyard and a large, private bath. My father was asleep in his bed and across from him was a sofa, a coffee table, and Babette, standing lost by the walk-in closet, with her wild hair and her bony arms.

"Oh, Molly," she said. "Molly, we can stay here with him. The sofa pulls out. We can sleep in it together."

I went over to him and gazed down at his sleeping face, the hollowed cheeks, his mouth a little open.

"That's okay," I said. "I'll come back in the morning."

"But what if he?"

"I'll come back in the morning," I said, a little too forcefully, imagining her cigarette reek next to me in the bed—I always showered before I went to sleep—and for the first time in my life I saw her glare at me, the way she'd always glared at the others, as if she meant to claw at me.

In the morning he was sitting up and a pretty little blonde nurse was feeding him oatmeal. Babette was in the bathroom, showering.

Another false alarm, I thought, bitterly; but the nurse turned aside so I could reach him and I leaned down and kissed his cool, spotted forehead.

"Daddy," I said, and he made kissing motions into the air, his old mouth puckering weakly, and pins and needles rushed into my body, like when I'm driving and I swerve into the wrong lane or fail to see a stop sign.

I kissed his head again.

"You have a nice family," the nurse said, too loudly, as if he were feeble-minded, or foreign, the way those wealthy housewives spoke to my mother when she begged them for clothes. The nurse turned to me then and said softly, "All your siblings have already been by. Your one sister stayed here—I just like to see a family come together at a time like this."

My father cleared his throat. "I'm not deaf," he said, but his speech was raspy and labored. "You don't have to—" He paused. "Raise your voice—for me. Dying is not—" He gave up, shook his head.

"That's all right, Mr. Moore," the nurse half shouted.

"Judge," I murmured.

"Is that right? You were a judge, Mr. Moore?"

"Is," I said. "He is a judge."

"My," she said, with proper appreciation.

"I can feed him," I said. "I'm sure you have other things to tend to."

"Oh? Oh, well, okay. I'm going to let your daughter feed you, Mr. Moore." Then once more she lowered her voice for me. "Your sister was afraid to. She thought she'd do something wrong, but we like for the families to participate."

I smiled at her and took her seat and lifted the gluey oatmeal to his lips. Spoonful after spoonful I fed him while he gazed at me, and I felt the old animal pleasure I'd felt with Zim: the satisfaction of getting the spoon into his mouth and catching what fell out and scraping the bowl clean. But to what end? If he ate, if he got his strength back—I'd have to come back when he was really dying.

After awhile I could feel Babette, standing in the doorway to the bathroom, watching me.

"Weren't you scared?" she asked, when I was done and had swung the tray away from his bed.

"Of what?"

"Accidentally choking him."

"Don't talk," my father said, straining to form the words.

"I'm sorry," I began.

"About me—in—the third—"

"Sorry, Daddy."

"Not you—Babette. You are a good—nurse."

"Babette has taken very good care of you," I said, with a firmness I had only ever used before with Zim, when he was acting up.

"I'm going to go," Babette said softly, her eyes red-rimmed. "I have some errands."

I followed her into the hallway and she began to cry again, finger-
ing the hem of my tee-shirt. "I can't stand to see him like this," she
said. "I just can't stand it. I don't want him to be alone, but I can't."

"It's okay," I said. "I'll stay."

And so I did, all through that long, quiet day, and the next, and the
next and the ones after that. Babette spent the nights with him and the
twins and Ted dropped by during the day, but mostly I sat alone with
him in his dim room. It took almost three weeks for him to die and I
thought I'd never go home, never hold Zim in my arms again. Every
night I called Tyler's mother and she put Zim on the phone and I told
him I loved him so much and I'd be home soon, but all he really cared
about was that no human being should ever die, and so every night I
told him just how really strong his grandpa was and wasn't that a great
thing? He was still breathing so well.

I fed my father and held a straw to his lips so he could sip some
lemonade and now and then he managed to say something about his
diaries and I promised yes, yes, of course Daddy and then one day he
stopped eating and drinking and talking and still I sat with him and
still he breathed, and if I kissed his forehead, he still puckered his
mouth in return. The days fractured, fell apart, and there was no
sequence to them.

Every evening I drove back to the old house and every evening it looked
newly sad and forgotten. There was still no one in any yard, no sound
anywhere. I smoked a while in the back yard and then I turned in. We
were going to sell the house—his other assets had been bequeathed to
various Quaker charities—but the house was so dilapidated it would
only get a fraction of what it was worth; once you divided that by five,
it wasn't a fortune. Still, it needed a deep cleaning and I'd told the
others I'd take care of it since I wasn't going to stick around for moving
day; every evening I gazed at the broken vacuum cleaner, the old
containers of Ajax and Lemon Pledge.

At last I went to my father's study, thinking I'd start there. I sat at
his desk and stared out the window at the neighbor's softly curtained
windows, at the fine dust covering everything. Behind my father's
heavy, wood-veneer desk was a wall of cheap, metal bookcases, the kind

you'd find in the most anonymous of office buildings. The books, though, the books were the most beautiful thing in the house. None were leather-bound, but all were old and heavy, with embossed covers and gold-leaf titles. Shakespeare, Yeats, Milton, Chaucer, Plato, Sophocles, Cicero, Coleridge, Moliere, Balzac, the books went on and on: shelves of legal tomes and biographies and autobiographies and histories and art books and at the very bottom, almost hidden, two rows of small composition books, which I began to read.

In his tight, slanting script, he'd made a thousand tedious entries, recording everything from the time of his bowel movements to the pages he'd read in a particular book on a particular day. From this we were supposed to deduce the formation of the man? What time he had risen and what he had eaten and how many miles he had run? Even in high school, he was preoccupied with his digestion.

In college, he noted every grade he received and quoted the comments professors had written on his essays. The essays were there, too—I'd look at them later.

There was no diary from the war, but on June 20, 1948, the day he married my mother, he wrote: *08:00: A breakfast of soft-boiled eggs, plain toast, coffee, followed by mild diarrhea. 10:00 Interesting conversation with Betty, $10 plus $5 room fee at the Riverside Inn. 11:40: Intercourse.*

I couldn't stop, as compulsive in my reading as he had been in the writing.

15:00 Wedding at St. Thomas Moore's. (I have not converted.)

When his children were born, he noted the road conditions on the way to the hospital, the weight of his offspring, the snacks he had eaten in the cafeteria and what he had read to pass the time—I couldn't find any mention of graduations or weddings, of our eventual departures.

I turned at last to the night of Kate's death. Before I'd even read the words, I saw the hours and minutes all laid out, the evening ordered with such detached precision my ears rang as if he'd boxed them.

I imagined that a bird flapped in the eaves of his brain, swooping everywhere, upsetting everything, a small, wild bird, desperate to get out—how else to explain what he could not see? There should have been a single line—*I killed her. I raped her and then I killed her, I have committed a crime*—nothing else.

21:10 Thirty-two degrees Fahrenheit and falling, icy precipitation, the roads perilous. Offered to take Kate Lopez to a motel to warm up. There had been a motel, then. The book was trembling in my hands. *Indigestion from earlier in the evening still noticeable.*

21:30 Arrival and check-in at the Comfort Inn. $50 non-smoking room fee.

21:40 A request for $1,000 from the sullen Kate. Declined. Rather than talk, she went to bed without undressing or removing her shoes.

For an instant my heart lifted: she'd wanted a thousand dollars; I might have mis-imagined the whole night.

21:45 Two TUMS.

21:40 Despite earlier proposals, Kate denied interest in sex.

21:50 Intercourse.

22:20 Hershey's bar and coffee from vending machine, $2.50. Kate refused food and drink.

What was that flapping bird? He had no conscience at all. How was that possible? He didn't know that what he'd done was rape—what rape was. He had no idea what constituted a crime.

I closed my eyes. I would have driven to the church and woken up the priest, confessed it all as my own sin, because I had imagined it, but I couldn't move. *Judge Moore was only trying to help*, the paper said.

Poor man, you might think. Trying to help and now he's got to feel bad for the rest of his life. It's sad about the prostitute, but still.

But he doesn't—he doesn't feel bad about a thing!

23:00 Lost control of the car on Mo-Pac near 35th. Arm badly bruised. Kate Lopez killed instantly.

23:04 Used cell phone to dial 911.

What was that wild bird? Something was trying to get out, stunned and beating itself against the walls, but were they the walls of my brain or his?

No conscience at all. How was such a thing possible? Like a circus trick, a contortionist.

I stood still, listening to my breath, and then I tore the pages out of each and every book. All 105 volumes—no one would ever discover the formation of the man. My arms were shaking—1939, 1977, 2001—the older books fell apart easily, the bindings already loose. I tore his sentences in half: *pp72-180 Yarb ough's Biogr A lu ch of Crisp an cheese Ju ice Brennan, in his cal the electri insomn twelve I c ld not a bre zy day*; then I tore without looking.

When I was done, I took down all the other books, the marble-edged volumes and the books with yellowed pages, the art books with their sheets of tissue, Fisher's *Drawing Room Scrap-Book* and *Grunenwald's Sketches*, and the collections—Disraeli's gold-embossed *Works*, with their small, elegant type, their smell of dust and stone, somehow, of comfort—I tore those pages, too. The books I loved and the books I'd never read. All those pages, tearing my hands as I ripped them—even Blake, even his beautiful little drawings—because everything had to go, every last trace—his clothes, too, the spare robe and the suits and the perfectly polished shoes. His manicure kit, his comb, an old bottle of Grecian Formula. What was flammable, I burned. His files and notes and papers and the torn pages of all those books, I carried to the tub and set on fire. Cleopatra ranting, *rather a ditch in Egypt be gentle grave unto me*—and Michelangelo's naked sketches and the uncut letters of Madame de Sevigné, because who could read them, all that paper curling and burning, and glossies from the Sistine Chapel turning the flames as bright as Christmas wrapping. Yeats, too. Poor Crazy Jane, railing against the bishop.

The books were full of silverfish, I'd say, when the others asked. *The clothes were moldy.* I worked all night, manning the fire in the tub, gathering the rest into garbage bags and hauling the bags out to the empty street. The next day the garbage collectors would come and throw the bags onto their truck and everything my father had loved would vanish, his old robe and his hair dye tossed into the Travis County landfill.

In the morning, he was still alive, still breathing. The nurse at the front desk told me and I thanked her and went outside to sit by the fountain; I didn't look into his room at all. I thought about landfills, the way they go on and on, all the different things rising to the surface and settling back down: a shoehorn, a handkerchief, a bar of soap.

CHAPTER fourteen

For days I sat by the fountain without looking in on him. The sun burned through a low, white sky and heat shimmered off the ground. I took to wearing clothes I'd worn in high school—tiny skirts and halter tops that had been hanging at the back of my closet for more than twenty years—and sat with my legs open, my arms dangling at my sides, to catch any breeze that might rise out of that sodden air. I didn't set foot in the nurses' station, or ask any more if he was still alive.

I could hardly breathe in that heat, though I smoked pack after pack. That's a different kind of breathing, and it's never too hot for that—never too hot to add a struck match to the city's record highs. I smoked like I'd never smoked in my life, like the way you'd drink if you'd run a hundred miles. Gulping it in, relishing.

I could have left. I could have gone home, to Zim, or at the very least to an air conditioned building, but I couldn't tear myself away. Sometimes I thought of Sharon Watkins with her awful husband who might be Zim's father, and their daughter's photograph turned to the wall. I never learned what crime she had committed to be made to face the wall, but I used to pick her photograph up, dust it, and wonder if it would be any consolation to her that they hadn't been able to throw the photograph away. I always hoped she *could* throw their photographs away.

When Babette arrived at night to sleep in my father's room, I pretended I'd sat with him all day, and in the morning, when I arrived, I waited until she came out and followed her back to her car, as if I wanted to have a little conversation with her before I began my bedside vigil. She always hurried away, so I could hurry back to him. "I just don't think he should be alone," she said. "Go on in, Molly. You wouldn't want him to be alone when he—if he—"

She barely registered what I said about the silver fish; it wasn't his books she was grieving.

A dream from college came back to me: I was at the funeral of a man I'd barely known and people were offering me their condolences. I didn't know what to say. Finally, an usher told me that the deceased was my father. There must be a mistake, I said. No, he said. Look. He showed me photographs of myself standing next to the dead man. I saw that I must be his child, after all: in every picture we were dressed alike in Harvard insignia clothing.

A joke dream, a dream to tell my college friends. *Fucking Harvard, can you believe it?*

His robes, the color of his hair, the care with which he ate his ice cream. What else did I know of him, finally?

One day, at last, I rose, went into the cool air of the nurses' station, and found Becky's number in the phone book. She lived at a perfectly good address on McCall and for a moment, while I dialed her number on the nurses' phone and waited for her to pick up, I wondered if my father had given her the money to move. My heart started pounding, afraid of some new crime I might discover he'd committed—and worse, some awful complicity of Becky's—but I knew that wasn't it. To my father, Becky was still the only girl whose mind had ever been worthy of his. Not once had he spoken of her in the fascinated, belittling way he spoke of the prostitutes with whom he had such interesting conversations—he only spoke the way a man would speak of a daughter for whom he'd had high hopes. But why, if she was living on McCall Road, wasn't he satisfied with what she'd made of herself?

She answered on the fourth ring and I couldn't speak, letting her ask, *Hello? Hello?* into the empty phone line.

"Becky," I said, getting a hold of myself. "Becky, this is Molly Moore." I had to work to keep my teeth from chattering.

"Molly?"

"I'm in town, in Austin. I was wondering if I could, I was hoping—" My face was drenched with tears. "Would you like to get together?"

"Well," she paused. "Molly. I—well, sure. Why not? Sure. Do you want—" She paused again. "Do you want to come over?" I felt as if I'd trapped her, as if I were a Jehovah's Witness, or my mother asking for clothes, but she gave me directions, her voice deeper than I remembered, and with more of a Texan accent.

"If this is a bad time," I began.

"It's okay. Come on over."

She lived in a nicely landscaped group of condos set back from the street and when she opened the door, she gave me a hug right off. I thought of a girl I'd known at Harvard whose brother had committed suicide when she was in eleventh grade. When she returned to school the following week, her friends were so embarrassed by her suddenly tragic home life that she took to hugging them every time she saw them; it made them feel useful, she said. I didn't know if Becky's hug was purely for my benefit, but the feel of her—her slender, muscular arms, her full breasts—electrified me: we had never touched before, never locked arms or sat on each other's laps the way girls do, and I would have held the embrace, but she pulled away and led me over to a leather sofa in her living room.

Her apartment was not bare after all, but filled with Mexican art and handmade wooden furniture and framed black and white photographs of Kate. Becky looked the way she had in high school, only a little heavier: the same dark auburn hair pulled into a ponytail, the scattering of freckles, the jeans and the boys' white tee-shirt, but her face had grown puffy, almost sallow.

We sat side by side, turned towards each other, and for a few minutes I just stared at my knees and listened to the hum of the refrigerator in the next room. At last we began to speak in the stilted way of blind dates about what we did, what our interests were. She was a self-taught computer programmer, she said, and then, as if to answer my question, she smiled a little—her teeth pure white now, bonded or bleached or capped or whatever it was people did to make their smile look like everyone else's. "Your father thought that was a terrible thing to be. He thought I should go to college, study philosophy. He was against computers, he said—but I guess you know all about that."

I hadn't known, and I thought of Ted, with his endless letters about his work. "Becky, I'm so sorry. About Kate. About my father."

She looked away.

"I'm sorry," I said again.

"You want something? A Coke? A beer? I might have a couple of beers left." She didn't say it like someone who fixated on her own supply of beverages—the way Babette did, always knowing to the last milliliter how much wine she had left—and it occurred to me that my father might have spun a whole story out of nothing, as the arresting officer must have done. She might drink a little too much—she looked like someone who might—but I could not believe she'd driven drunk. Even in high school she'd disparaged anyone who didn't know when to hand over the keys. She must have swerved to avoid a squirrel, or gone a little fast, or maybe her registration had expired; and the cop had insisted on a breathalyzer, because—she hadn't been willing to flirt with him? She would have refused out of pure irritation.

But it didn't matter. My father would have had no patience with her having a brush with the law, however innocent a brush it was. Not Becky, who could have been a philosopher, who might be the only person in all of Texas who wasn't, in his eyes, an idiot.

She was smart, I knew that, but I still couldn't make any sense of it. Unless he was like me—and I like him—and something in Becky's steadiness, her wry warmth, made us want her for our own. Made us want to *claim* her.

I'm sorry, Becky. I am so sorry. I wanted to say it over and over, the way I'd done with Buttercup, when my father kicked him, when I brought my own fist down on his soft yellow back. "I'd love a Coke."

She came back with the drinks—she was having a Coke, too—and said, "You haven't told me what you're doing in town."

"Oh? Oh, I—my father's dying. And, you know, I hadn't been here in a while," I added, as if I needed a better reason.

She sighed heavily, her shoulders dropping, and I had the feeling that she was going to roll up her sleeve or pull up her shirt—something—and show me a terrible bruise, a wound that wouldn't heal, like Jesus pulling open his chest to reveal his thorn-bound heart, something no one wanted to ask about but everyone wanted to see—*How do you manage? How do you get through the day?*

But what she said was, "That must be hard," and I shrugged, and then we were quiet again.

"How did you figure out—how did you teach yourself about computers?" I asked, finally. "I can't imagine."

She laughed a little. "You have to have a sense of direction, for starters. There's more to it than that, of course, but the first stage is like reading a map—and then drawing a better map. It's not all that interesting, but it's a living. You still get lost all the time?"

"There's only one road where I live."

"That's good."

I nodded. We kept going like that, little flares of conversation that died out quickly, until we had finished our Cokes. What had I expected? That I might comfort her? I should leave her in peace. "Thanks for the drink," I said. "It was great to see you."

We sat perfectly still, neither of us rising to go towards the door, as if I hadn't spoken. I stared back down at my knees, trying to think of something to say, some small, kind thing, but everything I thought of was too small.

At last she sighed again. "I blamed him for a long time, Molly, but he was just giving her a ride. It could have been anyone on a night like that—the roads were awful. The truth is, I did everything wrong with Kate."

"Oh, Becky." I had *reminded* her; there was no comfort in seeing me. Kate had been dead seven years and now I'd come and made her pick through her grief all over again.

But she kept going, her voice tired but steady—I hadn't reminded her of anything. Kate was everywhere, the black and white photographs—Kate as a toddler, naked at Barton Springs; gap-toothed on a swing set; dressed as a vampire for Halloween— displayed to be visible from every spot in the room. "I thought she was rebellious the way we were and that she would grow out of it. I didn't want her to get pregnant, but I was pretty sure she wouldn't. She was into being a virgin, not needing boys, so I figured she was safe on that front—I didn't realize she was out on the streets. She'd tell me she was spending the night at a friend's house and I believed her—but a car wreck. That can happen to anyone, can't it? Even if I'd done everything right?"

"Becky, you can't possibly blame yourself—my father, you know my father, my father was *driving*."

She shrugged, her eyes a little glazed. "I should have known. I should have paid more attention, locked her in at night if I had to. But I didn't want to squelch her. You know? I always liked the way your parents—the way they weren't in your face. I thought that was a good way to be and it worked for you, didn't it? You went to Harvard after all."

"Oh, Becky. I dropped out, actually."

"Oh?" she said, but how I or my parents had failed or succeeded made no difference to her. She had no idea what my father had done and that was good, I suppose, although I don't know, after you have lost a child, if pain has any degrees left in it. I suppose it does. It's better to imagine that your child died whole, unravaged—but the loss Becky had suffered made all other losses meaningless. Her puffiness had nothing to do with drink; it was just grief, and no amount of time would lighten it. She was perfectly sober, and it seemed to me as great a crime as any my father had committed, the way he'd re-invented her for his own purposes—the terrible failure, the wild drunk. Why? I wondered, though I knew full well; I must have always known: she hadn't just been like a daughter to him. He was in love with her, I thought, and my eyes welled up with tears. It was true that he never would have touched her, that he never thought of her the way he thought of other girls, women—she was above the rest, the prostitutes and boy-crazy girls whom he could safely harm—but still, she had rebuffed him. She hadn't followed his advice and so, in the way of spurned lovers, he'd changed her, made her a derelict, a woman unworthy of the admiration he'd so generously offered. He'd done to Kate what he couldn't do to Becky.

"You want to see her room?" Becky asked suddenly, and she led me up a flight of stairs behind the kitchen to a small, tidy room: on one side was a wide daybed covered with pink and white pillows, on the other a small desk and a white chest of drawers. The only signs that a teenager had once lived here were a piece of lace hung with earrings and a framed collage of gossip-magazine pictures.

"It's the guest room now, I guess," Becky said. "Though I never have guests." She hesitated. "It's where I sit and think of her—at first, after she died, I used to come up here and straighten her things. Just a little at first. She had all this makeup, all this beauty paraphernalia, and I'd organize the bottles of nail polish, or I'd clean the hair out of her brushes. As secretive as she was, she never minded if I tidied her things. She'd even thank me for it. She liked order, even if she didn't like cleaning. So I tidied. I kept doing the one thing that always soothed her, regardless of her mood. I folded all her clothes and put them away, I cleared drawer space for her makeup, I framed her collage—" She let out a small laugh. "I re-painted her room, finally, the way I'd been promising for years. And then one day, there was nothing left to clean."

Becky was standing in the middle of the room, staring a little blankly, the way she'd done in the halls of Austin High when she was pregnant with Kate. I imagined I could smell the sweet, harsh odor of dollar store makeup in that now spotless room—as if Kate might return at any moment and might, upon seeing all of Becky's efforts, brighten suddenly: *Mom, thank you. My room looks great.* As if her death had been no more than a terrible infraction—like shoplifting and getting caught—a miserable episode that had merely to be weathered.

Becky turned to go. "You want something to eat? Some cheese and crackers?"

I stayed for a long time and after awhile she offered me a glass of wine to go with our cheese and crackers and she burst out laughing at some point—I can't remember why—and it could almost have been an ordinary get together of women who had been friends long ago. What could she do, short of dying, besides go on? Though of course she hadn't gone on. However ordinary she seemed—asking me politely about Zim and teasing me about being a maid—there was nothing ordinary in anything she did. All the while that we were talking, she seemed preoccupied with some other, much more difficult activity, as if, in another room perhaps, she were balancing on a high wire, and everything she did with me—offering snacks, opening the bottle of wine—must be accomplished without forgetting herself and stepping

231

off into the empty air.

I told her I was sorry about Keith Miller, and even sorrier that I'd never apologized. She shook her head. "That was a long time ago. Mostly I was just jealous because you were going to Harvard and I wasn't—and then I had a baby and that was all I thought about." She sighed. "Keith was awful. He dumped me again right after graduation and I never heard a word from him until Kate died. His father sent me a monthly allowance, if you can believe that, but Keith didn't write a post card. Then Kate died and he came over here crying. He's so sorry, etc. He stayed for a few hours and after awhile I realized he wanted to start back up with me. I'd have shot him if I'd had a gun. That I didn't do something to him to land myself in prison—well, I would hardly call it a miracle, but it's something."

"Oh, God," I said.

She shrugged. "It gave me something to be mad about when I wanted to smash the world to nothing. I'm glad it's over, being mad that way. *Lisa*," she laughed softly. "That Lisa is not on Death Row *is* a miracle. She wanted to kill Keith every way a body can be killed."

Lisa, she said, had been married all these years to Charlie and was making hundreds of thousands of dollars a year in real estate. They didn't have any children, but they had a sailboat and a sixteen-year-old cat in diapers who slept in an honest-to-God bassinet by their bed.

Becky was seeing someone she'd been seeing now for four years—another programmer—and he wanted to get married, but she liked living alone. He had kids, anyway, and she didn't want someone else's kids. What she really felt like doing was traveling; she'd been in Texas way too long, she said. She'd always felt like Texas was a cess-pool, but she just couldn't get out.

"*The frog-spawn of a blind man's ditch,*" I said, absently, the wine having gone to my head.

"What?"

"Yeats."

"Oh God, you're like your father."

"No!"

"Oh, Molly, I'm kidding. I mean you might be, I don't know. I haven't seen you in so long. But it wouldn't be an insult, you know.

Your dad's not a bad guy. When I got over blaming him, I thought, at least Kate wasn't with some creep. At least she was in a warm car, and she must have felt safe."

My face froze, but she changed the subject again, going on in her quiet, gentle, deepened voice, as friendly a person as I have ever known, until it was time for her to go—she had a date with her programmer.

We hugged goodbye and this time she held me longer. "I was going to name her after you," she said suddenly. "Before we stopped hanging out." She laughed a little. "One day—I don't know how long we'd been friends, not very long—you showed me all the bedrooms in your house, like it was an art gallery or something. You remember that? You showed me your dad's closet, for Christ's sake, and I remember thinking how— I don't know—innocent you were. I loved that."

She stopped and I couldn't look at her—how much more kindness would she offer me? Better she had spat on me, broken every one of my bones. Mine and Daddy's, too. *All we ever did was fool people*—but I knew better: I'd never fooled Becky for a minute. She loved me, as I loved her.

"I was planning on Rebecca," I said. "Till I had a boy."

"So you settled on Zim," she said, chuckling, and kissed the side of my head goodbye.

———————

I resumed my nicotine-drenched vigil by the fountain. I sat beneath a small mimosa tree, moving as the shade moved, but still my skin blistered in the heat. Every day I thought of getting into my air conditioned car and driving back to the airport, but I never left.

Whatever he had done, I loved him. And yet, I thought, I could punish him. I could do that, at least. Let him die in there alone.

Below me, the feathery shadow of the mimosa swam over the flagstones; for a hundred dollars you could purchase one of the stones and have it engraved: *Benjamin Mills, 1919-2000, Beloved Husband and Father; Susanna Casey, Forever in our Hearts*. Sometimes I imagined they were grave markers, that I was sitting on layers of bones.

The twins came every few days, their differences put aside; they'd drive the four hours up from Houston early in the morning and hurry to get home before the evening traffic got too bad. "Aren't you hot?" they always asked, and then, "How is he?"

"The same," I answered, as if I'd just checked on him. Claire was composing his obituary and sometimes she read me a line or two, to see what I thought. I heard nothing. "That's great," I said. "Thanks for taking care of it."

Once, Pat put her hand on my shoulder and said, "Thank *you*, Molly, for sitting with him. Even when they're in a coma, they like having company."

Ted never asked how Daddy was, as if he knew I had no idea. He came every day and sat with me for a few minutes before going inside. Every day he tried to make a little conversation. "So," he might say. "What's up with Zim?" Or, "So, Molly, I haven't really talked to you in forever." Or, "Zimran—that's an unusual name."

Of all of us, Ted seemed the most at peace, and I didn't know how to act with him anymore. I'd felt sorry for him for so long, measuring myself against him: however small my handful of friends, at least I wasn't like Ted. I didn't know what to do, if I couldn't pity him.

He was just being nice to me, all my siblings were, stopping for a word or two on their way in to see Daddy. I might have been in a Dickens story, with all the characters of my childhood streaming past me, offering me tokens of kindness; but when Ted spoke, I stared at the ground. After a minute or two he went on inside, and I was alone again, with nothing to distract me but the heat and the inscriptions and the wavering shadow of the mimosa.

When Andy Newell appeared, I was as shocked as if my father had shown up, in suit and tie and shining shoes. He taught at UT, he told me, though I hadn't asked—he'd heard from Ted that I was in town.

"Ted?" I asked.

"He said I'd find you here."

"You and Ted are friends?"

"Well, sure. Of course. Since he moved back."

I stared at him, unable to speak, and then he said he'd come to apologize. He was balding, grey, and he clasped his hands and said how sorry he was, that he should have apologized long ago, but he'd been too ashamed.

Whatever had happened between Becky and me was too recent for an encore; I looked away. A different life, I thought, all those years ago in Amsterdam; but suddenly, as if I were still sitting on that narrow hotel bed, a whoosh of feeling flooded from between my legs. A sad arousal, *shamefool as sheet.* How had I imagined I'd felt nothing?

Andy went on: when he thought of how young I'd been, how he'd taken advantage of me, he just felt sick.

"Oh Andy," I said, desperate for him to hush. "You were pretty young yourself."

"Not that young, Molly."

"Please," I said. "It's all right." To change the subject, I asked him about his work, his students, and then he asked what I did—Ted was lousy for news, he said—so I told him: I'd dropped out of Harvard, become a maid, had a child whose father I didn't know. I laughed a little, and that water-stained hotel room, my clumsy childhood, faded.

He was quiet for awhile and then he said, "Molly Moore. You know what I remember about you? How concerned you always were about other people's happiness. Even when you were little. You were so *kind.* You still are."

"Oh—"

"I mean it."

"I don't know."

"Molly."

I wanted him now in a way that had nothing to do with being twelve, this man who'd loved Ted from the first, who could regret a single mistake for thirty years, who might hold me in that burning courtyard for however long it took for Daddy to stop breathing. I leaned forward, my hand reaching towards his arm, and then I glanced down and saw his wedding ring. "Thanks," I said. "It was so nice of you to come. Really nice. Thanks."

I was still blushing when he left, but I almost called after him to stay—suppose he wasn't happily married? Then I thought of Ted calling girls on the phone; even Ted had finally stopped.

But still he came to see Daddy, showing up day after day, with his pale, fragile skin, his gentleness. He was as decent a man as any; why should I be ashamed of our resemblance? I was like Ted and, like Ted, loved.

And yet Ted was no fool. He must have known for a long time what Daddy was. Why visit him then? I couldn't think of any reason, unless the merits of his own love had never troubled him. He visited because he had to, because the need to see Daddy--touch him, for all I knew-- was in his blood, a thing no more in his control than breathing. *We've always been the same, Ted and I.*

I didn't go straight to my father's bedside. I sat awhile in the corridor, watching the nurses come and go. The blonde had vanished and been replaced by women who were smart and kind, though they called him Henry—I could hear them from where I sat, and at last I followed them into his room and watched as they turned him over, side to side, two of them at a time lifting him with the sheet and positioning him so that he wouldn't get bedsores, making him as comfortable as they could for the time he had left.

Beneath his sheet my father was naked. He'd worn a hospital gown when he first arrived, but one night it was taken off and never put back on. "He told us when he got here that he could only sleep comfortably naked," one of the nurses told me. "We don't mind. Whatever a person wants."

I stared at his body—it was like any other man's—the skin hanging off his broad chest in tiny folds, his hipbones as stark as a young girl's, his penis hidden away. Personality fades, like a bruise; all that's left is the breath, the arcing ribs, the skull's bright curves. I gazed down into his gaping mouth, his eyelids thin as moth wings.

It won't be long, the nurse said, when she saw me kiss his cheek, his hands. *See how his jaw catches on each breath? How his knees have turned purple?*

He lived four more days and I only left him to go smoke. I realized during one of those cigarette breaks that I probably wouldn't be giving Roscoe any more blow jobs. As simple and sudden as that, I knew those days were over for me. I could stop without hurting his feelings— Roscoe, of anyone, would understand—but he would miss it and I'd be out fifty a week. It was the right thing to do—who wouldn't applaud a whore's conversion?—but I was sad to leave that broken world where a hen-pecked paraplegic and a middle-aged slut could provide for each other a little. It was how I'd lived, the life I'd made—I had no other prospects that I knew of—and when I got back into the halls of the Hospice—the change of light made me see spots—I squatted on the floor and wept, for Roscoe and me, for Becky.

I cried until my head ached and except for one young nurse who asked if anything was wrong, no one disturbed me. When I was done I wanted to curl up where I was and go to sleep, but I didn't move; I just watched the nurses' shoes come and go along the corridor, and it came to me suddenly that while I was at it—while I was giving things up—I could give up being a maid, too. If I wanted. I could use the money from the house to go to the community college and get a nursing degree. Or a beautician's license. Anything where you took care of people. Made them feel more beautiful or less afraid. I was good at that, at knowing what a person needed: a pretty haircut or a cool hand upon a forehead. A meadow to play in. I might have grown up in the empty spaces of my father's heart, taken shape from all that he was missing— but wasn't my heart, then, a negative of his?

When I went back in my father's room, he lifted himself up and moaned. He hadn't moved or made a sound in days and I ran to him and slipped my hand under his head; he breathed once more, a single, gurgling exhalation, ordinary-sounding as a drain.

I like to think he was waiting for me, but I only know that he died in my arms, his last breath caught in the curve of my shoulder.

I waited until all the dying beauty left him, and then I lay his head back on the pillow and went outside. It was dusk and I stood in the courtyard for a long time, until the fountain turned dark and the path lights came on beside the benches. The night cooled off a little and away in someone's yard a dog barked steadily—some yappy thing—but I imagined hounds: strong and lovely and tirelessly leaping.

When my first novel, LILI, was published, people asked my husband which character was based on him. I barely knew my husband when I was writing LILI—I had no idea we'd end up married—and, compelling as my own future is to me, he was the last thing on my mind when I was writing that novel, about a French woman born at the beginning of the twentieth century.

The relationship between fiction and memoir is fascinating. I'm fascinated by it. When I read my friends' novels, I want to know what really happened and who's based on whom. Some of my characters have a surface resemblance to real people; I might borrow someone's looks or occupation— I knew an honest roofer with a tilted shoulder once—but all of my characters' emotions are my own. My fears and desires animate the French woman surviving two world wars, her disabled son, Molly, Molly's lovers and family and her mean seventh grade teacher.

Like Molly, I had violent dreams when I was young. I was terrified of them until I read a book on dream interpretation and discovered to my huge relief that anyone I dreamt about was just a part of my own psyche. Novels, for me, bear the same relation to real life that dreams do. As in dreams, parts of my waking life appear, but they appear distorted, out of context, paired with the fantastical. And the dream is all about my own preoccupations.

I wanted to write about the problem of loving someone who has done great harm to another. When I began writing DOGS, I imagined a woman who discovers that the lost love of her life has killed someone. I went to North Carolina's Central Prison and interviewed a man on Death Row so that I could make the lover's character believable. The inmate I spoke with was kind to me, and it was easy to imagine someone loving him despite the awful crime he had committed; but in the midst of working on that version of the novel, I lost my father and became more interested in the father-daughter bond than in the bond between old lovers. Molly's father is nothing like mine, but the way she adores him grew out of my love for my father. What if my father had been a very different kind of person? What if he'd killed someone? How would I feel? Then, of course, I had to create a father who could believably do the things Molly's father does; and I had to imagine the kinds of relationships the daughter of such a man might have.

Here are the parts of DOGS that are real: my mother is French; her family was killed on D-day; I was born in 1959; I attended O'Henry Junior High; I spent my childhood summers in the Alps; my father and I both went to Harvard; my father died in hospice; I live in western North Carolina.

Here are a few differences between my life and Molly's: both my parents were theoretical physicists; they did not meet on D-day, but at the Princeton Institute for Advanced Studies; I only lived in Austin for one year; I finished college and went to graduate school; I have a daughter and two step-daughters and I am certain of their parentage.

But my husband does have a cameo role in this novel: he's the red-haired man at the free clinic. He never worked at a free clinic, and he doesn't have bad teeth, but that's what he looked like when he was young, the sort of man he was.

—Abigail DeWitt

Abigail DeWitt is a Michener Fellowship recipient and the author of the acclaimed novel *Lili*. Her short stories have appeared in *Salamander, The Journal,* and *The Carolina Quarterly*. She has lived and worked in France and throughout the United States where she teaches creative writing. She lives in North Carolina with her husband and daughter.